PRAISE FO

'Poignant, emotional, and b... _Us_, Olivia is running from something we've all feared and hope to never face. Carol Mason's effortless storytelling and exquisite writing will keep you turning the pages until the book's stunning and surprising ending. Bring tissues!'

> Kerry Lonsdale, Amazon Charts and _Wall Street Journal_
> bestselling author

'Acutely observed, emotionally honest, utterly brilliant writing, with a shocker of a twist that took my breath away.'

> Melissa Hill, bestselling author

'A beautifully written story of how we connect with each other in terrible crisis, told with wit and humanity – and one hell of a final twist. I loved it.'

> Louise Candlish, author of _Sunday Times_ bestseller _Our House_

'A skillful, compassionate journey into the aftereffects of trauma, _The Shadow Between Us_ deftly explores what happens when we hold tight to the secrets we keep, and they hold tight to us too.'

> Amy Hatvany, bestselling author

'A haunting, heartfelt exploration of guilt and hidden turmoil, of running away, of turning back to face the shadows. I loved it.'

> Charity Norman, bestselling author of _See You in September_

'I read *The Shadow Between Us* in two sittings. Carol Mason has created a fast-paced novel. At its centre is a woman whose heart has been broken. She is on the run from herself. Carol takes us on an emotional journey which keep us gripped right to the very last twist, which hit me in the solar plexus. I had not seen it coming.'

Carol Drinkwater, bestselling author and actress

'This book is a haunting exploration of the corrosive power of grief and the redemption to be found in understanding each other and ourselves.'

Caroline Bond, bestselling author of *The Second Child*

'Full of realistic emotional twists. The characters' reactions to the challenges they face are frank and unmelodramatic; there is a refreshing honesty about the numbness that comes from discovering an infidelity, and the shame that comes with perpetrating one. Equally affecting are the counterpoised sources of sadness in Jill's life. Her marriage has faltered because she and her husband can't have children and yet she must be a mother to her own parents in their old age; it's a poignant combination.'

Telegraph, UK

'A sweet, sad tale of love, loss, and the crazy way the world works to reclaim love again.'

Cosmopolitan, Australia

'What really goes on behind closed doors. Carol Mason unlocks life behind a marriage in this strong debut.'

Heat, UK

between
you
and me

OTHER TITLES BY CAROL MASON:

between
you
and me

CAROL MASON

LAKE UNION
PUBLISHING

Text copyright © 2021 by Carol Mason

Published by Lake Union Publishing, Seattle

www.apub.com

Amazon, the Amazon logo, and Lake Union Publishing are trademarks of Amazon.com, Inc., or its affiliates.

ISBN-13: 9781542004992
ISBN-10: 1542004993

Cover design by Emma Rogers

Printed in the United States of America

For my sister-in-law, Mary Capuccinello

ONE

December 2017, Santa Monica, California

The sun felt like anything but a winter one. I accessed the palm-treed pool deck with my room's key card, surprised to see there was one other person with the same intention. He looked up from his phone. He may have said, 'Good morning,' or 'Hi.' Nothing that demanded a reply. I shot one anyway in his general direction.

As he was occupying a lounger at the near side of the pool, I walked over to the far side, my laptop and notepad tucked under my arm. Parking myself under an umbrella, I stared out across the barely populated expanse of buttermilk sand, currently being groomed by two John Deere tractors. I watched them for a while as they performed their repetitive loops; a Los Angeles Police Department helicopter circled noisily overhead.

It was several hours later, in the mid-afternoon, when I heard a voice say, 'Would you like a drink?'

I had almost nodded off, and practically jumped out of my skin.

'Sorry,' he said. He was standing a few feet away. 'I didn't mean to startle you.' It seemed to entertain him. 'I just thought . . . it's cocktail hour. I'm ordering something, and I thought you might like one too.'

I sat up and looked at him. He was tall and slim, brownish hair flecked with grey at the temples. Older than me, maybe by a decade. And he was wearing a pair of aviator sunglasses. 'No thanks,' I said. 'I think I'm okay.'

He plucked off his glasses. It was a face that was neither forgettable in its ordinariness, nor straightforwardly handsome. More like somewhere in the interesting middle. 'Are you sure?' he said. There was a certain kindly tenacity in his gaze. 'Sounds like there's room for movement.'

Part of me thought, *Go on*, but what came out was, 'Thanks, I'm good.'

He gave a slightly helpless shrug and walked away. I immediately regretted not having been more sporting. Oh well . . . I reached for my laptop, tried to remember what I'd been doing before my thwarted attempt at a nap. Ten minutes or so later, a hand performed a wide arc around my shoulder.

'If I'm completely out of line, you don't have to drink it.' He was holding out a glass of some pale green concoction with a disk of lime on the rim.

'What is it?' I asked, staring at his long, slim, tapered fingers.

'A cucumber jalapeño margarita.'

'Uh-oh!' I quickly pushed it to arm's length. 'I'm deathly allergic to jalapeños.'

For a moment he looked mortified. 'You are?'

'Actually . . .' I tried to keep a straight face. 'No. I'm not. Sorry . . . I couldn't resist that.'

'Wow,' he said, after a little laugh. 'That's cruel!' He shook his head, seeming rather bemused. 'I think you might have just put me off asking a woman to have a drink with me ever again!'

We smiled at each other. I invited him to sit down on the lounger next to me.

'Well, if I'm not intruding . . .' He pulled the sunbed a foot or so away from me. 'You can tell me to leave any time.'

I raised an eyebrow. 'Be in no doubt, I will.'

He told me his name was Joe Johnson, and I told him mine was Lauren Matheson.

He asked me what I was doing here, in the magnificent Hotel Casa Del Mar. I explained I'd flown in from London to attend the wedding of a friend who had married a successful guy in the film business. That they'd insisted on putting me up in a hotel for a couple of nights, and that I'd been stunned when the Uber had dropped me off here, when I'd been expecting somewhere like the Holiday Inn.

'Nice friends!' he said. 'Keepers!'

He asked where my friend and I had met. I was surprised he was even interested, so I told him how we were at medical school together.

'You're a doctor?' A flare of intrigue lit up his eyes.

'Not yet. I graduate next year.'

'Wow! That's impressive.' He grilled me about my chosen career, listened with a certain exclusivity of attention that most people didn't give you these days. Did doctors usually garner such curiosity? If so, I hadn't been on the receiving end of it before.

I told him I was from northern England, that I'd always wanted to be a doctor but, oddly, had ended up doing a degree in history then becoming a travel rep for a couple of years. I said I decided to apply to study medicine after one of those watershed moments when I realised that what I was doing, and what I'd always seen myself doing, were two very different things, so I'd managed to get into Imperial College London. I told him that I currently volunteered at a certain hospital twice a week, that I finally felt like my life had purpose – and that, clearly, I talked way too much and was now totally out of breath!

3

He laughed. It was a great laugh. I found myself wanting to hear it again.

'So you're studying for your exams now?' He indicated my abandoned laptop and notepad.

'Actually, no. I'm trying to write an entry for the British Medical Association's annual short story competition. They give you a theme and you've got 750 words.'

'Wow! A scientist and a writer. Left-brained and right! That's a rare combination!'

'Hardly!' I smiled. 'Believe it or not, there's no scientific evidence to support that people are either left- or right-brained! In fact, if you performed a CT scan or MRI, or even an autopsy, on the brain of a mathematician and compared it to the brain of an artist, it's unlikely you'd find much difference. Even if you did the same for a thousand mathematicians and artists.'

His eyes made a rather fascinated study of my face. 'I stand corrected.' He pretended to look suitably disabused. 'I always sensed that whole thing was a little woo-woo.'

A laugh burst out of me. 'Enough of me,' I said. 'Where are you from in America? And what are you doing here?' I wanted to get him talking. I wasn't sure if it was his voice I liked, or his accent, or both. Or was it simply that I just liked *him?*

'Well, I'm from Chicago, originally. I'm in venture capital. We're winding up a project here.' He clasped his hands behind his head and I observed his bony elbows. 'I was supposed to go home this morning but changed my ticket last minute to give myself one more day to hang out.' He gestured in my direction with a hand. 'And now, of course, I'm very pleased that I did.'

A shot of dopamine hit my brain.

'So you said you're from Chicago originally. Where do you live now?'

'Well, here's the thing . . .' His eyes took on a slightly devilish quality. 'I live in London too.'

'Seriously?' I let this land.

'Yes.' His gaze held fast with mine. 'For the last twenty years.'

I had known a few Brits who had moved stateside, but I'd never seen it happen the other way round. 'Why England?' I asked.

'Oh, I got an internship in the City in finance when I was twenty-one. It was supposed to be for just a year. But then, as is often the way of these things . . . I met a girl, married her and stayed.'

'Right,' I said, after a beat.

I allowed this new detail to articulate itself. Had I assumed he wasn't married because he wasn't wearing a ring? Why had I even looked?

I watched him take a sip of his drink.

'So this American your friend married . . . is he a good guy, as well as a rich one?'

'I don't know,' I said. 'All I really heard him say were his vows. But he certainly said them enthusiastically.'

'Off to a good start then . . .'

The sun had shifted. We didn't seem inclined to move. We had covered so much in a single hour. Everything from Brexit to US health care, music, Netflix, our childhoods, our friends. He told me his favourite backstreets of London, many of which were mine too. How he loved great food but wasn't 'into preciousness'. How he always booked a large hotel suite because he needed 'to pace'. He said his favourite park was Kensington Gardens, and I said, actually, I'd enjoyed many a summer's day sitting in front of the palace at Round Pond.

He also said he had a thirteen-year-old daughter, and a three-year-old son. And a dinner reservation, shortly, with an old friend.

'I really wish I wasn't going to this thing now,' he said, after we'd walked off the pool deck and arrived at the lifts. 'If I hadn't been, maybe I'd have asked you to join me for dinner.'

I tried to picture it. Dinner. A nightcap. Then what? A kiss? An invitation to his room? Wrong for a million reasons, yet right for one: something had started that I didn't want to end.

'Yes. That would have been nice.' I reckoned I could admit it, given it wasn't going to happen.

When the lift arrived at his floor, I said it had been a pleasure, and I was sorry I'd attempted to ruin his classy attempt to buy me a drink. He told me there had been no ruining of anything, that I was charming, that he had enjoyed every minute of our conversation.

'I meant to ask you,' he said, just as he was about to step out. 'What's the theme of the story you're writing?'

I told him it was about regrets.

The door started to close. He surprised me by wedging a foot in. Then he took the little notepad from my hand, plucked the pen from my fingers.

'In case we ever find ourselves sitting at opposite sides of Round Pond and you want to alert me to the fact that if I look forty-five degrees to my right, I'll find you sitting there.'

He had written his name, phone number and his company name.

'Thank you.' I glanced at the tidy block capitals. 'I'll keep it handy on the off-chance.'

And then we said goodbye.

Later that evening, I sat on my own eating dinner, contemplating my failed romantic life, chance encounters and what-might-have-beens. Part of me thought, *Just be glad you met him; everyone enriches our experience in some way.* The other: *Why do people have* to pass through your life, make a big impression and then you never see them again?

The next morning, after a restless sleep, I told myself to think no more about him. He'd be checking out. I had one more day to fill. I didn't want to end up back at the pool, staring at an empty sun lounger, seeing him still sitting there in my mind's eye.

But when I opened my door, there, lying on the carpet, was a small white envelope with my name on it. Inside was a sheet of plain heavyweight stationery.

> *I thought long and hard about phoning your room after dinner and inviting you for a drink in the bar. I hope you know that I wanted to more than anything. But it's complicated.*
>
> *Joe.*

TWO

London, fourteen months later

The man in Bay 4 is handsome. And fit. And has no shirt on.

'Good morning,' I say, perfunctory but pleasant. 'I'm Dr Matheson.' One of these days there'll be an experimental drug for blushing, and I'm going to be the first to take it.

'Doctor?' His eyes go to my legs. 'Hmm . . . Interesting.'

It's usually just the oldies who somehow manage to reinforce your own regrettable case of Imposter Syndrome. I tug the blue curtain closed behind me. 'And you are?' I glance at his chart and answer my own question. 'Dave Wilson.'

'But you can call me darling.' He gives me the cheekiest grin.

I shake my head in feigned exasperation. 'So what brings you in here today, Dave Wilson?'

'Well, I'm not sure, Doctor,' he says. 'But believe me, if I'd known you worked here, I'd have got here a lot sooner.'

When I give him my *Okay! This is getting a little tiresome!* face, he says, 'Well . . . I was up a ladder – I'm in construction – then I fell.' He touches his right bicep. 'Done my arm in, I think.'

'Hmm . . .' I tap my pen on my clipboard. 'So how far did you fall, exactly, Mr Wilson?'

'Call me Dave. A couple of storeys. It's still a bit blurred.'

I ask him to perform certain movements with his arm. When he tries to move it ninety degrees, he winces. 'Lose your balance?' I gently squeeze all the way down to his wrist and when I get to his hand, he upturns his palm to mine.

He stares at our hands touching for a split second before I retract mine. 'Not really sure how it happened. I must have. Or something.'

'Do you suffer from dizzy spells . . . Dave?'

'Nope.'

'Blackouts? Headaches? Migraines?'

'Aren't those for girls? *Honey, I've got a headache?* When he sees my face he says, 'Sorry, that was a really crap joke . . .' He briefly looks down, blushes. 'I have had a few headaches lately. Mostly in the morning. Maybe because I'm not sleeping very well these days.'

'Do you take recreational drugs or drink alcohol?'

'No!' he says, a touch defensive. 'I mean . . . few beers on the weekend. But drugs have never been my thing. Mess with your brain, don't they?'

'Prescription medication?'

'I just finished a course of antibiotics. Do they count?'

'What were they for?'

'Family doc thought I might have an ear infection.'

'Symptoms?'

He reels off a few, mentions this niggly headache again. Interesting, I think. Not sure I'd have been so quick to diagnose an ear infection.

'Can I look in your ears?' I move in closer.

'If you tell me you're single, then definitely. If you're married, I have to think about it.'

'I'm married.' I take hold of the pinna and give it a deliberate little tug.

'Ouch! How long, if you don't mind me asking?'

I peer in there. 'Since December.'

'Just two months! Suppose he hasn't had time to foul up yet, has he? Not boding too well for my chances now.'

I smirk. 'Believe me, they weren't all that high before.'

'Would you go out with me anyway? Call it keeping your options open. Like any sensible person would.'

'I've got a better idea. I'd like to get your shoulder X-rayed. Plus I'm going to order a CT scan of your head.'

'Head?' He frowns. 'Why?'

'Just being thorough. You can't say we don't look after you in here!' I make some notes on his chart. 'Let's start with that, shall we. I'll be back to see you in a bit. Okay?'

'That's the only good thing you've said so far.'

I step outside the curtain and walk back to my computer feeling a little warm, my brain ticking hard. Even though I'm beginning my second rotation in Foundation Year 1, it still often feels like I'm fumbling in the dark. My role is no longer just to observe and learn. Now I'm hands-on, dealing with new symptoms, puzzling test results, equipment malfunctions, consultants testing me with tricky questions. Sometimes I'm the only doctor on my shift. It can be daunting. I hope ordering the CT scan is the right thing to do. On the positive side, I don't think anyone got sacked for *over*-ordering tests . . .

I sit on my stool and make some notes on my jobs list, do the appropriate requisitions. Some bloods are back for Mrs Shipman, the eighty-year-old who was admitted with sudden onset confusion and auditory hallucinations. Her inflammatory markers haven't gone up so that rules out my first suspicion of a bladder infection. One of the nurses was convinced it's dementia but I haven't seen it present like this. I decide to get the duty psychiatrist to weigh in. I'm just filling up a glass of water at the cooler when Paul, one of the residents, taps my back. 'Have you been for lunch yet?'

'Lunch? Oh! That thing!' I look at the clock for possibly the first time today. Six hours. No break. No wonder he's asking; he can probably hear my stomach growling a mile away. Time flies in A&E. If I were to work here permanently I wonder if that would be a good thing, or would I feel my life was passing too quickly? Everybody needs a bit of healthy boredom, right?

'Go,' he says. 'It's quiet but we don't want to jinx it.'

I could use a dose of fresh air, so I pull on my wool coat, dig out a flattened relic of a peanut butter sandwich from the nether-world of my bag and stuff it into my mouth as I head through the maze of shiny-floored corridors that leads out to a square of manu-factured green space with a few benches dotted here and there. I sit down, feeling the damp penetrate my coat, and pluck open a bag of salt and vinegar crisps. I'm just stuffing the last handful into my mouth when my mobile pings. A text.

All good?

I quickly reply, Just gone on break! Call me! Joe never phones me at work in case he's interrupting.

No sooner is it sent, my phone rings. 'Good timing!' I tell him.

'Must be that special GPS I put in your handbag that detects handsome predatory doctors.'

I chuckle. 'Is *that* what that thing was? I was wondering!'

'It's got a special shoot-to-paralyse mode that can be activated remotely.'

'I'll keep that in mind. If they start dropping like flies . . .'

He does his endearing masculine, three-beat laugh.

'Are you still taking me out for dinner tonight?' Sometimes I still feel like we're newly dating rather than newly wed.

'Do you want to go?'

I think about this, shove my rubbish back into my bag and pull my coat around me tightly. On any given shift I never know what's

11

coming through the door, or how wiped out I'll be by the time I'm done. 'Can I reserve the right to just stay at home?'

There's a small delay, an interval where I can almost feel him smiling. Then he says, 'I love when you say that word *home*.'

The afternoon flies by. I deal with a fractured hip, a head pain that should have required a trip to the dentist, not A&E, and then on a slightly more challenging note, an elderly man with a bowel blockage and an eight-year-old boy with severe stomach pains. Kelly Kimpson, the duty psych, confirms Mrs Shipman had an acute psychotic episode, not dementia, and we send her home with a prescription for Risperidone. And then David Wilson's CT scan comes back. I stare at it on the monitor, along with the radiologist's report.

My usual drill is to hop on the bus from the hospital to East Croydon station. But tonight I need to walk even though it adds half an hour to my journey. It's a route that takes me through the neighbourhoods where kids in hoodies loiter on corners and cease conversation to give me solid stares as I pass them. Where I'll get hit up for spare change, or occasionally offered drugs. Where, a while ago, I had my bag ripped clean off my shoulder – I didn't even feel him behind me until it happened. The shock somehow came a distant second to the fact that it was the fantastic jade green suede bag I'd bought in France; I was in love with that thing.

Tonight I keep my head down, my hands planted deep in my coat pockets, and push out clouds of breath into the damp air.

On the train to Victoria Station I try to pay attention to my audio book. Usually I can get lost in a good historical yarn, and the hour or so it takes to get home, door to door, vanishes. But today, I don't hear a single word. Eleven minutes later I'm off the train, trotting along the platform, then crossing the concourse to the entrance of the underground, losing myself in the rhythmic click of my heels, in the practised art of cutting a path through the wave of commuters coming at me, heading south. Out into the fresh air briefly, then I canter down the twenty or so steps to the Tube, push through turnstiles, disappear down long escalators to the platform, where I wait briefly for the train that will shuttle me to north London.

At Hampstead, where I emerge, he is standing there with Mozart, the kids' Portuguese Water Dog. A lone and graceful figure, long legs in dark jeans, a form-fitting black collarless windbreaker. The second he sees me, his face breaks into a smile.

This is our routine. I text him every night as I leave work. I've told him he doesn't need to come and meet me just because it's dark; I'm of tough northern stock – there's very little that makes me quake in my boots. But I know this is a novelty for him. He'll disguise how much he loves it by saying *It's no big deal. Motz gets to go for a pee. I get to stretch my legs.*

He once told me that he never knew when Meredith was getting home, never had any sense of them coming together as a married couple at the end of the day. He said it was a bit like she just returned to base, a necessary transition to take her into the next work day.

'You're late and you didn't text or reply. I was worried.' He kisses me on the mouth. His face is warm and he smells of faded aftershave that's found its way on to the wool of his scarf.

'Sorry. I must have forgotten to turn my ringer on.' I briefly rest my head on his shoulder. 'Bad day.'

'Tell me about it,' he says, as we take a sharp right and meander up the steep and windy incline to our home, Mozart leading the way.

And so I do.

I'm still talking about it when we're in bed a couple of hours later. He made me some scrambled eggs because I couldn't face the seafood and chorizo hotpot he'd pulled together after we'd agreed to stay home. Joe is an amazing cook. Until I met him, I'd never known a guy who could even boil an egg, let alone care about whether I was eating something nourishing and healthy. 'I just love feeding my people!' he once said, in his big, rather extravagant Chicagoan way. And I loved knowing I was one of them.

'I don't know why I wasn't prepared for it,' I tell him. 'People get ill, die . . . I've been trained for this. I've seen this.'

I didn't want to bring it home with me; I remember a professor telling us that no matter what happened on the ward, when you leave it you must 'return to your world'.

'Because he's your age,' he says. 'Because you guys had a bit of banter . . . Hell, you liked the guy!'

He's right. I appreciated his messy charm. In another life he might have even been someone I dated.

'Look . . .' He draws me into him, tightly. 'No one wants to tell someone they've got a brain tumour – certainly not someone virtually your own age. It's an unthinkably horrible position you're in.'

'But if I'm like this every time I've got to break bad news . . .'

'Don't be silly. You won't be.' He turns my chin, makes me meet his eyes. 'Lauren, you're caring and kind, and you feel things on a very deep level. That's an *asset*! It makes you *you*. It doesn't make you less strong, or less professional. In fact, it makes you a much-needed addition to this cold, cold world.'

I am embraced by this rare ability he has of always saying the right thing. And maybe I will eventually grow a thick skin and stop being so riddled with self-doubt.

'Think of him before you go to sleep!' he says, with a certain bright humanity. 'Send him a dose of the fighter spirit.'

14

'I will,' I tell him, touched that he has the capacity to feel empathy for someone he's never met, to let some other man be the last person on my mind as I fall asleep.

Four months after we met in Santa Monica, I had arrived on the ward as usual to start my volunteer shift. One of the admins looked up from her computer and said, 'Oh, some post just came for you.' She rooted through a pile and handed me an envelope.

It was addressed to Lauren Matheson c/o my hospital. I recognised the neat block capitals instantly.

Dear Lauren,

This could perhaps be a wild goose chase in more ways than one. But in case by some miracle this does actually manage to find you, and if there is even the remotest chance that, after all this time, you still vaguely remember me, I wanted to say that it's not complicated anymore and I would love to take you to dinner.

Joe Johnson.

THREE

Grace is sitting at the dinner table tinkering with her phone when I come in. She's wearing an oversized denim shirt, and her long, bare legs are drawn up into a yogic half lotus.

'Hi,' I chirp, noting I'm a bubblier version of myself when I'm around Joe's daughter – almost like my inner teenager is compelled to come out in a rather feeble attempt to relate to hers.

She doesn't look up.

As I pass her chair I can see that behind a curtain of silky, honey-coloured hair, she's immersed in watching one of her own vlog posts – an entertaining tutorial on how to get the designer T-shirt look for under ten pounds. What you do is, you buy the cheapest, plainest one you can find from H&M, then slash holes in it. I'd sneakily watched her go to town with a pair of scissors the other day.

'How's your day?' I ask, fascinated that she can find herself so enthralling. As I glance back at her again, I realise I can see right up her shirt – and it doesn't look like she's wearing any underwear. I make a point of looking away, set the shopping bags down on the Carrara marble counter. Joe and Meredith's custody arrangement has the kids staying with us Sunday to Tuesday, and alternate Saturdays. 'How did your exam go?'

'Fine,' she mumbles.

I wait for more, but nothing is forthcoming. That's okay. If she doesn't want to talk, I'm not really in the mood to drag conversation out of her. I haven't had the best day. A consultant gave me a telling-off for something that was actually another junior doctor's error, not mine. Instead of putting him straight, I took one for the team. But I've spent the rest of the day berating myself for being spineless.

I start setting out vegetables and pulling things from the fridge. We live in a charming garden-level Victorian conversion that Joe rented, at vast cost, after his marriage broke up. It's one of those civilised, spacious, serenely decorated spaces in tones of cream and elephant grey that's ideal for a couple who earn enough to afford the luxury of the square footage, but it's not the most practical place for a family, being rather open-plan – pretty much one big living space – and free of escape hatches. Last week Joe told Grace off for always walking in the door and disappearing straight to her room. So I'm assuming this is why she's dutifully sitting here now.

'It'll be a while before dinner . . . You know . . . if you've got things to do,' I say, trying to give her the green light to leave, but I might as well be talking to myself.

To fill the awkward silence, I pop on my playlist and start humming along to Billie Jo Spears's '(Hey, Won't You Play) Another Somebody Done Somebody Wrong Song' – one of those rare and catchy melodies that even the most tone-deaf among us can sing along to.

After a time I hear her say, 'Do you have any idea where my dad went?'

She has plucked out an earbud and is staring at me with a certain idle curiosity.

'I don't know,' I say. 'Isn't he just out picking up Toby with Mozart?'

No answer.

'Are you hungry?' I ask. 'I bought stuff to make tacos.' I've noticed in the past that if I buy chicken, she wants beef. If I get us fish, she wants chicken. So this time I thought, *Right. I'm going to buy the lot!* 'I thought I'd set it all up as a bar and we can build our own.'

'Build our own?' There is no mistaking her disdain.

Hmm. I've the internet to thank for this particular brainchild. How to make meal times entertaining for kids of all ages. They should have said *but not teenage girls who seem determined to hate what you cook for them anyway.*

Her phone pings.

Saved by the bell!

As she reads her message I watch her smirk, her pretty, coral-painted lips turning up at the corners to show charmingly uneven teeth, the eye-teeth a slightly deeper ivory than the rest, the hint of a silver filling in the upper left. Grace is a truly gorgeous girl. She mostly looks like a mini version of her mother, though she has many of her dad's mannerisms. But it's her confidence, not normally seen in girls her age, that is no small part of her allure. At one point, as she's firing off a reply, she looks up and catches me watching her. I'm given the *WTF?* face again, then she slides off her stool and relocates to the sofa – tossing a cushion out of her way.

Okay. I'm going to cook my meal, and everyone can just dig in without me trying to turn us into an episode of *The Durrells.*

I start up Billie Jo Spears again, and sing along. Joe told me I don't need to prove I'm an amazing chef just because Grace informed me her mother is. Then he added, 'It's actually a load of crap. Meredith had never so much as roasted a chicken until we got our new Wolf stove. And then she stuck her head in there and nearly blasted her eyebrows off.'

In no time, Joe walks in with the dog, Toby hoisted high on his shoulder. 'Well, hello!' His smile is refreshingly saucy and lights me up. Toby is wearing his cute little burgundy blazer, his bare legs dangling from his grey shorts, the evidence of an old scrape on his knee. I go over to them.

'Hello,' I say to Joe, aware that Grace is watching us. I turn my cheek when he aims for my lips, and he seems a little puzzled by the gentle rebuff. Mozart runs to his water bowl. I rub Toby's head and crouch to help him off with his coat and mittens. 'Hi there, little fellow. How was school today? Did you have a good time?'

'No,' he says. 'It was a rubbish-ish time, and now I want to play on my iPad!'

He bullets towards the sofa, but Joe calls him back. 'Hey, Tobes. Can you please give Lauren a hug first?'

I'm about to say, *Oh, that's all right!* but to my delight, Toby does a U-turn, runs back and rugby tackles me. 'No running inside the flat!' Joe calls, but it's too late. Toby glues himself to my lower body, his arms tight around my hips, which makes me smile.

'School was awesome! I can count to twenty and I know what a noun is!'

Joe catches my eye again and mouths, 'Bullshit.'

I chuckle.

'Would you like some tortilla chips and dip?' I ask him.

'Chips and dip? Wow! Yes please, and thank you!' You would think I'd offered him a trip to the moon on a rocket. He stands to attention like a keen little toy soldier.

I'm about to pass him the bowl but Joe intercepts it. 'How about some apple and cottage cheese instead?'

When I must look confused, he says in a hushed tone, 'Toby got a pharyngeal abrasion with one of these things not so long ago, because he doesn't always chew properly. They can be sharp for a kid.'

'Oh,' I say, cringing a little. I would never, ever, have thought of that in a million years. 'Sorry . . .'

Toby pouts but doesn't burst into the fit of tears I'm anticipating.

'How was your exam?' Joe asks Grace, who does an exaggerated duck-walk towards him, then slumps her full weight on to him, hanging there like a rag doll.

'That bad? Huh?' He laughs, and gently pushes her away.

She starts to tell him how her friend Phoebe faked feeling ill – or Grace thought she was faking, until the girl actually puked on her exam paper. The story goes on at length. As I return to the meal prep, I listen to the theatrical delivery, the cultivated Queen's English that comes with an expensive private education – though not a boarding school one; Joe refused to send her away from home, a battle he had to fight with Meredith. Then she moves on to another friend's high jinks in France, and I can't read whether Joe is genuinely interested in all this, or angling to get away.

Right then, Toby charges around the room fencing with an imaginary foe. Joe cuts Grace off. 'Tobes! How many times have I told you . . . No running indoors!' He catches my eye and shakes his head in good-natured despair.

'I'm ravenous!' Grace sashays over to the breakfast bar where I've set out onion, peppers and tomatoes, grated white and yellow cheese, seasoned fish with chilli and lime, cubed chicken breast and sautéed slices of steak.

I watch her peer down her nose at it – like a property owner inspecting a fresh deposit of shit on her lawn. Then she says, '*Que desastre!* Please tell me we can order a pizza!'

I glance at Joe, expecting him to give her some sort of ticking off, but all he says is, 'Well, I, for one, think Lauren's done a very good job here and I'm going to enjoy diving in.'

Then he dips a finger in the sour cream, pops it in his mouth, and smiles at me with his eyes.

FOUR

April 2018

I would love to continue our conversation soon.

His text came about ten minutes after he'd dropped me off at my door. Our very first date.

I'd only got as far as the bathroom with the intention of taking off my make-up, but had found myself gazing at my face in the mirror. Was this what 'in love' looked like? The sensible streak in me said, *Come on! You can't fall for someone this fast. It's just a strong – very potent – like.*

Could we possibly have more to say? I responded.

The date had lasted five hours. Until the staff began upturning stools on to tables, and Joe said, 'Do you think they're trying to tell us something?'

I've a feeling I could talk to you forever, Lauren, and it still wouldn't feel like too much.

I smiled. Actually . . . ditto.

The dots came again.

To be honest . . . I haven't enjoyed talking to someone this much in a very, very long time. Not for four months, to be precise!!!

It was true. We'd clicked as seamlessly as on the day we first met. As though then and now had known no interruption – almost like we had a history behind us, not just an hour in the sun. I had heard about this kind of connection; I'd certainly never even come close to experiencing it. I wasn't looking for Joe, yet in a way it felt like I'd been on course to meet him my whole life.

Still, my instinct was to keep it light. Safe.

Clearly you don't get out much!

The doctor in me had an almost existential fear of the unknown. I was so far out of my depth, yet I had a sense that my life and priorities were about to shift in some profound way, which was as exhilarating as it was terrifying.

Believe me, I do. This is rare. Rare and wonderful. The inappropriate truth . . . I was dying to kiss you in the car.

Hmm . . . What stopped you?

Fear of coming on too strong? Past mistakes? Mainly . . . I don't want to rush this.

I wondered what he meant by *past mistakes*.

Two meetings in four months? Not exactly hasty by anyone's standards!

Haha . . . I'm an old guy, remember? I move slowly. Bones are creaking just writing this.

I loved his humour. But I knew why he was moving slowly. Joe wasn't even officially divorced. He hadn't had time to process the end of a relationship, let alone contemplate a new one.

I felt the need to make something clear.

I'm not in a rush either.

I was still in medical school, still had so much to accomplish in my immediate future. A heavy romantic commitment wasn't really on my agenda – not yet.

Good, he replied. And then, Wise. And then, You should know the much older man is very patient. A rare trait in a world of instant and sometimes false gratification. Throughout his extremely long life

22

this has proven to be a rewarding and ultimately long-term winning strategy.

Patience is a fine quality . . . I replied.

He didn't respond right away.

Where are you now? I wrote, eager to keep this going. You surely can't be home already?

Pulled over at side of the road.

His unabashed confession made me laugh out loud. I thought it was lovely. I pictured him sitting there in his white Lexus – somewhere – a silhouette carved by the light of his phone. I'd just been reading F. Scott Fitzgerald's *This Side of Paradise*, and the words '*They slipped briskly into an intimacy from which they never recovered*' buzzed in my head.

This was us, surely. Or so it felt.

Maybe you should get yourself home!

Having trouble. Clearly!! You're hard to walk away from!

After a moment, I typed, Then don't walk away.

That was it. No more dots. Damn it. I'd shown my hand. Made it known I was feeling the depth, length and significance of us – something that was way too premature, or presumptuous, to articulate.

This was what I hated about romantic involvements. The second-guessing. The worrying that, with one misstep or wrong word, you might undo another's faith or feelings.

I was convinced I'd never hear from him again. I agonised about it all night.

At around 2 a.m., just as I was drifting into a shallow, unsettled sleep, my phone pinged.

No intention of walking, he wrote.

FIVE

Our turn to have the kids stay over on Saturday rolls around quickly. This particular Saturday, I have to work. It's a gruelling day, emotionally. A six-year-old boy is admitted with cardiac arrest. Our tests show he suffers from long QT syndrome, a heart rhythm disorder that can cause fast and chaotic heart beats. It's not uncommon for the condition to go unnoticed until it's too late. He dies while I'm on a call with a consultant on a different matter. So, on my way home I wish it was just me and Joe tonight, so I can curl up on the sofa and just feel what I need to feel, and think what I need to think. To try to watch the telly while I relive every second of that kid's face, and the faces of his parents. Right now, that's what I need to do to process this. But when I get in Joe tells me Toby is waiting up for his story.

I find him sitting propped up in his bed by his Freddy the Frog pillow.

'Hey, little fella!' I say.

Staring at him, I have to make a massive effort to push thoughts of a dead little boy to the back of my mind, and to remember what the prof said about returning to your world.

'Hiya, Lauren,' he says.

It's so cute how he can't pronounce his r's. Lau*w*en.

I always enjoy storytime. I read to him a combination of the tales I loved as a kid, and popular ones a website informs me are essential reading for children.

We're just getting to the part where Jack hacks down the beanstalk and the giant tumbles to his death when Joe pops his head around the door. 'Nightcap?'

To get myself out of the habit of reaching for a glass of wine at the end of the day, stressed and tired, I've instituted a policy of booze-free weekdays, wine only on weekends. But last Sunday, Grace gawked at me as I was walking from the fridge holding a wine glass and said, 'Were you – like – born with one of those in your hand?' So I was going to give alcohol a miss tonight to show her that actually, no, I wasn't. But suddenly, with the day it's been, all my good intentions fly out of the window. 'Please,' I say. 'I'd love one.'

'Hey, bud,' Joe says to Toby. 'Why did Jack hack down the beanstalk?'

Toby just looks at him blankly.

'Wasn't the giant chasing Jack, or something, Toby?' I gently prompt him, conscious of Grace appearing in the background. She's dressed in an oversized T-shirt and is standing on one leg like a pelican, the sole of her left foot pressed against her right inner knee. 'Remember the goose who laid the golden egg?' I say.

Toby pushes away my hand with the book in it. 'I don't like this stupid story!'

'We don't have to read anymore,' I tell him. He's tired.

Grace briefly meets my eye, and I see a glint of mischief in her expression. 'It really is a stupid story. And completely inappropriate for children, actually. You know . . . unless you want to teach them it's okay to steal, murder, then live happily off the spoils of their crimes.'

'What?' At first I think she must be joking.

Joe looks at me, shrugs. 'Hey,' he says light-heartedly, 'for what it's worth, I think it's a great story!'

'My favourite is *The Wonky Donkey*!' Toby chimes in, seeming happy again.

'The Wonky Donkey is funny, isn't he?' I'm disproportionately thrilled he loves a story I introduced him to, and feel an impish sense of satisfaction because Joe once let it drop that whenever Meredith bothered reading to the kids she'd fall asleep before they did.

'Maybe it's funny if you're fine poking fun at people with disabilities,' Grace says, tartly.

'But the donkey isn't a person. He's a farm animal,' I tell her.

'So we don't need to respect animals?'

'Of course we do. But it's a children's story. It's designed to be amusing. To instil in kids the concept of rhyme.'

'Perfect. Let's ridicule him and but still respect him.'

It's very odd behaviour, so keen-edged and antagonistic. Anyone would think she was thirty-four, not fourteen.

I look to Joe for help, but he seems oblivious. 'Why is he wonky anyway?' he asks.

'Because he's got a gammy leg,' she answers for me. 'And he's missing an eye. So they call him a winky wonky donkey. Oh . . . and he's got a cleft palate!'

'No, he doesn't!' I exclaim.

'But – really – he might as well have. And on top of everything, he's anorexic. So they call him a *lanky* winky wonky donkey! All he needs now is to stink, then he'd be a lame, half-starved, one-eyed homeless person.'

I'm about to say this is ridiculous, but she flits out of the room.

Joe and I look at each other. 'That nightcap? Can you make it a big one?' I ask.

'I thought you might say that.'

In bed, while Joe lies beside me answering emails, I surf my phone, still feeling more than a little puzzled about what just happened. I wonder if I should say something to him. But given he didn't exactly bat an eyelid, I suppose it's possible I just took it the wrong way. Perhaps because of the day I've had my sense of humour has taken a leave of absence. I decide it's best to let it go.

For no reason in particular, other than raw curiosity, I find myself punching into Google the words: Step-parenting. Challenges. Stepmothers.

> The feeling of being an outsider and wondering if it will ever go away is almost universal for every childless stepmother.
>
> How to protect your marriage – and save your sanity – in a step family.
>
> I love him but not his kids.
>
> —Life and Style. The Guardian.

Joe is immersed in typing, his long, slim fingers dancing over the keyboard. He must sense me watching because he suddenly turns his head, meets my eyes, gives an inquiring little smile.

I send one back, then we return to our respective devices.

There's a lot to read, and I won't be able to get my head around it. Nor do I really want to. I'm just about to click off when a link to a blog catches my eye:

> S'MOTHERHOOD: Coping with an instant family.

I click on it.

> Have you suddenly acquired another person's kids? Does your husband have an intimidating ex? Resentful offspring who seem to hate you? Have you had moments of feeling like an outsider? Frustrated? Worried this will never change? Welcome to the wonderful world of stepmotherhood! Guess what? Nothing can prepare you for what you thought you signed up for. But we can help you navigate the future. Join us and you'll have like-minded friends to offer you the benefit of their experience – or, if nothing else, a safe place to have a good rant.

There's a link to the forum but I have to register to gain access. Part of me thinks, *This is for other people, not me*, and I'm about to exit. But my finger hovers over the back button, and I find myself saving it to *favourites*.

Joe slaps his laptop shut, reaches across and places it on the night table. I watch the long flex of muscle down his bare back, then the way his hand settles, suggestively, in a space an inch from my leg. Our eyes meet; a frisson of anticipation. 'What are you reading?' he asks.

'Nothing,' I say. 'Nothing very important.'

He smiles. 'That's the right answer.'

SIX

On Sundays I usually try to make myself scarce for a few hours to give the kids – Grace in particular – a bit of quality time alone with their dad. Sometimes, I meet my friends Sophie and Charlie for lunch, but today they're out of town so I decide to go on a shopping expedition.

Last weekend Toby forgot to bring Godfrey the Giraffe when he came to stay. When we tried to put him to bed, he threw the tantrum from hell. 'I want Godfrey! I want Godfrey!'

He thrashed and screamed and cried, until Joe said, 'If I don't go and get goddamn Godfrey I'm going to slit my throat with a carving knife.'

It's a beautiful day, so first I take the Tube to Marble Arch then have a wander through Hyde Park towards the Serpentine cafe where I nurse a coffee and a piece of walnut cake and watch kids feeding the ducks, families picnicking on the grass, a dad taking his son out on a pedal boat. Afterwards, I head back the way I came and take my time walking the length of Oxford Street, popping into a few shops and a clutch of cute boutiques in one of my favourite little hidden backwaters, St Christopher's Place. As I have to make my way down Regent Street to Hamleys, I decide to pop into Topshop at Oxford Circus first, because I can hardly go home with a gift for Toby and nothing for Grace.

Just the very idea of choosing something for her reminds me of the first time I bought the kids gifts.

Joe decided on afternoon tea at a posh hotel for me to meet his children. I'd heard how advanced Toby was for his age, had pictured a nerdy boy wonder, a member of the London Mensa chapter with an IQ of 250. A child who, when most of us are just discovering our toes and learning that food is supposed to go in the mouth, had already become fluent in eight languages and could find the cubed root of 456,667,235 in less than six seconds. I knew Grace was a YouTube 'influencer' as Joe said she described herself, and he surprisingly said it with a straight face. So I decided to buy them books. Ripley's *Believe It or Not* for Toby, and, for Grace, *How to Be a Hepburn in a Kardashian World*.

When I arrived at the Dorchester's Palm Court, I spotted them at a table near a grand piano. It was odd seeing Joe in the context of father – with two lives he had created with another woman, both of whom looked every bit like him and nothing like him at the same time. But they did look very much a unit, and at ease in their privileged surroundings. Even though I knew he earned well, drove a beautiful car and stayed in nice hotels, I had still thought of him as a down-to-earth bloke from Chicago who was as comfortable talking to a politician as to a parking attendant.

It was almost like I was seeing someone else.

Joe made stiff introductions, and before I handed Grace her book I bigged it up a little too much. There was suddenly something withering in her expression that made me want to actually eat the book rather than give it to her, to just push it sideways into my mouth and chew until there was no evidence of it. But instead I handed it over. She went on staring at me like I had two heads and one was growing a beard. Then she placed it on the floor, like a wet umbrella, and said, 'Kim Kardashian is just one of those tacky yesterday people.'

Toby's book was a big, glossy hardcover. His dad had taken his glasses from him and was cleaning them with a napkin, and when I handed it to him somehow the sharp edge went right into his eye. He erupted with gurgling cries.

I was mortified, and made a great big dog's dinner of apologising. No one was really listening. Grace began tinkering on her phone like nothing was going on. The more Joe tried to pacify Toby, the more he howled. I could have offered my help. I was a doctor to be, after all. But I just sat there, useless and squirming.

The manager came over. The place was full of wealthy Arabs and elderly English upper class types – we were spoiling their pleasure. The pianist was playing 'The Shadow of Your Smile' – one of my favourites – and he sent me a look of sympathy.

'I think I'm going to take him outside,' Joe said, and he thrust two twenty-pound notes at the waiter – grossly overpaying for their tea and orange juice. As we were leaving I watched a couple of Arabs almost tip from their chairs to stare at Grace's legs in her white pleated mini-skirt.

'They were very thoughtful gifts,' Joe said in that magnanimous way of his, as he tried to juggle an ill-tempered Toby and the stupid books in his arms.

Outside, he hailed a taxi, then took a while getting Toby settled into the back seat. Grace slid in after without so much as a glance or goodbye. Then there was an awkward moment where Joe was waiting for me to climb in.

He indicated the empty space with a hand.

It was a pivotal moment. I could get in the taxi, move on to some other phase of the day with the three of them, hope to correct a bad first impression. Or . . .

'I think I'd like to walk,' I said.

He seemed so disappointed. 'Please,' he said, when I clearly wasn't budging. 'At the very least, let us drop you off somewhere.'

'I really would just like the air,' I said.

Eventually he gave up. But his eyes reflected exactly what I was feeling: this was a let-down, not how we'd envisaged things would go at all.

As I stood there alone and watched the taxi merge into traffic, it felt symbolic. This bubble we'd existed in until now was something we'd zealously constructed, negating, in the process, everything that fell outside of it. The bubble wasn't real. Joe had a life I wasn't part of. There was a side to him I'd never witnessed – Joe the father. Until now I was aware his children were a big aspect of his life, but they somehow felt peripheral to my idea of him.

Now I saw it: as he had once tried to tell me, his children were *who he was*.

A few weeks later, I spent my very first night at Joe's place when he had the kids staying. We sat through a stiff dinner. Afterwards I got up to fill the dishwasher and Grace said, 'Why are you always cleaning up? Are you auditioning to be our housekeeper?'

'Lauren is a tidy person!' Joe sent me a fond look. 'You could try taking a leaf out of her book,' he said, and gave me a playful wink.

We went to bed. I got up around 2 a.m. to go into the kitchen for some water. We hadn't made love. Joe said it felt too weird with the kids around. I hadn't pushed it. I loved him enough to let him adapt to all this in his own time.

When I walked into the kitchen, there was a banana skin lying in the middle of the breakfast table. It hadn't been there when we'd gone to bed. I picked it up and put it in the bin.

And there, lying on top of the day's rubbish, was *How to Be a Hepburn in a Kardashian World*.

Grace's perfectly staged *Fuck you*.

It's late afternoon by the time I put my key in the door; finding something for Grace was more of a chore than I'd expected. They are playing Jenga. I can hear wooden blocks crashing to the floor, Grace clapping and cheering. No one hears me come in except Mozart who runs to me, offering up a gruff bark – something I've noticed he often does until he realises it's me and not an armed robber.

When I walk into the room, they are sitting on the floor among the rubble of their game. There's an air of cosy domesticity the place lacks when it's just the two of us. As though the flat has two distinct personalities and might favour this one.

'Hi!' Joe gets up and walks over to give me a kiss.

'Hi guys!' I say cheerily, even though I can feel the charge run out of their collective battery with my arrival.

I go over to give Toby a kiss but he shrinks into himself. 'No! Don't touch me!'

Grace messes with her phone. Not so much as a hello.

'Grace, Lauren just spoke to you.' Joe glares at the top of her head.

She reluctantly glances my way, says a grudging, 'Hi.'

'Why don't you tell Lauren what we got up to today, Tobes?' Joe says, playfully nudging Toby with his foot.

Toby scrunches up his face. 'Because I don't want to, that's why!'

'It's okay,' I say. 'Why don't you guys play another round? I'm going to get some water.'

A look of apology crosses Joe's face. I send him one that says: *It's totally fine!*

I walk over to the kitchen area, a little relieved. Just as I'm noting the state of the countertops – food and rubbish all over the place; items on the bench that should have been put back in the fridge; an enormous uncovered block of cheese that's on its way to becoming a dried-out barnacle – Joe comes up behind me. 'Don't worry about the mess. Grace and I are going to take care of it.' He moves my hair to drop a kiss on the nape of my neck, obviously designed to make light of everything, and somehow it does. 'How was your day? We missed you.' Then he whispers, 'My God, this has been never-ending! I was dying for you to walk in that door.' Joe is not fond of the Sunday plan where I disappear for a few hours. 'Doesn't it matter that *I* want you with us?' he pouted when I first insisted on it. But it didn't. I was doing this for the kids.

I smile, pour myself some water from the filter in the fridge. 'It's nice to be missed!'

'What's in here?' He mooches through the bags. I tell him I got a little something for Toby – and for Grace, of course.

'Hey, Tobes,' he hollers, 'Lauren's got you a present.'

Toby rushes at me like a rocket, tries to grab the bag from his dad's hands. 'No snatching!' Joe holds it aloft, out of his reach.

'Sorry,' Toby says, and stands still. 'Sorry for snatching!' He looks at me. 'Can I have my gift, please?'

I smile. Joe hands it to him.

'What is it?' He excitedly dives into the bag. 'Oh.'

'Toby has Godfrey already.' Grace is suddenly standing right behind me.

'I know,' I tell her brightly, trying to ignore the fact that Toby looks like he woke up believing it was Christmas morning, only to learn it's next week. 'But now he's got one for each house.'

'That's amazingly thoughtful.' Joe puts his arm around me and pulls me in for another kiss. 'A Godfrey for each home.' He says it like it's the most endearing thing he's ever heard. He tells Toby to thank me for the gift and Toby rugby tackles me, almost sending me off balance.

'I bought you something too,' I say to Grace. 'I hope you like it.' I hand her the Topshop bag.

She takes it without a word. Then, incuriously, she reaches into the bag and pulls out the red and black lumberjack shirt I actually spent over an hour choosing. 'Thanks.' She inspects it with the same disinterest. 'Oh my God . . . this totally reminds me . . . I've cleaned out my wardrobe and have put some old junk in a bag for the charity shop. I'll leave it down here in case anybody's got anything to add to it.' She flings the shirt on to the chair and sashays off towards her room.

'Great thinking,' Joe says. 'I might have some shirts too. I'll take a look in a minute.'

'I think I'm going to take a bath,' I tell them, not quite believing he didn't notice her cheap shot.

'You should,' he says. 'Then if you want, later, the three of us can watch a movie together.'

I nod. 'Sounds good.'

In our bedroom, I scrutinise my face in the mirror, wondering if this might be what trying too hard looks like. As I prep my bath, I can't help but think, *Oh well, only one more hour until Toby falls asleep*, and hopefully Grace would rather pluck out her own eyeballs and eat them than watch a movie with me. Then we'll be one night down; two to go . . . then four days of freedom.

As I lie there, my chin floating above the bath water, I hear a tap on the door.

'Lauren?'

For a moment I freeze. 'Er . . . yes, Grace?'

There's a suspenseful pause then she says, 'Dad wanted me to bring you a glass of wine. Can I come in?'

Without waiting for my reply she opens the door and I lunge for the towel draped over the side of the tub. There's a moment where she just steadily observes the sight of me hiding behind it, my head and fingers peeking over the top.

'Where shall I put it?' she asks.

'Maybe just on the floor.'

She sets the glass down like a listless waitress.

'That's kind of you,' I say. 'Thank you.'

'Not a problem,' she replies. 'Don't forget it's there and stand on it, or you know . . . you might glass yourself.'

SEVEN

When Joe said, 'Meredith wants to meet you,' it came out of the blue.

We'd been introduced once before, when she'd come to drop the kids off and I'd slept over. 'Meredith, this is . . .'

Joe never did get my name out. Meredith's phone rang. She said a curt, 'I have to take this,' then strode back down the path to her car.

'She wondered if you might want to meet for a drink this Thursday,' he said.

It was early October. We had been dating almost six months, but in some ways it had felt like a lifetime.

I had to stop myself from saying, 'Er . . . why?' But perhaps my face said it anyway, because he quickly added, 'Don't worry. She doesn't bite. It's just that, you know, it might not hurt if you guys get to know each other a little . . .'

He left it hanging there. An implication of something he was perhaps hedging around articulating, which I was left to guess at.

'Okay,' I said.

I was early.

She was earlier.

She was typing on her phone, thumbs flying, head bowed in concentration. It gave me a chance to compose my features into something that resembled ease. As I approached, she looked up, like she sensed me. Neither surprise nor acknowledgement.

'Sorry.' She glanced vaguely in my direction. 'I have to take this.'

'Of course,' I said, a little stymied by the lack of eye contact.

I perched on the stool next to her, pulling it slightly out of her personal space.

Her dark blonde hair was fashioned into a well-cut bob that went askew at the back due to an annoying natural curl, much like my own. Her fingernails were short and painted red, with a dried smudge of colour on the thumb pad. And beneath the sleeve of her oyster pink silk blouse, I caught a glimpse of one of those watches that probably cost as much as my father had ever earned in a year.

Through a hearty spot of googling, I knew a lot more about Meredith than I'd ever let on to Joe. I knew she was an outstanding interlocutor who rarely lost a case, that she was passionate about family law and always fought for the underdog. That her father was Sir William Baxter, a former chief executive at the Bank of England. That she went to Marlborough College, where the Duchess of Cambridge studied, then Oxford, where she achieved a first-class degree in law. I believed, too, that she had recently become a QC – the highest achievement and accolade in the legal profession. Joe said something about it being a lifelong ambition.

I doubted she'd have afforded me the same curiosity.

'Done.' She finally clicked off. 'Oh my God, I'm in a trial right now and it's utterly consuming me. Terrible case of malicious mother syndrome. This evil little bitch is claiming her ex-husband sexually and physically abused their kids – all because he met some-one else.'

She plucked the cocktail stick from her martini glass, pulled off a fat green olive with her front teeth, then lowered her face and slurped unselfconsciously. And in two seconds flat I could already tell what would have attracted Joe. She was sexy, confident, and she didn't give a shit. Oddly enough, the opposite of me.

'Malicious mother syndrome? Is that an actual *thing*?' I asked.

'It's a *thing* . . . and more common than you'd imagine.'

'And you're convinced he didn't do it?' I wasn't sure if it was wrong for me to ask.

'One hundred per cent. The entire case is premised on two key pieces of evidence: the mother saying she was aware of the abuse, and the testimony of her friend who claims she told her about it – right before both women went off to Barcelona and the friend left her own children in his care!' She met my gaze with those serious, soulful, almost woeful eyes that were so brown they were almost black. 'You don't understand . . . this man has lost his job, his family, friends. Not to mention that he's facing game-changing legal bills. And for two years he hasn't been able to see or talk to his children.' She looked at me as though she was only just seeing me for the first time. 'Can you imagine subjecting innocent kids to intimate examinations? The humiliation they suffered at school? Forcing them to lie and choose one parent over another? Their young minds grappling with what they know versus what they're being told . . . Can you imagine doing that, as a parent, to your child – out of *revenge*?'

'No,' I said. 'How awful.' The insufficiency of my response sat there. It seemed odd she would divulge so much. Wasn't there lawyer/client confidentiality?

She fished out the remaining olives from the glass. 'Anyway, enough of this.' She flourished a hand my way. 'Lauren . . . look at you. You're young, beautiful and a doctor. My God, what are you doing with Joe?'

She said it with a certain vapid affection, neither a compliment nor a disparagement, but it still threw me. Even without really knowing exactly why their marriage broke down, I couldn't imagine she was oblivious to the fact that Joe was a catch.

It was a little icebreaker, though, so I laughed, oddly admiring her straight way of talking. 'I don't know how I'm supposed to answer that! I don't always feel young, and I'm just a very, very junior doctor for now.'

I had tried to imagine how she might see me: the younger woman he met poolside on a business trip, before he was even divorced; someone he'd introduced to his kids already. I was sure she must recognise the anomaly – Joe was spontaneous in life's little things, but not normally in the big. She might feel extremely mistrustful of me.

'By the way,' I said, to change the subject. 'Congratulations! I think Joe mentioned you recently became a QC!'

She studied me through a long-held pause. Then she said a rather blunt, 'I think you need a drink.' She raised a hand and immediately commanded the young barman's attention, which I sensed was probably a good indicator of how Meredith moved through life.

'I always enjoy watching them make cocktails, don't you . . . ?' she said, focusing on the young guy's toned torso rather than the drink. 'The almost conceited way they thrash that ice around the shaker . . .'

I was convinced she was about to poke fun at him, but she just looked back at me and asked if I wanted what she was having or something else.

For ease I said, 'What you're having sounds great.' As she ordered for us, I felt relieved just knowing that alcohol was on its way, so I told her how I'd passed this hotel a million times and never realised how beautiful it was inside.

'I know! I've been coming here for years. I used to pop in often when we lived in our first house in Brighton, many years ago, if I'd missed a train. Then after that I'd usually end up missing three of them.'

She managed a short laugh, and I noticed something unusual. She was way more attractive when straight-faced. When she smiled she showed quite a lot of upper gum and her eyes didn't smile with her, which made her look slightly ghoulish, though I felt rotten for thinking that.

'That doesn't sound like a bad way of ending a day,' I said, trying not to see a picture in my mind's eye of her and Joe excitedly putting an offer in on their very first house. The thrilling moment when they were handed the keys. Their first cosy night under its roof.

'Anyway, you were telling me about yourself,' she said. 'Joe says you like to write. You were writing some sort of story the day he met you by the pool.'

'Yes, I was,' I said, a little disappointed he'd have shared what felt like rather personal details with her – *our* moment. 'It was for a competition run by the GMC. The topic was on regrets. I didn't win, so clearly my regrets couldn't have been all that profound.' My attempted humour fell flat.

We held eyes briefly and then she said, 'Well . . . let's hope they never are.'

I rattled on about how I was from the small market town of Alnwick in Northumberland, but she already seemed to know that too, that my mother was a nurse and my dad a telecom service technician. That I was an only child, that five years ago my parents retired to an ex-pat community in southern Spain. The alcohol on a near-empty stomach must have been what made me also blurt

41

out that I'd had two serious relationships – one with a great-looking loser, and one with a decent guy who was just the wrong one for me.

'And now you're involved with a much older man, with two children.'

I was about to say I never really thought of Joe as twelve years older, maybe because he was energetic and fun, and passionate about life and his achievements – and everyone else's, for that matter. But I didn't know if that would go down well, so I settled for, 'Children can be very rewarding!'

'Mine?' She looked like she was going to cough up an olive. 'Have you ever been involved with a man with kids before, Lauren? Because that comment makes me think you haven't.'

'No,' I said. 'I've mostly dated in my own age group, and they tend not to come with ready-made families. But I love kids. What woman doesn't?'

'Plenty. Me, sometimes. Me, a lot of the time, in fact.' She wagged a cocktail stick at me. 'But I can tell you one thing. It's way easier to love your own than someone else's.'

'Well, I suppose I'll have to take your word for that!' I tried to laugh it off but there was an awkward strain in the air. 'Look, Meredith . . .' I said. 'And I hope I am not getting ahead of things here, but whatever happens with Joe, I will be going into it with my eyes fully open.'

'I'm sure you will,' she said, after a hesitation, like she wasn't sure of any such thing. I couldn't tell if she was being genuine or a little pillorying.

'What I mean is, I know things won't always . . .' I didn't know how best to put it as it felt so premature. 'I mean that anyone getting involved with someone who has children has to know that the children will always be a priority. They won't have the luxury of everything always being just about them.'

'No,' she said. 'You can say that again.'

My palms had broken a sweat. I discreetly clutched my skirt. 'What I mean is, I love Joe, so if we do end up . . . I know I can love his children, and—'

'Great sentiments.' She waved the bartender over and asked for some water.

Clearly I'd over-schmaltzed it. *Over-egged the pudding* as my mother was fond of saying.

'Anyway,' she said. 'While we seem to be going down this path, I suppose there's a few things I'd like you to know, too.'

She latched on to my eyes in that serious way of hers again, and then I knew I was about to learn the real reason why I'd been invited here.

'Joe's a good person. I care about him. He's the father of my kids. I've known him most of my adult life. But I don't want him back.' Her gaze held mine. 'We didn't work for a reason, but I bear him no ill will – or you for that matter.'

I opened my mouth to cut in, but she pressed on. 'If I'm honest, though, I'm feeling a little circumspect about all this. The fact is, I didn't exactly see Joe getting together with someone this fast. I never imagined we'd be here, in this place, for a very long time. And while I accept you're going to be in the lives of my children, I've never had to contemplate sharing them before – in any capacity, not even a purely practical one.'

I wasn't listening. I just kept thinking how odd it was that we were both talking like it was a foregone conclusion that Joe and I were going to be married – when Joe and I hadn't even had the conversation yet.

'What I'm trying to say is I hope you'll remember that the kids don't need a mother, because they have one already. And, as their mother, I will always have a voice. It might not agree with yours. But it can't ever be undermined.'

'But—'

'Look, whatever happens going forward, I know you'll always take Joe's side, Lauren, because you're young and you're in love and that's what any woman in your situation would do. But remember that if you haven't heard something straight from me, then keep in mind that there are two sides to every story. Joe is a good person and he doesn't bad-mouth people, but, well, he has his way of seeing things and I have mine.'

She stopped there, finished off the dregs of her nth martini. My eyes dashed around her face, not sure what I was thinking or feeling any longer, or what I was supposed to say.

'Anyway . . .' she said with a note of finality, 'I just hope that whatever arises, you will always come to me, talk to me. If there's a problem, let's hash it out. I say this to the people I work with, you know . . . don't let it sit there and grow into something . . . into a big *thing*.' She threw up her hands a little theatrically. 'I can promise you I am not a perfect mother – as I'm sure Joe will have already told you – but I can assure you that ultimately, nothing and no one comes before my children, and they never will.' She met my eyes again, her face a little slack from the booze. But the implicit warning sat there.

I was about to speak but she held up the palm of her hand. 'I think we've said all we need to say. But I'm glad we had the conversation.'

With that, she swiftly asked for the bill. She pulled out her credit card and I scrambled to do the same.

As we walked out, shoulder to shoulder – her so much taller than me – she turned and looked down at me. 'I just think it'll be easier for all of us if we don't start out as enemies.' Her mouth stretched into one of her slightly ghoulish smiles. And then she added, 'Or become them.'

EIGHT

The Orange Public House is packed. I spot Sophie and Charlie at the end of the bar. There's an empty seat next to them, saved for me.

There is a moment, before they notice me, when I'm flooded with a memory I'd rather forget.

The night I met up with them soon after I'd got back from Santa Monica.

Same bar. Almost same seats.

'So . . . !' Sophie gave me that suspenseful, loaded look the minute I'd sat down, before my coat was even off.

'What?'

'Come on then. Spill the beans.' She rubbed her hands together, like she was trying to start a fire. 'You've met someone!'

I'm sure that my beaming from ear to ear was all the confirmation she needed.

It was true I'd flitted through the week with nothing but Joe on my mind. I'd found myself staring into space and smiling, only paying scant attention to conversations. Little episodes of human interaction that would have annoyed me failed to penetrate my happiness. I had gone to bed thinking about him and woke up thinking about him, and I was thinking about him every minute in between. But she didn't know any of this.

I was dying to tell her. But *her* – my friend; not her husband too. Sophie and I have been close since the first year of medical school. And then, a couple of years ago, she met Charlie, who is also a junior doctor, on a work placement, and since then he always seemed to be *there,* tagging along. I have never fully understood, nor have I managed to bring myself to ask, why he doesn't have mates of his own. Or is it a sign of possessiveness? Maybe he worries we're going to sit there talking about him . . . I have nothing against him personally, but I miss the good old days when I could talk to someone who knows me well without it going through the filter of someone who doesn't.

Nevertheless, I told them about meeting Joe by the pool. Every detail, from first word to last.

When I was done, there was a moment where they both just stared at me blankly.

'What?' I said.

Sophie looked slightly bemused. 'Well, you're obviously not going to contact him, are you? I mean . . . he's married.' It wasn't really a question, more a judgement that was a little out of character for her.

'No,' I said. 'I have no intention of contacting him. But that doesn't mean I can't think about him for a while – before I let him go and never think about him again. Does it?'

They exchanged a look.

'Well,' Charlie said, 'even if he'd been divorced, no one wants to get involved with an older man with two kids. So you had a lucky escape.'

'Why do you say that?' I asked.

'Er . . .' He looked at Sophie again. 'Because that's an absolutely humungous commitment. Other people's children. You're not just a wife, you're a stepmother and we all know how the world loves a stepmother.'

I knew Charlie had a bit of an issue with commitment, having somewhat mysteriously bailed out of his wedding to Sophie just a week before the big day. I also remembered meeting his stepmother at the registry office a month or so later when he changed his mind back again.

'You loved yours,' I pointed out.

'It took years.'

'I would have years,' I said. 'Anyway, it's a non-issue, isn't it? He's gone and it's hardly likely that I'll ever see him again!'

I expected that to be it. But then Charlie said, 'But he left you his number. So he's not entirely gone if you don't want him to be . . .' Then he added, 'He wouldn't have done that if he didn't want to have an affair with you.'

'I'm inclined to agree,' Sophie said.

'How do you make that out?' I was slightly offended – how did they know what Joe did and didn't want? 'If he'd just been after sex, then why didn't he ring my room after dinner? If he was determined to pursue an affair, why didn't he ask for my number instead of just giving me his?'

'Maybe he met someone else while he was out for the night!' Charlie said.

It was flippant. Just a bit of cheap Charlie humour. Said. Done with. Forgotten.

Except that I didn't forget it.

As I approach them now, Sophie spots me and waves. With the enthusiasm of her gesture, there's an instant again where I miss the good old days of our friendship, before Charlie came along.

I remember on one of my first dates with Joe in London, asking him, 'Why did you give me your phone number in Santa Monica?' And him saying, after a lot of thought, 'I don't really know. I just

47

think that, for the time it took me to write it down, I liked to imagine that we weren't *done*.'

I had loved that answer – but hated that I'd only asked the question because my friends had put doubts in my head.

I shrug off my drenched raincoat and sit down.

'Are you always this wet or are you just happy to see us?' Charlie grins, raising his pint glass in a toast to his own wit.

'Ha ha. Very funny.' I try to position myself so I can see them both without having to turn my head back and forth. 'Oh God, it's been a nightmare of a day!'

I tell them that a middle-aged woman came in with chest pain. I was the only doctor there at the time. I suspected a clot on her lung, popped a drip in her hand and took some blood. I stepped away to give her bloods to the lab only to then hear the piercing sound of the emergency buzzer. When I returned to the ward, I found her slumped forward, pale, eyes open, unresponsive. In my sudden panic I couldn't find a pulse so I ordered the crash trolley and defibrillator. I was just about to start chest compressions when a consultant happened to be passing and intervened.

'This woman has a pulse,' he said, and then pointedly added, 'Doctor.' The patient had come to. She'd just fainted.

'My God!' Charlie slaps a hand to his forehead. 'Don't you just hate that!' He then tells me how he had a similarly humiliating experience at the hands of a 'bastard consultant'. 'Let it go,' he says. 'Don't let one prick like that shatter your confidence or your belief in yourself.'

'Thanks,' I say. 'You're right.' I'm just ordering a white wine when my phone pings. 'Ooh, it's Meredith!' I pretend to look daunted.

Grace wants to return that shirt. You could go with her tomorrow night after school.

48

Hmm . . . We don't have the kids on Thursdays. Tomorrow is also my one day off after six straight shifts. I think my way around a tactful reply. Happy to! Should we wait until next week when she's staying with us, perhaps?

She fires back, I have a function tmw night. Sitter for Toby, but thought Grace might rather be with her dad than endless hrs on her own.

Hmm . . . Not *you* and her dad. Not, do you mind if she comes over on one of your free nights? Not, do you have any other plans?

I don't, as it happens. So in the spirit of cooperation, I say: Okay, can meet at Oxford Circus after school. Will text her tmw to arrange.

She sends a thumbs up, and for some odd reason that little icon makes me pleased with myself.

When I click off, two pairs of eyes are fixed on me.

'What's Manifesto Meredith want then?' Charlie asks.

Hmm . . . This joke has got a little stale now. 'I suppose you're never going to stop calling her that, are you?' Sometimes I regret telling them all about that night when I met Meredith for a drink, shortly before Joe proposed. What is it with friends, alcohol and the urge to overshare?

'Probably not.'

I stare at his overfed, cherubic face, the cupid's bow top lip. Charlie has a certain *Downton Abbey* public schoolboy charm and a certain endearing pompousness that goes with it – at least, sometimes it's endearing. I tell them about the text.

'Isn't that a bit annoying?' Sophie says. 'Expecting you to drop everything because she's got somewhere else to be – when it's not even your night to have them?'

'Yeah, can't Grace take the shirt back herself?' Charlie chimes in. 'Why do you have to be involved?'

'Maybe Meredith thought it could be bonding for us to go together.'

Charlie sends me a raised eyebrow.

'Ah . . . I can see that, I suppose,' Sophie says. 'Nothing like a girls' expedition to Topshop to right the wrongs of the world.'

'Well, I can understand why she'd rather Grace isn't just hanging out by herself all night at home,' I say.

'She's not by herself!' Charlie says. 'She's with her brother! And the hired help!'

'She's fourteen. He's four. They've hardly got oodles in common.'

'Well, maybe her parents should have thought of that before they had them so far apart.' He says it in passing, like an aside. Then he adds, 'Why did they have them so far apart, by the way? Do you know? Toby was obviously an accident. Don't have to be a rocket scientist there.'

'Actually,' I say. 'I've never asked.' I take a sip of my wine. 'I didn't really think it was any of my business.' *So it's certainly none of yours . . .*

Sophie must sense I'm turning a little defensive because she says, 'Where's Joe tonight?'

I smile. I wonder if she ever feels eclipsed by Charlie's enormous shadow. 'At a client dinner.'

'So he *says*,' Charlie says darkly to his wife – as though I am not there.

I'm just about to take another drink but my hand goes still. 'Sorry, er . . . what's that supposed to mean?' I stare at him a little too hard.

'He's only pulling your leg,' Sophie pats my arm. And then she says, 'Char . . . lie!' The drawn-out syllables being her version of a telling-off, I assume.

To try to get past the awkwardness, I click through my camera roll and show them an adorable picture of Toby I snapped when he'd stepped out of the bath and I'd wrapped him in a fluffy pink towel.

'Cute!' Sophie's face lights up. 'Ah! He's handsome! Looks so much like his dad, doesn't he? Same chin. Same eyes.'

'Handsome?' Charlie scowls. 'Joe? Hmm . . . Maybe for a geriatric.'

Hearing that word, I think of all the other times they've brought up his age like it's a *thing*. Always conveniently getting it wrong – despite them both being highly numerate, with good enough memories to get them through medical school.

What is he? Forty-five now?

How many years between you? Fifteen, is it?

When you're a generation apart . . .

They have called him old, older, senior, silver fox (despite his hair being nowhere near silver), 'getting on', 'middle-aged', and 'almost over the hill'.

Geriatric takes the biscuit.

I should tell Charlie, 'Joe said you were "on track for a heart attack"!' I am sure that would wipe the smile off his face. But I can't bring myself to come down to his level.

So instead of dignifying it, I show them Grace's latest vlog.

'Oh. My God,' Charlie says, slapping a hand to his mouth. 'She's beautiful, self-possessed and fourteen! Fancy giving birth to that!'

One day, I've a feeling I'm going to have it out with them. There's a need in me to say, *Why are you two always so negative? Why is it that from the minute I met Joe you seemed to be unable to do anything but distrust and disparage?* But for now I tell them about the charity bag comment and the *glass yourself* dig. Predictably, they dissolve into hysterics.

'Anyway . . .' I feel bad. Joe would think I was very disloyal for getting a laugh at his kids' expense. 'She's young and she's probably still just getting used to her mum and dad not being together, without the addition of me in her life. It can't be easy,' I say.

'She's not that young, you know,' Sophie says, carefully. 'Fourteen is old enough to know you have to treat people with respect.'

'It's true,' Charlie chimes in. 'I was younger than Grace when I got that drilled into me by my stepmother.' Then he adds, 'Unless her parents never taught her the R word.'

'You're quite an expert on parenting,' I tell him. 'You know – for a childless gastroenterologist.'

Sophie chuckles but then seems to stiffen and turn a violent red. After a long pause she says, 'Well, it sounds like you're coping with everything, so that's the main thing.'

She doesn't exactly sound like she's applauding me or cheering me on. I find myself looking at her and feeling like you do when two people are at opposite ends of a divide, and at least one of them just longs to be back on the same side.

'I don't think I could do it,' she adds. 'Someone else's children . . . It's a testament to your love for him, I suppose.' For an instant she looks downhearted. She glances at Charlie and he briefly lowers his eyes and turns very still – a bit like the last person sitting on the bench who didn't get picked for the sports team. An uncomfortable silence falls over us again. I make an excuse about feeling exhausted so I don't have to stay for a second drink.

Neither of them tries to twist my arm.

When I get home, Joe is hanging up his suit jacket in the walk-in.

'I just got in a minute ago!' he says. 'Good night? You're early.'

I kick off my shoes, go and give him a kiss, then perch on the end of the bed, pulling my feet up and clutching them. 'Not particularly.' I watch as he carefully places his jacket back among the dozen or so other suits he owns – all Italian, and all in various shades of blue. And I hear an echo of Sophie's words right after she first met him: *He really cares about his appearance, doesn't he?*

He glances over his shoulder. 'Why? What happened? You seem flat.'

I stare into a blank space for a second or two. 'I don't know, really . . . Nothing exactly happened . . .' I try to think what it is. 'I suppose I don't always feel connected to Sophie like I used to, and at times it can be a bit sad.'

He stops what he's doing, tilts his head. 'Since the husband came along you feel you've lost a friend.'

I smile. Joe is impressively intuitive for a guy. 'Yeah. In some respects.' Is that how Sophie feels since I met Joe?

He resumes undressing. 'So what vacation are they not going on this time?'

This makes me chuckle. Since they've had to pay back Sophie's parents for the cost of the wedding, they've had to cancel all their holidays. 'Ha. They don't really talk about themselves very much anymore, actually.'

'So what do they talk about then?'

I can hardly say *Mostly you, and how wrong they seem to think you are for me.* 'Work. That's pretty much it.'

'That doesn't sound like fun.'

'No,' I say. 'Not fun at all. So how was your night?'

He reaches for another hanger. 'Oh, it was okay. Wasn't really into it. Sometimes those events get a bit like a frat party.' He turns and smiles. 'Drank more than I'd intended. I'd much rather have stayed home with you, to be honest.'

'I know the feeling,' I tell him, though I don't really know what a frat party is like.

I watch his thick, well-cut, attractively dishevelled hair, the slim line of his back in his crisp white dress shirt. I can still hear

53

Charlie's words that day in the bar when I first told them about him. *Of course he wanted to buy you a drink at the pool! You're young and lovely, and he was a million miles away from his wife and family!*

I remember how the whole encounter felt sullied after that – illogically so. When I later learned that Joe had actually been separated for over a year when we met – not 'still married' – I took great delight in telling them. But it didn't seem to change their minds. Their beliefs seemed cemented at that point.

I put it down to my theory that when people listen to your story, they're secretly searching for a reflection of their own experience. If they can't find it, then a part of them will be inclined to deny you yours. It's a mixed-up survival instinct.

Oh well . . .

I tell him about Grace staying over tomorrow, Meredith's text.

He looks a little puzzled at first. 'That's okay . . . I suppose. I mean . . . is it?'

'Of course,' I say.

He yawns and starts to unbutton his shirt. Watching him undress reminds me of the first time we were close, how I'd been dying to undo every single one of those buttons, and when the moment came, I'd never been so attuned to a man standing before me, to his skin as I peeled back the crisp cotton, to a heart beating beneath the palm of my hand – to my own need to have him possess me.

'What?'

'Nothing . . .' I smile a little. 'I just like watching you undress.'

His eyes slowly look me over. 'Believe me, it's mutual.'

Suddenly I don't much care that my evening was a washout. Or what other people think.

I stand, reach for the hem of my top, and whip it off over my head. 'Prove it, then.'

NINE

Grace is already there when I arrive at Oxford Circus, standing against a wall, head dipped, tinkering with her phone.

'Hiya!' I say.

She looks up like I've been there all along. 'Hi.'

'Do you want a sandwich or something before we get stuck into the shops?' I try to sound like it's a regular girls' outing and I'm on board for a barrel of laughs.

'I wouldn't mind a hot chocolate.'

I was banking on being shot down so I'm disproportionately happy about this. 'Let's cross over then,' I say. 'There's a Costa on Argyll Street.'

The queue at Costa is snaking out of the door. We tag on to the end. Grace returns to tinkering with her phone. When it's our turn I order two hot chocolates and a raspberry almond square to share.

Once we're seated, Grace shrugs off her long coat, sinks her face in the cloud of whipping cream, then comes back up and snaps selfies from various angles. I watch her zoom in, assess herself, smirk, and then post it to Snapchat. I'm about to tell her that I'm actually following her vlog, that I find her daily posts about healthy eating, fashion, streetbeats from Camden Market, the top of the Shard rather entertaining. But something about her self-absorption right now makes me reluctant to fuel it. Oh well! I decide if you can't beat them, join them, so I settle for hauling out my own phone, taking a furtive picture of Grace pouting with her 'moustache' of whipped cream, and send it to Soph. A minute or two later she texts back three laughing emojis. Having fun?

Fun might be a stretch.

LOL. This is the bonding session, right?

Yup. It's working a treat.

More laughing emojis.

After a bit, I hear Grace say, 'Erm . . . Are you done yet? Can we go?' She is staring at me like a teacher who has just cottoned on to the fact that I'm not paying attention in class.

We leave, cross back over the road again and enter the shop. 'Do you want to look around a bit first?' I ask.

'Not really. Can we just do the return?'

We join the long line. Finally Grace slides the shirt across the counter and gets thirty pounds. 'There's your money.'

I stare at the notes. 'I don't want it back. Why don't you pick something else with it?'

I'm waiting for her to say, *But that means I'll have to hang out you with even longer!* But instead she says, 'Cool.'

I conclude that it couldn't possibly be anything other than sarcasm, but we wander off and peruse the racks. 'What do you think of this?' I ask, holding up a cute little white blouse. But when I glance over my shoulder I'm talking to thin air. She's gone.

They are playing '80s music. I hum along and wander around for a bit, but then start to feel hot, and parched from that hot chocolate. I text her, Where R U?

Just when my patience is starting to run out, I hear, 'I'm going to try all this lot on.' She is right behind me. I do a quick scan of the mountain of clothing in her arms – at this rate we'll be here until next Christmas. Among the pile of dark stuff I spot a unique-looking electric green waistcoat with black polka dots.

'That's quite a haul,' I say. 'You'll be bankrupt by the time you pay for all that!'

'Who says I'm paying for it?' she asks with a certain disdain.

That's true. I suppose that's what Joe is there for. It makes me think of my old Saturday job at the library when I was her age, and how I'd have to save for a month to afford a new pair of jeans. 'Want me to come with you for a second opinion?'

I don't get an answer but decide to follow anyway. She disappears inside the changing room. The music is grating now, and I am mega thirsty. I am starting to feel utterly drained when Joe's text pops up.

Where are you? Still shopping?

Yup!

Hope she's being nice?

Nope! She's being a self-absorbed little madam. Of course! Having a fun time!

I saved you some dinner.

Thank you. Looking forward to coming home.

He sends a red heart.

Eventually, Grace emerges and I watch her hand back a few things to the attendant. I can't see the green waistcoat, though. Perhaps she left it behind in the changing room.

'You're buying all that?' I say, as she walks over to me with her arms full.

'Nope. None of it.'

'Oh . . . So why didn't you give it back to the assistant then?'

'Because back then I was still deciding.'

She walks off ahead. I watch her go over to where the mirrors are, and then she dumps the lot on the floor. 'Okay, then. Let's go.'

I feel like I should say something but right now I can't be bothered. Outside, I'm so relieved to breathe fresh air. 'Your dad's saved us some dinner,' I say, partly wishing we didn't have to suffer through a long Tube ride home.

She gives me her best withering look. 'Don't get me wrong, this has been a blast. But I'm off to meet some friends now.'

'Oh,' I say. 'Does your dad know about this?' I'm not sure if she should be wandering around town on her own.

'Does he have to?' she says. 'I'm fourteen, not four.'

Before I can respond she sings, 'Bye!' in her famous *Fuck off and drown in a ditch* tone. I watch her stride off towards Tottenham Court Road. Some young lads turn and check her out as she passes.

'It's 8 p.m. and a school night!' Joe says when I get back home. 'You shouldn't have let her just go off like that!'

I must look a little stunned. Joe has never really been short with me before. I feel like saying, *How, exactly, was I supposed to stop her? Put her in a headlock?* Instead I say, 'She seemed to think she's allowed. So how was I to know any different?'

He scowls. 'Allowed? By whom?' Then he adds, 'Has she even done her homework? I mean, do you even know?'

I know he's had a bad day. A deal he's been working on for months was threatening to go sideways. He slept very little last night and was virtually monosyllabic over breakfast. But I don't appreciate his tone. I bend over to scratch Mozart behind his ears.

'Lauren,' he says. When I look up, he is standing there gazing at me. 'I just asked you a question.'

'I have no idea,' I say. I straighten up and meet his eyes. 'I was at work all day . . .' *In case you hadn't noticed.* 'Anyway, wouldn't

58

it have been her mother's responsibility to ensure she'd done her homework before she met me?'

He seems momentarily lost for words, then says, 'Whoever's responsibility it is . . . she can't just do whatever she damned wants. Not on a school night . . . You can't just let her get her way all the time.'

Oh . . . I feel like saying. *You mean like you do?*

'I'm going to get changed,' I say.

As I walk to our bedroom, I'm completely mystified by his attitude. I can hear him muttering away under his breath. And then moments later, 'Jesus Christ, Grace. You're not responding to my damned texts. Call me back.'

I shut the door.

A few minutes later, as I'm getting into my tracksuit bottoms and T-shirt, I hear a tap.

'Sorry,' he says, popping his head around the door and giving me an apologetic raise of his brows. 'I didn't mean to snap at you. I haven't had the best day.'

'It's okay,' I tell him.

'It's actually not okay. Not at all fair for me to take it out on you.'

We hold eyes. I am not going to correct him on that.

'All I meant was, Grace can be a bit of a law unto herself, in case you hadn't noticed. So sometimes . . . well, it's perfectly okay for you to stand up to her.'

'All right,' I say, pleased, at least, that he's just given me this green light. 'I'll be sure to keep that in mind in the future.'

TEN

My new yoga class is hard work, but I need it. Especially after my weekly one-hour Facetime with my parents in Spain, where all we talked about was Brexit. I reach forward, wrapping my hands around the soles of my feet, rest my cheek on my knees and try to breathe out from my stomach. The fan spins rapidly on the ceiling, cooling the hair on the back of my neck.

'Great class!' the woman next to me says, and I watch her as she deftly rolls up her yoga mat.

I reluctantly unfurl from my lovely position. 'I definitely feel so much better than when I came in!'

'Have you been coming here long? I haven't seen you before, I don't think.'

'No,' I tell her, admiring her perfectly honed figure in pink-and-purple Sweaty Betty leggings. She's around Joe's age, I'd say, with expertly highlighted red hair in a high pony tail, and the sort of dewy complexion that has less to do with a yoga session and more to do with the sort of make-up that should have its own repayment plan. 'It's actually my first time. I only moved to the area fairly recently. But I intend to come more regularly, if my shifts allow.'

She smiles. 'What do you do?'

'I work in a hospital.'

'Oh! I truly admire nurses. Wouldn't want to be one, but you guys do a great job . . .' She holds out a hand. 'I'm Lucy. I've been coming here a couple of years now. My sanity saver.' We shake. She glances at our instructor, who is demonstrating an exercise to an older lady, correcting her form. 'You should look out for Elena. She's fantastic. I take all her classes if I can. I practically stalk her.' She chuckles.

I tell her my name, thank her for the tip, and say that I'm sure I'll see her again some time.

Outside, I feel a refreshment is in order, so I start off in the direction of the high street, relishing the rare treat of no work and the rest of the afternoon ahead of me to fill as I see fit. I'm just walking into the coffee shop when my phone rings.

Joe.

'Hey, Lauren . . . What are you doing right this second?'

I can tell he's not after idle chit chat. 'Not much,' I say. 'I just finished a yoga class and am about to get a coffee.'

'Sounds . . . wonderful.'

'What's wrong?' I ask, detecting something in his tone.

'Oh . . . Nothing. Just in a bit of a bind. Been roped into a meeting across town so I can't collect Toby from school. Shooting over there now. Traffic's insane.'

'Oh,' I say. 'That's fine. I'll go and get him!'

We live in Hampstead Heath. Meredith lives in Primrose Hill. Toby goes to school in Chalk Farm – close enough, almost equidistant. It's a pleasant enough walk on a nice day, or a shortish bus or car ride. Either way, I want to help.

'I hate asking . . .' He sounds like he truly does. 'You were enjoying your day off.'

'You're not asking. I'm volunteering . . . I'll pick him up and maybe take him to the park for a bit.'

'Are you sure?' he says, sounding uncomfortable.

'Positive!'

'It's very kind of you. You're amazing.'

'This is true.'

He laughs.

I hear traffic, the blast of his horn, him swear under his breath. I look at my watch. Clearly I won't have time for that coffee. 'I'd better get going,' I tell him. 'I'll pop back home quickly and let Mozart out for a pee.'

'Thank you. You're a life-saver.' Then he adds, 'Oh, if you're taking Toby to the park, don't forget his trainers.'

'I won't,' I say.

'Where's Daddy?' Toby asks, when he comes bulleting out of his classroom door and sees me. There is a second where his face falls and I try not to feel disappointed by his disappointment.

'Daddy can't make it so he sent me – if you'll do me the honour of letting me escort you home.'

I hold out my hand but he clasps his behind his back.

'I thought Daddy was coming!'

'I thought we could go to the park. Maybe get an ice cream after!'

His eyes widen and I sense the possibility of a meltdown subsiding. 'Can we? The one with the swings? Not the one with the birds and the ducks! And can I have chocolate ice cream once we're done?'

'Of course. Would you like a little snack now? Are you hungry? I brought you something.' When I'd popped back home to let the dog out, I cut up some grapes and grabbed a banana. But, in my hurry, I now realise I completely forgot his trainers.

'I can wait. We can eat after we play. If that's okay. Then I'll be hungry because I'll have worked up an appetite. Mummy says I'm always hungry because I burn a lot of nenergy.' We start walking and he reaches up, and his warm little hand finds mine.

'It's good to burn nenergy,' I tell him, and give his hand a little squeeze.

There's no one in the park. Toby dashes straight to the swings. 'Will you push me higher and higher and higher so I go over the bars?'

'Hmm . . .' I hurry after him. 'That's not a very good idea.'

He climbs on to a seat. I stand behind him, and give him a gentle push. His legs flail out, his feet moving like he's pedalling a bicycle.

'I want to go over and over and have the ground be upside down like I'm flying.'

'That would be impossible, Toby. Swings aren't designed that way.'

'Why not?'

'It's just . . . It's part of the design mechanism.'

'What's a designmcinizm?'

I smile. 'It's just the way things are meant to be built. You can't go over the bars because then the park wouldn't be safe. Children would hurt themselves.'

'Byron hates swings because he fell and cracked his head.'

'Who's Byron?' I ask. Joe tells me that Toby has a lot of friends but a great many of them are imaginary.

'Byron is my friend. Byron has an egg on his head.'

'An egg?'

'Because he fell off the swings!'

'Ah! A bump the size of an egg.'

'Mummy says it's an egg.'

'Well, whatever it is, I hope he heals soon.'

'If I jumped from all the way up here would I get an egg on my head like Byron?'

A shiver trickles down my spine at the thought of him jumping. Or falling. Or hurting himself in any way. 'Yes. And it would be very painful. So that's why you're not going to jump.'

'But what if I WANT to? To see if I can fly?'

'Can we not talk about jumping, please, Toby? Can we talk about something else?'

'What else?' The swing returns to my hands, and he lies back, almost horizontal, looking up at the sky. 'Would I tip upside down when I went over the bars, do you think?'

'I have no idea, Toby.' This conversation is wearing thin.

'I don't really want to go on the slide because it's so small. Not like the one at the waterpark that Daddy takes me to.'

'Did your mummy go with you to the waterpark too?' I ask.

'No,' he says. 'She never comes. Because, you see, Daddy can take me all by himself, so that's why she doesn't need to come.' There's a lull, then he says, 'Will you come next time we go?'

'I'd like that!' I say. 'I also think we should go now. It's getting really cold and damp.'

'What does damp mean?'

'Damp is when it's not raining, but it's not sunny either. You're not warm, but you're not wet. But the air feels heavy, like you're extra aware of it. Like it can get through your clothing and go straight to your bones.'

'I'm not cold! And I'm not damp.'

'Good for you, Toby.'

'It's cold where Daddy lives in Chicago. It's really cold there.'

'Have you been to Chicago, Toby?'

'When I was very small. But I don't remember. But I remember it was very cold there.'

'Well, maybe you have to go in the summer when it's nice and warm.'

'Mummy hates going to Chicago. But Daddy had a girlfriend and that's why Mummy left him so Mummy won't go to Chicago anymore.'

The blood freezes in my veins. The swing returns to me but my arms can't push. I can't move. 'Who told you that Daddy had a girlfriend, Toby?'

'Grace told me,' he says.

I watch his little body move away from me, and then towards me again. The swing, without me pushing it, gradually slows.

'I really think we should go home now, Toby.' I am suddenly – horribly – cold.

He rattles on but I'm no longer hearing him. Every distrusting thing Sophie and Charlie have said about Joe is rushing back. Is there something I have failed to see? 'Your daddy just texted,' I lie. 'He wants us to go home now. He's missing you.'

'Okay,' he says, disappointed.

When it's safe for him to jump off, I steady the swing, and he does a pretend leap through the air.

'One quick go on the slide!' he says, running towards it.

'No,' I call out. But it's too late. Before I can muster up another word, Toby has run around to the base of the slide. He stuffs his hands in his pockets and says, 'Look, I can walk up it with no hands!'

As he begins to walk up the slide, I know what's going to happen about a split second before it does.

His shoes slip and Toby pitches forward.

There is a moment of silence after his face makes contact with the metal. And then he screams.

65

When we walk in the door I can hear Joe on the phone. The moment he sees us, he lowers his voice, turns his back and walks out of range.

Grace is sitting cross-legged on the sofa and looks up from her phone. 'Ugh,' she says to Toby. 'That looks nasty.'

Toby's nose is red and there's a crust of dried blood around his nostrils. I did my best to stave off the swelling by applying a bag of frozen peas. He seems to be taking the whole thing in his stride though.

'Hey, little bud,' Joe falls to his knees to inspect his son's face, at the same time handing me his phone. 'It's Meredith. She wants to speak to you.'

As I take it from him, dread scurries up my spine.

'Why would you let him walk up a slide with his hands in his pockets?' she says. Her voice is eerily quiet and calm.

Her apparent bewilderment throws me. 'Er, I . . . I'm sorry, I—'

'What was he wearing anyway? Did he have his trainers on?'

My face blazes with a hot, potent embarrassment. 'Erm . . . No. No, he didn't . . . Actually, unfortunately . . . I forgot them.'

I glance at Joe but he redirects his gaze to the floor. In the background I can hear Toby excitedly telling Grace how we went to the shop and bought a bag of frozen peas, 'Because Lauren said it'll stop it being swelled, but they made my hands cold!'

Meredith says, 'You can't take a kid to a park in his school shoes, Lauren. And you can't take your eyes off him while he's there.'

'But I didn't take my eyes off him!' I blurt out.

Her tone is measured again. 'Well – clearly – you did.'

A hollow, suspenseful silence follows. Like that of a crowd at a beheading, before the guillotine comes down.

'Meredith.' I clear my throat. 'I really am sorry . . .' She's got a right to be annoyed. I can't believe I forgot the damned trainers. 'I promise next time I'll try to be more alert . . .'

I think I hear her snigger. 'Look . . . I'm not really interested in next times. You should have taken him to A&E. He needs to be assessed by a doctor.'

This takes me aback. *Er! What?* The insult stings. I say, quite firmly, 'Meredith . . . he didn't need a hospital. I assessed him myself and—'

'What about an X-ray? What if his nose is broken? He could have lost a front tooth. You do know that if they lose one at this age they won't get their adult teeth for two or three years? You know that? Right?'

The blood whips up in my veins. 'But he didn't lose a tooth.' I try to mimic her earlier composure and not show I'm rattled. 'There's a bit of swelling, but even if he went to hospital they wouldn't know anything until some of the—'

'I'd rather a doctor make that call, if you don't mind. At a hospital.'

I glance at Joe, who is still staring impassively at the floor, then at Toby, who is watching me with a face full of curiosity.

'Would you like to speak to Toby?' I say. 'He's right here.'

'Put Joe back on,' she says sharply.

I hand the phone back to Joe. Grace and I meet eyes but she swiftly glances away. But not before I catch a hint of mischief in her expression. Of course! I bet she rang her mother the second I rang Joe and told him.

Joe strides off to the other end of the room again.

I stand there feeling a bit like the elephant in it.

'Look . . .' I hear him say plaintively. 'He doesn't need to go to hospital. I checked him out. He's perfectly fine . . .'

I stare at his back, annoyance pulsing in my veins.

'Yes, yes, I know . . . You're right. It could have been a lot worse. But it wasn't. Like I said . . . it bled a little and it's tender, but he's going to be okay.'

Toby chimes in, 'Tell Mummy about me and the peas!'

I reach a hand and touch the top of his head, my eyes still locked on Joe's back.

'Meredith. Look . . . Believe me, I know what a broken nose looks like . . . !' He sighs. 'Like I just said . . . he doesn't need an X-ray. I'll decide tomorrow. If I think he needs one, I'll take him in then.'

He seems to have no idea how he's just undermined me.

Suddenly, he turns and looks at me, a long-suffering expression in his eyes – as though his medical knowledge gets called upon on an all-too-regular basis and it can be tiring.

Right. Clearly I'm not needed. I turn and walk out of the room.

Hours later, we have come to bed.

'I'm sorry I forgot his trainers,' I say. It occurred to me a little earlier that while I've been silently fuming the entire evening, I seem to have forgotten that Toby was the one who got hurt. My thoughts should only be of him, and of how guilty I feel, not how pissed off I am at Joe, or my wounded pride. Nonetheless, I can't resist exhuming this.

I watch him close his laptop, reach over and place it on the night table.

'It's fine,' he says, without exactly looking at me. 'You can't be expected to remember everything.'

I wait for more. But nothing comes.

'You know . . . if I'd thought he needed to go to hospital I'd have taken him,' I say, quietly but not without edge.

He glances at me, almost a little defensively. 'I know.' And then he says a firm, 'I know that. Are you upset?'

When it comes down to it, I'm not sure I feel like clashing with him over it. 'No,' I say, after a small time out. 'I'm not upset.'

'That's good, then . . .' He leans over and pops a conciliatory kiss on my cheek.

Daddy had a girlfriend and that's why Mummy left him. I hear Toby's voice, right as I feel the warm press of Joe's lips on my skin.

My blood runs cold.

ELEVEN

My shift at work starts off uneventfully. I'm able to catch up on some paperwork, even have a bit of fun with some of the nurses. But in the afternoon we're swamped. Among other cases, I see a ninety-year-old with a fractured radius, a woman who suffered a violent reaction to an over-the-counter hair colour, and an extremely agitated twenty-one-year-old who is convinced that a weekend bender has given her cirrhosis of the liver. She holds up her orange palms and bursts into a trembling fit of tears, barely able to get her words out. Once we establish that she received a Vitamix for her birthday and the orange palms are actually due to the increased levels of beta-carotene in her bloodstream from all the carrot juice she's consumed, she leaps off the bed and hugs me. I lie and tell her no, she's not an idiot, loads of people jump to that same conclusion, and I make her promise me that if she suddenly goes on a beetroot-eating craze she won't worry herself incoherent thinking she's got bladder cancer. She laughs, then hurries to ring her boyfriend to break the good news that she's not dying.

After my shift, Joe meets me at Victoria, as he was in the area for work this afternoon. I walk across the concourse to find him standing near the Caffè Nero, head down, absorbed by his phone. Blue suit, as usual. Crisp white dress shirt. He once told me that in his field people rarely wear suits anymore. But he respects the act of doing business, the interaction, the time. If he's coming to meet you, he wants you to know he didn't just come from a knockaround in the park.

He looks so utterly handsome and I get a strangely sinking feeling that there might be something in his past behaviour that he should have told me about.

As I'm watching him, trying to picture him being a cheater, he looks up, his very serious expression suddenly transformed by a smile. 'Well hello,' he says, in that winning way of his, and when I approach he kisses me with a certain zealous appreciation on the mouth.

We go to an eatery at the back of the station, one that's known for its great cocktails. As Joe orders us some appetizers and drinks, the young waitress flirts with him, virtually ignoring me. I watch the easy way he handles the attention, with a certain 'conscious immunity'. For some reason I remember a remark Sophie made ages ago, when I confided that Joe hadn't really divulged much about why he and Meredith divorced. *He's attractive, successful and charismatic. I'd not rule out the possibility of him being a player.*

Our concoction of gin, St Germain and green chartreuse arrives. As I sip I think, *Okay, Joe is not cavalier with people's feelings, and has never been disloyal to Meredith in his words. If he really did cheat he must have had a very good reason.*

We pick at the appetizers and talk about our respective days. Joe is always fascinated by my job and I'm as intrigued by his work because it's so different from my own. Sadly, though, our pizza comes out a little too crispy and burnt at the edges, the tomato sauce scant and dry. I tell him we should send it back, but he just says, 'It's fine. We can always just order something else.' When the waitress comes over to ask if everything's okay, the thought of paying sixteen quid for something inedible really bothers me, so I tell

71

her it's dried out and we can't eat it. Joe brushes off my complaint with an embarrassed apology that leaves me looking like I've made a fuss about nothing.

'Why did you do that?' I ask him, when she's taken the burnt offering away.

He shoots me a glance, seems slightly put out by my question. 'It's not her fault, is it? I just hate sending things back . . . making a fuss about *food*.' He frowns. 'No one wants to be that guy!'

Hmm . . . I do recall him once having no problem telling a male Starbucks barista that his coffee was cold.

I try to push this unpleasant cocktail of thoughts to the back of my mind. But when we've moved on to sharing a perfectly cooked order of truffle mac and cheese, I find myself saying, 'Why did you and Meredith divorce?'

His forkful of food freezes on its way to his mouth. 'Why would you ask that?' he says, after a study of me. 'I mean, you know why. I told you.'

I stare at the chunk of pancetta in the cheese sauce. 'She was never there. You were just occupying the same space. You were like strangers.' I repeat the words exactly as he'd said them when we were first dating. I remember at the time thinking, *Joe seems to want to know everything about me – to deep-sea dive for my darkest secrets – and yet he gives away very little in return. In fact, he might well be the most secretive – or should I say guarded – man I've ever met.*

'Yes,' he says, taking a drink of water. 'For the most part. That's right.'

In the back of my mind I think about secrets and our entitlement to know them. If Joe has cheated, do I, as his new wife, really have a right to know the ins and outs of that situation? What purpose does it serve? Is he not allowed to keep his past exactly where some would say it belongs?

'You had an affair,' I say. Somehow I can't resist it.

He looks me over like he's seeing an alien. 'An affair? What? No. Why would you say that?'

There's an instant where I find myself trying to determine whether the slight outrage of his reaction means I should assume it's genuine.

I can hardly say *Toby said you did.* So I say, 'I don't know. Just that . . . isn't infidelity one of the main reasons why marriages break up?'

He shrugs. 'Maybe. Probably. But they break up for lots of other reasons too.'

'Do they?' I recognise a hint of devil's advocate in my tone. 'Like what, for example?'

His jaw drops a little. 'Well . . . I don't know off the top of my head! Why don't you google it if you're so curious?'

'It was just a question.' I try to shrug it off, like he's doing. 'You've just never really talked much about it, that's all.'

He shakes his head, and I can tell he's a little exasperated. 'It's because I never really thought there was anything *to* talk about.' Then he adds, 'But I'm sorry you came to the conclusion that I must have cheated.' He puts his fork down. 'Pretty disappointed, actually.'

Something between us is changed. A wall has gone up around him and now he seems to be dwelling silently – petulantly – on the other side. I find myself overly scrutinising his words, combing back over his reaction, only to conclude that he really does seem offended, like I've hurt him.

Either that, or he's a very good actor.

'Sorry,' I say. 'I didn't really mean to imply—' On some level it is a bit unlikely. If Joe had cheated, why would he and Meredith have managed to stay friends? She hardly comes across as the forgiving type.

'It's fine,' he says. But he won't look at me again.

We eat in silence now. His eyes cast around the room. The moment our plates are empty and the waitress is in earshot, he flags her down and asks for the bill.

∞

We Uber home, not in silence, but without any of our usual post-night-out rapport. He reads on his phone and I stare at the space between our legs. We're not making physical contact; not a single part of us is touching. And I can't help but be reminded of Uber rides in the past, when we were first dating, where I would find myself enjoying the sight of our hands locked together, the feeling of Joe's fingers entwined through mine. That giddy sense of us being an indivisible unit.

Given the evening has somehow flatlined, I decide to go straight to bed. But as I'm walking towards the bedroom he says, 'Feel like a brandy?'

'Sure,' I say, grateful for this small concession. 'Might as well.'

After I wash off my make-up and slip into my nightgown, I walk back out of the bathroom and see the brandy is sitting on my night table. His, on the other side.

I get into bed and pull my Kindle from the drawer while he takes one of his lengthy showers. I listen to the water running, contemplating the concept of what it means to truly know another person – and whether you ever can. Or whether we all go through life just giving – even to the people who are closest to us – only that which we allow them to know.

'Reading?' He jumps in beside me a while later, buoyant again. 'Maybe for a bit.'

He doesn't say anything, just watches me, expectantly, and I think he's going to initiate something – to cement the fact that we are okay in the wake of that rather strange conversation. But then he pulls out his phone.

'Oh, look at this,' he says, after a moment.

He turns the screen around and presses 'play'.

It's some sort of karaoke of Queen's 'Fat Bottomed Girls'. It takes me a moment to realise, actually, it's not a karaoke; it's Grace and her friend putting on a performance. They're rocking out, front of frame, with guitars – belting out their patchy grasp of the lyrics then folding in fits of laughter. The friend is dressed in a skinny white tank top, has her hair greased back and a thick black moustache under her nose. And Grace is sporting a giant shock of long, dark, poodle-like curls. Brian May!

'Oh to be a teenager again.' He chuckles.

'Indeed,' I say.

But all I can focus on is Grace – in the electric green waistcoat from Topshop.

TWELVE

I mull over my options for a few days. If I tell Joe, then I'm ratting her out – and I don't even know for certain that she didn't go back and buy it. But nor can I let my eagerness to think the best of her cause me to doubt what I'm pretty certain I know.

Finally, on Saturday night, while Joe is out walking Mozart on the Heath with Toby, I pop my head around her bedroom door. 'Hiya, Grace. Is it okay if we have a little chat?'

She is sitting on her bed, long bare legs drawn up like a tent. She's wearing another of her oversized T-shirts that scarcely covers her bottom, and no knickers. She looks up from her phone. 'What about?' she asks.

I venture inside, despite not being given an actual invitation, and perch on the end of her bed.

'The fact that I think you may have taken a green waistcoat from Topshop without paying for it,' I say, as unthreateningly as I can.

There is a moment where her jaw drops, the pretty little pink bud of a bottom lip falling away from the top. And then she says, 'What?' But her face turns beetroot red.

'I saw you go into the changing room with it, and you left without it. And then I saw you wearing it when you were doing your Brian May act the other night – which was very good, by the way.'

I am fully expecting her to deny it, but after a spell of staring at me like I just landed from Mars, she says a flippant, 'So?'

I'm thrown a little off course by her admission and sense she knows this. I don't want to turn this adversarial by asking her why she stole the thing when she's more than capable of affording it. So instead I say, 'How did you do it? I mean, everything has electronic tags these days. I don't get how you could pull that off.'

She seems to measure me for a long moment. I'm pretty sure she's going to back-pedal or shut the conversation down but instead, a glint of mischief – almost triumph – appears in her honey-brown eyes. 'Actually, you'd be surprised. Not everything is theft-proof these days. If you scrutinise the rails hard enough, you'll find loads of stuff that's not been retagged after returns. But if you do encounter one of those nasty little fuckers . . . there's always this.'

She springs off the bed almost coltishly, and something about the action reminds me that despite her ability to come across as a little too grown-up and smart-alecky at times, she really is just a kid.

I watch her root around in her bag that's hanging on a small wicker rocking chair that's laden with a pile of discarded clothes that could rival Mount Everest.

'*Voila!*' She presents me with a clunky plastic contraption.

'What is it?' I ask.

'What does it look like?'

I take it from her, inspect it. 'I think if I knew that, I'd not be asking.'

She snatches it off me. 'It's a magnet, duh! No pesky little security tag will ever escape this puppy.'

'Hang on . . . you have an actual device to help you shoplift? This wasn't a one-off. You've taken other things?'

She gives me the *Puleese!* face again, her forehead rippling with a host of cute little wrinkles like a Shar-Pei. Then she leaps back on to her bed and crosses her legs.

'How long has it been going on?' I can't work out why she's being so open about it.

'Er . . . let me think now . . .' She gazes at the ceiling, eyes ablaze with roguery again. 'Since I was nine.'

'Nine.' *What was so special about nine?*

'Just little things at first, like bubblegum or a hairbrush, or I'd swipe some make-up or a necklace or something. You know . . . from *Primark*, not Tiffany's.' Her tone says, clearly, if it's Primark and not Tiffany, that makes it okay.

I try not to overly react – in case this is all just a game to get a rise out of me. 'So when did it become clothes?'

'Erm . . . Around the same time it became bags and shoes.'

I must look entirely gobsmacked. 'This is a joke, right? You haven't really stolen bags and shoes.'

She wags an index finger at her wardrobe. 'If you look in there, about forty per cent of everything you see is lifted. And I've got an even bigger stash at Mum's.'

I did think she had a lot of *stuff*. I put that down to her having parents who spoil her outlandishly.

'What makes you think you can do that and get away with it?' I ask. 'What gives you the right to take things that other people have to pay for?'

She hugs her knees with her arms, rests her chin on them. 'Because unlike other people, I'm a brand ambassador, aren't I?'

'A what?'

'My vlog! People see me in that cool green waistcoat or those Bally ankle boots, and they run out and buy the exact same thing. Because I gave it *eminence*.'

I almost cough up my spleen. I wait for her to say *I'm just pulling your leg! None of this is true!* But nothing about her delivery says she's anything other than serious. 'Grace . . .' I say, 'I hate to enlighten you . . . Taking stuff without paying for it doesn't make you a brand ambassador. It makes you a kleptomaniac.'

Suddenly the bravado falls away and she looks at me like I've mortally offended her. 'Tell me, Lauren,' she says, and I realise she's never actually called me by my name before. I've never made it past pronoun status. 'Do you think for one minute that any member of the royal family pays for the stuff they wear? Everything on their back is an advert for something or someone. British designers no one's heard of have had their entire careers made because Kate happens to wear their raincoat or their walking boots, otherwise they'd still be nobodies! Do you think they make *her* go and buy a pair?'

'No,' I say. 'But she didn't nick them either!' This is insane. 'Kate is a brand ambassador because she's a member of the royal family. You are not Kate.'

She tuts. 'Yes, I know that. And I wouldn't want to be! She's old and not even remotely relevant to my generation.'

'But *you* are relevant to your generation?'

'Of course.' She has absolutely no idea I'm ribbing her.

I let out a disbelieving gasp.

'So what are you going to do with all this new knowledge you have about me?' she asks, and something in the air changes. I feel we are getting down to what lies behind this conversation. 'Run and tell Daddy, I'm guessing.' For an instant she looks a little vulnerable.

'Do you want me to?' I ask.

She studies me, then drops her gaze.

'No,' I say, though I didn't actually know this was my decision until right this second. 'Not this time I'm not.'

She assesses me again, eyes loaded with suspicion. 'Why not?'

It suddenly dawns on me what might lie at the root of her behaviour. 'Because I think deep down you know stealing isn't the way to get attention, and that it's wrong, and that if you get caught, you'll have more attention than you're looking for – you'll have a criminal record as well.' I try not to say it judgementally. 'I doubt your fans would see you having much *eminence* when it comes out that you're a common thief.'

She drops her gaze again, blushes, stares unblinking at her kneecaps.

'Believe me, Grace, I know you've been through a lot recently,' I say carefully, after a close study of her, of how still she has become. 'You were an only child for a very long time . . .'

It suddenly comes to me. Of course. Nine. Around the time her mother would have fallen pregnant with Toby.

'Out of the blue you acquire a baby brother. Then your mum and dad split up. Your dad is now with me. You've got two homes. Two sets of everything. Schedules and school work . . .'

She looks up, and I feel the heat of her curiosity. This is a new me she's seeing.

'I know you have good friends. But . . . well, I only know from my own experience, there are things you can talk to your friends about and things you can't. Some things, unless people have been through them, they're never going to understand. So sometimes we end up bottling them up and carrying them around, and that's not always healthy.'

By the slight parting of her lips I think she's going to roll her eyes or say something sarcastic, but it never comes. We just look at each other, held captive in a surprising moment of truth.

'If you ever wanted to talk – about anything . . . I know some-one . . . a colleague who—'

'Oh my God.' Something in her expression seems to calcify. 'You want me to see a quack!'

'He's not a quack.'

'What is he then? A doctor who specialises in children's problems? Mental health problems?' She contracts into a ball, pulling back towards her pillow. 'I'm not crackers! I'm just . . .' Another jolt of movement; she jumps off the bed. 'Done with this weird conversation!'

I open my mouth, but she marches to the door, yanks it open. 'And by the way, can you please stop looking up my clothing? Anyone would think it's *you* who needs to go and see the quack.'

I play this back. 'What did you just say?' My cheeks burn with embarrassment.

She stands there, not looking at me, just holding her door open. 'You're a weirdo!'

The blood pounds in my face. 'Grace . . .' I suddenly feel confused, and hurt and insulted. I get to my feet. 'I'm not deliberately looking up your clothes. But as you go around the flat with no knickers on half the time, it's hard not to notice.'

We meet eyes. Her face blazes red. 'So you're the underwear police now? As well as everything else?'

'No,' I say, hating that I've been wrong-footed. 'I'm not the underwear police . . . But I don't see anything wrong in wearing knickers – especially outside of your bedroom.'

'Oh my God.' She almost laughs. 'Did you really just say that? No wonder Mummy said she can't tell by looking at you whether you're twenty-five or forty-five! You're from the Jane Austen era! Even Caroline Bingley was more exciting than you!'

It's a double punch. I'm not sure which hurts more. Did Meredith really say that about me? Is that how I come across? I know people have often told me I'm an old soul, but do I look like one too?

She is still staring daggers at me. But beneath the false front I can tell she's way more wounded than she's letting on. 'Can you, like, go now?'

I don't want to go. I want to take it all back, say it differently, or not say it at all.

'Get out of my room,' she says, still hanging on to the door.

'I'm sorry,' I say. 'Grace . . .'

'Just fucking go.'

As I pass her, she sharply turns her face away from me.

I keep my eyes down until I am out of her room, down the hall, and can bring myself to let out an excruciating breath.

THIRTEEN

The class is full by the time I arrive. I search for a place to set down my yoga mat and then see a hand waving at me. Lucy's. She pats the floor beside her.

'Thank you,' I whisper, as I carefully roll out my mat and try to slide, unnoticed, into my first downward dog. We go through the flow for forty-five minutes, occasionally sending each other smiles. I try to focus on the choreography of movement, on the therapeutic power of my breath, but I can't shake Grace and the ugly turn of our conversation from my mind. When Elena says, 'Namaste' and I'm finally lying on my back, staring up at the ceiling, I turn to catch Lucy studying me.

'We should go for coffee sometime,' she says.

'That sounds really nice!'

'Can't today though. Got a couple of appointments in Mayfair. But next week perhaps? If you turn up.'

I smile. 'I know. I haven't been the best at getting into a routine. I do shift work and there are times when no matter how much I know I should, I just can't drag myself off the sofa.'

She looks me over analytically. 'I believe it. Nursing's got to be hard work.'

We roll up our mats. 'Actually . . . I'm a doctor.'

I glance at her in time to see her face flood with colour. 'Oh. I . . .' There's a second where she laughs to hide her discomfort. 'I'm so sorry, I have absolutely no idea why I assumed . . .'

'It's fine!' I laugh a little too. 'I just thought maybe I should set you straight.' Then I tell her how I went through med school letting another student call me Laura for four years because it always felt like it had gone on too long to correct her.

'That's funny,' she says. 'It's a shame I haven't time today for that coffee . . .'

'Well, I'm going to make an effort to be here next week,' I tell her. 'I feel like a new person right now.'

'Me too! When I became single again, I had so many hang-ups about being back out in the world – you know – as a newly dating woman, walking a path I never thought I'd go down again in my life . . .' She looks wistful for a spell. 'Yoga saved my sanity.' She glances at her watch. 'Going to have to flee. I have to rush home and dress . . . See you next week?'

I smile. 'Stay sane.'

She chuckles and runs.

I go back to the flat, picking up a ready-made sandwich and a juice from a cute little cafe on the high street. Mozart is full of excitement when I walk in, so I pop on his lead and take him for a pee break, returning to have a quick shower and put on fresh clothes. I have a meeting with my clinical supervisor at 3 p.m., so I head over to the hospital early, which gives me the chance to have a coffee with a couple of the other house officers I get along well with. After my meeting I walk back to the train and am just crossing the concourse at Victoria station when Joe texts.

Taking Toby to his first karate lesson!! Grace home now. Should be back by 7.

Ugh. The thought of Grace and me alone until seven o'clock rolls around makes my stomach churn. Want me to pick up stuff for dinner?

No need. Leftover casserole in fridge.

I send a smiley face.

At the sound of my key in the door, the dog comes running to greet me. 'Hi, little fella.' I bend to stroke him and in the background I can hear Grace on the phone and her saying, 'Oh God. I better go.'

As I walk into the living room, she barges past me. 'Hello. Goodbye.'

'Grace . . .' I am caught in the draught of her exit. 'Where are you going? Look, please don't . . .'

'I'd have thought it was obvious,' she says. 'Anywhere but where you are!' She makes off in the direction of her bedroom.

'For heaven's sake!' I stare after her, noting that instead of just her long T-shirt and bare legs, she's wearing a pair of fluffy tracksuit bottoms. I suddenly feel horrible all over again about the underwear comment. 'Grace . . . look . . . can we stop this? Please. I think we should talk.'

She halts by her bedroom door, turns and meets my eyes, the sting in her own subsiding slightly. 'Er . . . Yes, that's appealing!'

'Look,' I say. 'I'm sorry I mentioned your clothing. I truly am. It didn't come out the way I intended. In fact, I really don't even know how I intended it . . .' I try not to sound emotional, or as utterly out of my depth and hopeless as I suddenly feel. 'I really, really don't want us to be at each other all the time . . . and I cannot believe that you do either.'

She goes on observing me, as though weighing this unexpected peace offering and contemplating whether to accept it or wage war.

But then she just seems to crumble. 'I'm sick of this!' she says. 'Just so, so sick of it! You don't want me here, and I don't want to be here – I don't want to be anywhere near you! I'm just so, so sick of it.' She gulps air. 'I just want my life back the way it was!'

Despite the weight of her words, she doesn't sound melodramatic, but more straightforwardly honest, which feels way more awful.

'I'm sick of this as well, actually,' I say, quietly. 'And there are days when I too just want my life back the way it was.'

She gawks at me, almost does a double-take. I slip my bag from my shoulder and let it drop into the chair. It lands with the heavy clunk of defeat. 'Grace . . .' I remind myself she's a kid and try to say it without enmity. 'You barely say a civil word to me. You hardly ever look in my direction. You rat me out to your mother at the first opportunity . . . How do you think that makes me feel? I am trying my best here, but I'm tired of finding tripwires everywhere I turn.'

We hold eyes. Hers have filled with tears.

'You're hating this?' I say. 'I get it. I understand. But guess what? Right now, *I'm* hating this too. But unlike you, I can't live between two places. I don't have two homes to go to.' Then I find myself adding, 'Sometimes I don't even feel like I've got one.' By the time I'm done I am almost breathless with anxiety.

There's an astonished pause, then she says, 'All this is you attempting to make the best of it? You could have fooled me!'

Once again, I am struck by how much older than her years she seems, like she bypassed childhood and joined the ranks of the cynical and misunderstood. But I am worn out by her – by this. 'Ah . . .' I throw up my hands. 'Whatever,' I say, and I walk towards the kitchen.

She hurries after me. 'What does that mean? *Whatever?* Like you're some kid . . .'

In one regretful, angry blast, I swing around. 'I am not the child.' I dig my finger into my own chest. '*You* are the child. And this is my home, and you need to show me some respect.' I glare at her, unrelenting. I have never, even slightly raised my voice to her. She looks stunned, mystified, and then I see the tears fall.

My heart is banging. She focuses on the ground, her body managing to look steeled and defenceless at the same time. Despite everything, a part of me wants to hug her, to force some kind of interaction that's not a brutal one. But instead my arms fall helplessly by my sides.

'Grace,' I say, when I really can't bear her being this upset any longer. 'Can we please, please, please try to get along? I am begging you.' Then I add, 'It's all I want in the world.'

She looks up, meets my gaze, and I think I see a slight thaw in her eyes.

Then she swipes a wrist across her running nose. 'It's never going to happen.'

FOURTEEN

The article is stored in my Favourites. I click on it, and read the description again. Join us and you'll have like-minded friends who can offer you the benefit of their experience – or, if nothing else, a safe place to have a good rant.

First things first: I have to set up a bogus Gmail account. This part isn't all that tricky. Next I have to give myself a name. Hmm . . . Harder.

I decide to call myself what I'm feeling right this second.

Miserable.

A few minutes and . . . *voila!* I'm in!

The forum is organised into a bunch of categories: Your story. Speak Out. Bitch Session. Positive Advice Only. Plus links to useful books and resources, and ideas for activities and fun.

I click on Speak Out, and scan all the post headings:

Enough is Enough

I hate my SKIDS!!

End of my Rope

Disgruntled.

Invisible.

Furious.

Fed up!

I read some of the posts, familiarise myself with the acronyms. BM: biological mother. OH: other half. DH: dear husband. SS: stepson. SD: stepdaughter . . .

I click on Disgruntled.

> Today was SS 7th birthday. OH took the kids to their grandparents for a party. I wasn't invited. Understand I'm new to the family and not exactly welcomed by all, but what will this mean for Easter, Christmas etc? Am I always going to be saying it's okay, I've got other stuff to do anyway? So disheartening!

Second Best replies:

> I went through this with my in-laws! Sat down with them, had the conversation. Things got better over time. Was worth it for me! Try it!

Invisible who *Can't Stand This Child!!!* writes:

> So we had SS, the snotty-faced, mollycoddled, money-grabbing little monster, again this week-end! This kid is nine years old. 'Why can't we do this? Why do I have to eat that?' Fucker got freaked out by the wind and jumped into bed because he wanted Daddy! Despite previous

conversation with OH about bedroom being off limits, OH can't resist being needed. I tell him but he doesn't get it. My space = my sanity! Sorry but I just don't feel comfortable sharing a bed with my masturbating SS! Okay?!!! We've been married less than a year – I only want to share a bed with my bloke!

PushingTheLimits replies:

This child is 9? That is way too old to be sleeping with daddy! Kid needs to be taught boundaries and OH too! What he did before you moved in was his choice, but this is your house too now and your rules have to count as much as his.

BloodBoil replies:

Same here! Told OH no more kids in our bed, or no more blow jobs. He got the message pretty quick!

It's like really bad reality TV. I want to click off. I should click off. But I can't look away, and click on another thread.

Moanie Minnie:

So sick of smelly, sulky stepson! This kid is 11 years old and hasn't even basic manners! DH and I get on so well when he's not here but we are fighting all the time now because he says I need to be more understanding. I'm always the baddie! He will never find fault with his son! Wish this kid would vaporise!

KatyG replies:

This is your home, and your SKID doesn't get to rule it. You need to have a talk with OH about the custody arrangement and your role in the family. And your OH needs to have a talk with his son about his manners.

I read on. And on. And on. Among all the negativity, there are some really constructive questions and some insightful replies. When I look up from my phone, half my coffee is still sitting there, cold. Looking out of the window, I can see it's started to rain. At the bottom of the page there's a link to start a new topic. I click on it. My alias pops up, along with an invitation to type a subject and a message. I ponder for a bit, and then start typing.

Dear all,

I am a new stepmother – a few months in. Having a very hard time bonding with DH's 14-year-old daughter. She can be sullen, silent, a bit of a tell-tale and troublemaker, and quite angry at times. I have tried to give her space, befriend her, give her alone-time with her dad . . . all to no avail. She won't eat what I cook, doesn't like my gifts,

leaves the room when I walk in. My worry is –
what if it will always be like this? If I can never
bond, or feel part of this family? I am starting
to dread the nights when they stay with us and
I feel so guilty! Not at all what I imagined! Any
and all input would be appreciated!

Signed,

Miserable.

FIFTEEN

When I log on to the S'MOTHERHOOD forum during my dinner break at work, I have quite a few replies.

The first is from Patience of a Saint:

> Dear Miserable. Stop trying to please her. She's not upset with you. This is not about you. It's about changes in her family. She doesn't want to get to know you because you represent this change. Your goal should not be to bond with her but to have a degree of agreeability between you. Being rude is not okay though. I would insist DH speaks with her. She doesn't have to love you but she has to be polite.

Too Much Mothering says:

> I echo Patience of a Saint. When I came on scene, SS was 15. It was horrible! 5 years later, things are great. But it takes time. Just stop trying so hard. She doesn't eat? Don't cook for her – she knows where the fridge is. She hates

your gifts? Spend your money on yourself! You don't need to try to win her over. Please don't be so hard on yourself! BTW, you don't mention how OH is and what BM is like . . .

Mumstheword:

SKIDS are pond life and stink like fetid water. You will never love them, so don't even try. You need a big talk with OH. It's his job to speak to his kids. Yes, there's going to be confrontation. If he can't do that for you then he's not worth being in your life. IMHO.

The last one is from Odd One Out:

I understand everything you're saying and feeling. I don't believe stepkids are inherently horrible and that you'll never love them – that's so cynical in my view. They're trying to feel their way around some big changes. Like Patience of a Saint said, it's not about you. My strategy, for what it's worth, avoid confrontation with OH for now. Try to take one small step in the right direction each visit. Aim low: one short 'normal' conversation. Deciding on a TV show you can watch together . . . Stay positive. Give it time. Hate the cliché but Rome wasn't built in a day!

I read them several times. Odd One Out sounds the most sensible. But even then, I'm not exactly uplifted. I take a few minutes to craft my reply.

> Dear everyone. Thank you for your honesty. Like Odd One Out, I don't want to assume I'm never going to love them! That's so sad! To answer your questions, DH is generally a fair guy, though he's not always perfect. We haven't had any sort of confrontation about his kids and I hope we never will. I certainly never want him to have to feel he's got to take sides. BM – as you ask – was never there – always working. DH was the main parent. BM is fine I suppose. Wouldn't want to be on her wrong side. Thanks again for the input! I remain optimistic.

After about twenty minutes I see that F$%KthisShit has replied to my reply:

> What is this, the 1950s????!!! You don't want to put DH in the position of having to take sides because he's a great guy and you want to give him the impression you love his kids and you're so under his big manly thumb that you can't even speak up for yourself?!! WTF!! I mean, sorry, but this takes the pathetic biscuit! Attitudes like this from women these days just make me puke! I'm, like, is this person for real???? I might be the lone wolf here . . . but hon, my serious advice, GROW A PAIR is all.

Too Much Mothering replies:

> F$%KthisShit – don't comment if you can't be
> helpful. Clearly Miserable is a decent person.
> I perfectly understand her not wanting to cre-
> ate a rift already. I still think Miserable should
> try putting herself first, focus more on herself
> and less on others. Hoping the rest will fall into
> place. If not, we are all here for you to vent –
> even if some of us say stupid things and maybe
> we shouldn't be in this forum if we can't control
> ourselves!!!!

I reread F$%KthisShit's reply. And while she's obviously some
sort of angry, disenchanted nutter, her words bother me. Why am
I so afraid of confrontation?

I'm just about to sign off when a new reply pops up. From
Odd One Out:

> Ignore the haters! Their sad life is not yours!
> You're doing fine as you are. You say your OH
> can be a fair person. Sounds like he's married
> to one too! Stay the course!

I quickly reply:

> Odd One Out – thanks!

SIXTEEN

On Saturday I work 8 a.m. to 8 p.m. Fortunately we're not busy, so I manage to keep a fairly low profile and catch up on some paperwork, even taking a full hour for lunch and a catch-up FaceTime call with Sophie.

'Maybe we can go for dinner next week?' I say, after we've talked a while.

'I'd love that!' She smiles. 'Charlie's been doing quite a few late shifts lately. Let me see when he's got a night off.'

'Or we could just go ourselves this time. Like the good old days.'

'Sure,' she says, after a tiny hesitation. 'That would be great.'

I have no idea if she truly wants him to always be joining us. Has it become a bit of a habit that she's not sure she can break now? Or are they so disapproving of my relationship that she feels she needs an ally around for whenever the topic comes up?

'Okay,' I say, weakly, because I'm not sensing oodles of enthusiasm and don't quite know how to address it. 'Give some thought to the best night for it and text me tomorrow.'

When I get home, too late to read Toby his bedtime story, Joe is sitting on the sofa listening to a podcast. He sees me but doesn't get up to kiss me.

'Everything okay?' I ask. 'Where's Grace?'

Instead of answering he indicates the opposite chair for me to sit.

'What's wrong?' I say.

It takes a moment before he meets my eyes. 'Did you have a conversation with Grace about her underwear, by any chance?'

His face is stoic, his awkwardness palpable. My blood heats up to a thousand degrees. 'What?'

'There was some insinuation that you felt that she was dressing *inappropriately* . . .' Then, like he's got some horrible smell under his nose, he adds, 'Around *me* . . . Some reference to her being Lolita and me some sort of . . .' He doesn't finish.

'Oh my God! I . . . No . . . I never said any such thing! There must be—'

'But you talked to her about her clothes.'

'Well, yes, but . . . it's absolutely *not* what you seem to be implying!' My tongue is suddenly sticking to the roof of my mouth. 'I . . . I definitely didn't say she was Lolita or . . . or anything about you. How could anyone . . . How could you even think that?'

He doesn't answer. His mouth flexes. A seed has been planted that I've implied something unsavoury about his daughter – and him. And not a seed Joe wants in his fragrant garden. Then he says, levelly, 'I'm just not sure why Grace's clothing had to be a topic at all, to be honest. I mean, it's not really your place, is it? To tell my daughter what she can and can't wear?'

This blows me back like a bomb blast. 'But I—'

He gets up and walks over to the window, stares out, his back to me.

'Grace is very upset. She doesn't want to stay here anymore. And Meredith is pretty furious. She was ready to march over here and have it out with you, but I persuaded her to let me talk to you first.'

Of course Grace told her mother. And her mother told Joe. I try to picture them all dissecting it. Dissecting me. What happened to, *If there's a problem, let's talk about it?*

'This is ridiculous,' I say, thinking *Grace is upset? How about me being upset about her telling a pack of lies?* 'It's a huge overreaction . . . I don't know what was said, but Grace obviously blew it way out of proportion.'

'Of course. She would, wouldn't she?' He turns and meets my eyes. 'Because you are never to blame, are you?'

I am stunned. What is he even referring to?

I go to try to articulate this, but my heart just drops. 'Wow. That's really hurtful . . .' I try to swallow my sadness down. 'I mean . . . Don't you want to hear my side, at least?'

'I think you just stated it.' There is a certain finality in his tone.

He walks back over to the sofa. 'Anyway, this is not about taking sides, Lauren. It's about speaking out of turn when you've got no business. You can't just say hurtful things to her. She's got feelings. She's never had an adult tell her what she can and can't wear before. And frankly nor should she.'

My heart is blazing at all these mixed messages he's sending. One minute I'm being encouraged to stand up to her, and the next I'm *speaking out of turn.*

A surge of defeat rushes at me from the ground up.

'I think you should apologise to her,' he says. 'And let's hope Meredith will leave it at that.'

Me apologise? I am suddenly furious at this threat of Meredith coming over to chew me out, like she's some sort of dog he's trying to call off, for which I should be grateful. 'I did already,' I say, firmly. 'We had a conversation.'

He meets my eyes. 'Well, clearly you need to have another one.' His tone is cutting and superior.

Half an hour later, I am still rattling with the injustice of it. I should have insisted he get Grace on the phone so I could have this out with her while everyone was listening. Instead, I just got defensive.

When I can't sit here any longer, with him shut away in his office, I grab Mozart's lead and my jacket, and take him for a walk around the block, sucking in big breaths of fresh air.

But it won't go.

I cannot believe how 'put in my place' he made me feel. It makes me think of what that woman in the forum said: *What is this, the 1950s?* Urgh!

Mozart goes to poo and I almost walk on. I've practically forgotten he's there.

Calm down, I think, as I wait for him to go, my heart hammering. *Keep it in perspective.* Surely Joe must know that Grace doesn't always speak the truth. But if he does, he clearly wasn't going to entertain the idea that she might have just overreacted. His daughter's word is inviolate.

And I'm expected to apologise!

But then a part of me thinks that if I don't, then this isn't going away. Grace will stand her ground – refuse to come and stay with us – and I'll be the bad guy.

And so, before we reach our gate, I dial her number.

When she doesn't answer, I text her: Grace, I'd like to talk. Can you please pick up?

No reply.

I try calling her again, and as each unanswered ring passes, I feel more peeved, and less inclined to eat humble pie.

Finally, it clicks on to her voicemail. So I suck it up and say, 'Grace . . . Look . . . your dad is very upset.' I can hear the jag of nerves in my voice. '*I'm* very upset by all this . . . Believe me. I had no idea that what I said offended you to the extent it did. I thought I'd already apologised, but obviously it wasn't clear.' I take a breath, try to swallow my humiliation. 'I'm sorry for what I said – for embarrassing you. It was thoughtless of me. I truly – truly – hope we can get past this. We want you to come back and stay with us – this weekend, and every weekend, for that matter! It's your home . . .' I feel an inexplicable surge of emotion. 'Can we please try to move on? Please come over tomorrow. If you don't, our weekend will not be the same without you.'

When I hang up, I realise I'm almost breathless. But it's over.

But I don't open our gate and walk blithely up to our front door. Instead I stand there, lifeless, staring at the light on in the living room.

Perhaps I can put Grace's behaviour down to her being a hormonal teenager who's carrying a lot of baggage that somebody needs to help her unpack. But I can't feel the same nod of charity towards Joe. He has sunk in my estimation – like he did once before, when I glimpsed a trait in him that I didn't like.

When I go inside, everything is quiet. Feeling oddly displaced, I hang up my coat, take off Mozart's lead, top up his water bowl and pour myself a glass of water.

Joe is sitting up in bed, working on his laptop, when I go into our room. He briefly glances my way, and then his eyes return to his keyboard, but he'd doesn't resume typing.

When it's obvious he's not going to be the first to say something, I tell him I rang Grace and left a message when she didn't pick up.

There's a stretch of silence, then his index fingers start pecking the keyboard again.

Fine.

I walk over to our wardrobe, slipping off my cardigan. The typing stops again. As I reach for a hanger I can feel his eyes on me.

And then he says, 'I know.'

I turn to look at him.

'She just texted me. She seems fine. I'm going to pick her up in the morning. Bring her over here.' And then, as though this had only been a trifling matter, perhaps a favour I needed to do for him, he adds, 'Thanks.'

I have no idea what to say to that – what I can civilly say to that – so I say nothing.

I undress and pluck my nightgown from behind the bedroom door. In bed I tug the covers over my shoulders, lie there on my side, barely moving, barely blinking, the whole thing going through my mind on an endless loop.

Grace might be fine, but *this* is not fine.

His letter said, *it's not complicated anymore.*

But it was.

SEVENTEEN

The weekend is uncomfortable. But – somehow – only for me. Grace seems very much her normal self when Joe collects her from her mother's on Sunday morning. Joe acts like nothing's happened. In the morning, I build a fort with Toby on the patio, and try very hard to look Grace in the eye and not think of the pack of lies she told about me. Later in the day, I take a walk to Regent's Park to give them time with their dad. When I return home, after a forced attempt at civility, I make my excuses about having to update my e-portfolio, then take a long bath. Come Monday, I am worn out by the undercurrent of bad energy that only I seem to be able to feel.

The second they are both off to school, and Joe has left for a meeting, I refill a big mug of coffee and take a notepad and pen to the chair by the window.

In our second year of med school we learned about the Gibbs reflective cycle, one of the models of reflection that is used in the health care industry to learn from good and bad experiences and to apply that knowledge to future situations. Very simply, you first describe in detail an objective account of what happened. You then state exactly how you felt about it, moving on to what you might have done differently, and what you will do when something similar arises again.

On my pad I begin by writing the key headings: *Description. Feelings. Evaluation. Analysis. Conclusion. Action Plan.* I then spend about half an hour writing up as much as I can, coherently, for each section. When I'm done I am pleased with my head versus heart approach.

But somehow, it still doesn't feel half as satisfying as a good natter with an old friend – on what ails you, or on just about any other topic, for that matter.

I pull out my phone and text Sophie, remembering she never did get back to me about our dinner plans.

Free of kids Weds night. Dinner? Pig's Ear?

I try to coax her with the name of one of our old favourite pubs.

When half an hour passes and she still hasn't texted back – perhaps she's at work – I find myself irresistibly drawn back to the forum. Within minutes, I've typed a new post.

> Dear all,
>
> Do you ever get days where you feel a little lonely in your marriage? As though your OH and his kids form a unit you'll never be part of?

I very briefly explain the gist of what happened. And then I end it with,

> I thought I'd married a man who would always have my back. Now I feel that his support is something I will continually have to earn and negotiate. Any input is welcome!

Within fifteen minutes, I have twelve replies. Half of them are outraged and say if I turn a blind eye it will only happen again. And again. Three suggest I call Grace out for lying. Two say this is life – their life too – and I should have known it when I married a man with kids. And then Odd One Out pops up again.

> Hi there. Me again. Try to move past the anger. My strategy? I fester for a day, then start afresh tomorrow. You said before that OH is fair, so this sense of betrayal is big for you. Okay, he never promised you a rose garden, but he owes it to you to not disappoint you as a human being. Talk to him. Keep it friendly.

The lyrics of one of my favourite Billie Jo Spears's songs spring to mind: '(I Never Promised You A) Rose Garden'.

> Odd One Out – thank you. What you say makes sense – and, as an aside, that just happens to be one of my favourite songs! Anyway, not sure I'll master the art of staying friendly but appreciate the reminder to try!

Ten minutes later she replies:

> I hear you. Then do what's comfortable for you. Remember, you didn't marry Prince Charming. Sometimes OH will be slow to find fault with his daughter. It's easier to find it with you, sadly. But it doesn't mean he doesn't love you, or value you, or want to make you happy. You may just have to slowly coax him out of this

behaviour. Also, you're not Pollyanna playing 'the glad game' – hope you get this reference! – this is life, and you chose it, warts and all. But you don't have to stick it out. If it's truly intolerable, you can change it and the world will still go on. Anyway. I am no expert. Clearly. Or I'd not be on this forum! Wishing you luck!

I google the reference to Pollyanna and 'the glad game': a fictional heroine who was taught by her father to find something in every situation to be glad about – who then went on to spread good cheer to the common folk wherever she went.

But who then became synonymous with blind optimism.

EIGHTEEN

'Shit.' Joe walks out of the bathroom with a towel around his waist and his mobile in his hand. 'Toby's come down with something and needs to go to the doctor. Meredith's in court and I've got to get to a meeting.'

'What's wrong with him?' I ask.

He digs in the drawer for his underwear and socks. 'Fever, stomach ache, headache . . . She's been up half the night with him, gave him a couple of aspirin. Rosamie can take him to the doctor's this morning, but she won't be free to watch him until much later in the day because she's taking her sick daughter to an appointment.'

'She probably doesn't want to give him aspirin,' I say, and carefully tell him why. 'Calpol would be better.'

He sighs. Types.

'Oh . . . maybe don't tell her that!'

'Too late.' He tosses his phone on to the bed but it pings right away. He picks it up, reads. 'Urgh!' He clicks off.

I perch on the end of the bed as he disappears into the walk-in wardrobe and then emerges in navy suit trousers and his trademark crisp white dress shirt.

'I can probably help out,' I say. 'I'm not due into work until four . . . I could take him to see his family doctor if Meredith likes, instead of the housekeeper. Then he can come back here with me before I head into work. So long as she can find someone to collect him before three.' Perhaps it will be a chance to get back into Meredith's good books.

'Thanks,' he says. 'That's thoughtful, but I don't want to be an imposition.'

The formality of the word strikes me as a little odd. 'It's not an imposition,' I say, noting how tired he looks. He tossed and turned in bed last night, something that's common when he's stressed about work. 'Please let me do it.'

He seems to hesitate, then says, 'Well, let me check with Meredith, then.' He reaches for his phone again, and is already texting her before I can suggest that I just sort it out with her instead.

I hover there, while the topic bounces back and forth. Then he finally looks up. 'Okay. That's great. If you can make your way to the surgery – Meredith still wants Rosamie to be the one to take Toby in to see his doctor . . . Then you can collect him and bring him back here.' He tells me he'll text me Rosamie's phone number just in case there's any confusion.

'That's fine,' I say, trying not to fixate on Meredith's wishes. I tell him I'll follow up with Rosamie in the afternoon to sort out the arrangements.

'Thank you for this,' he says. 'It's a big help.'

A coffee thrown down, he's rushing out the door. 'Oh . . . take the Lexus. If you're going to be doing all this driving . . . I'll grab an Uber.'

'I'd rather just take my car, actually,' I say. I know he's big on airbags, but I'm probably safer driving a car I know than a strange

SUV with too many bells and whistles. But it's too late. He's already thrown me the key fob and, as a reflex, I've caught it.

Toby has chickenpox. It's pretty obvious the second I set eyes on him.

'Oh, little man!' I pluck him from Rosamie's arms, introducing myself to her and thanking her at the same time. 'I know . . . the itching's awful.'

Someone has dressed him in a pair of yellow-and-black striped pyjamas. I think he's supposed to look like a bumble bee, but somehow looks more like a tiny inmate at a maximum-security penitentiary. Rosamie tells me that she will probably be available to collect Toby later this afternoon – in time for me to get to work.

Back at the car, he fusses and fidgets as I try to secure him into his booster seat, flailing a fist and catching me on the nose.

'It's okay!' I struggle to get his seat belt fastened. 'Please don't scratch your face, Toby. Can you do that for me?'

'Itchy! I'm itchy!' He makes a gruesome gurgling noise.

'I know,' I tell him, feeling his pain and frustration – and a little of my own. 'But if you scratch you'll only make it worse.' I try to push away a small surge of helplessness as his hands fly up to his face again. 'Please don't do that.'

'No!' he screeches, as I gently attempt to take his hand away. Then he wails, 'I want to sit in the front seat, not this seat!'

'You can't sit in the front seat, Toby. It's not allowed. It isn't safe.'

'Mummy lets me! I want to! Want to!' He screams harder, struggles like he's trying to escape.

'You can't sit in the front seat. That's not negotiable. But we can stop off and get you a chocolate bar if you like!'

There's a moment where his cries seem less frenetic and I think, *Thank God!* I walk around to the driver's seat, get in, and take a moment to try to just breathe. Once I start up the car I see we're very low on petrol. Damn. I pull out of the parking spot, glance in the rear view, see him tearing into his neck. 'Please, Toby!' Tension and helplessness clutch at my chest. 'Please don't do that! You're going to make it so much worse. Please don't scratch!'

I am suddenly boiling hot, and I roll down the window. I can't immediately think where the nearest petrol station is so I pull over again and try to work out how to punch it into Joe's fancy sat nav. Damn. I keep mis-keying.

'I want my mummy! I'm hungry and I want to go home.'

'We are going home soon, Toby.' Finally, I manage to get the thing going. 'Just as soon as I get petrol . . .'

'I don't want to go with you! I want my mummy.' He lets out another grisly gurgle and through the rear view I see him tug at the neck of his pyjamas to get at his skin.

I think I want my mummy too.

Once we get to the garage, I badly just want to get him his treat to shut him up, so I decide to go straight to the shop. There's no one else in there, so I could probably be in and out in two minutes. But I can't exactly leave him in the car, so we go through a similar rigmarole again as I haul him out of his seat and carry him inside.

'Mummy! Mummy! Mummy!' he wails. 'I want Mummy! Why are you taking me in here?'

'What snack would you like, Toby? You can have anything you want, okay?'

The woman manning the till is on the phone and looks up briefly. I pull a juice from the fridge and grab a Twirl when he won't select anything for himself.

'I want to go home,' he wails when I try to pacify him by showing him the chocolate bar – one of his favourites that his dad lets him have.

'I know, Toby.'

He thrashes his arms and legs. His glasses fall off. I struggle to bend and pick them up while wrestling with the weight of him in my arms.

The woman is still on the phone. She doesn't want her daughter's boyfriend coming over anymore on Sunday nights. Her daughter isn't happy.

'Excuse me,' I say.

After a moment or two – reluctantly – she hangs up. 'We're having a problem with our system at the moment so we can only take cash,' she says when I pull out my credit card.

Damn! 'I haven't got cash,' I say. 'At least, I don't think . . .' I sit Toby on the counter and root around in my purse, pulling out all the loose change I can find.

'You're 51p short.'

Her face doesn't emote. I observe the deep wrinkles, the smoker's lines puckering her lips.

'Is there any way you could you take my card? Please. My stepson has chickenpox and I badly need to get him home.'

She stares at Toby, and I think a mite of sympathy is breaking through. 'I told you, no cards. We're working on getting it fixed. It should be working again soon . . .'

I have the most ridiculous urge to burst into tears. 'Look,' I say, trying to remember I'm an adult, not a big baby. I slip the credit card into my coat pocket. 'Can I come back later with the 51p? It would have to be tomorrow, but . . . I can give you my name and address, even tell you where I work.' I tell her I'm a doctor, for whatever that's worth, and I say the name of my hospital.

Her face softens a bit. 'It's fine.' She waves a hand at the two items as though she's got a grievance against them. 'Just take them.'

'I can't just take them. Won't you get into trouble?'

'No worries. I'll pay. 51p isn't going to change my life. Get your stepson home.' She looks me up and down. 'Oh, and I gave mine baking soda baths when they had chickenpox. Worked a charm.'

I thank her profusely, gather my stuff and a whimpering Toby. I'm just getting to the door when she says, 'My Archie has had a searing pain running down his right leg for a while now. Do you think it could be a thrombosis?'

I try not to look aghast. 'I'm sorry,' I say, attempting to glance back over my shoulder. 'I can't diagnose someone without examining him. I'd encourage him to see his family doctor.'

'He can't go to the doctor. He's always working, isn't he?' she says as I struggle out of the door.

The sky has suddenly gone dark and I feel a few big droplets of rain as we hurry under cover. I throw my bag on to the driver's seat, then we go through the same palaver of getting him back in his seat – thankfully he's a tiny bit more compliant now that I've given him his chocolate bar. I reach into my coat pocket for my credit card so I can fill up the petrol, shut the car door and . . .

It locks.

What?

My heart gives one enormous kick of terror.

I try again. Nothing.

Where's the fob? Did I leave it in my bag? I can't think straight. I pat my coat pockets, dig my hands inside. My fingers land on it. The fob! In my pocket! Toby, in his little convict's pyjamas, peers out of the window.

I click on the *open* icon . . . Nothing happens.

'Shit!'

Toby starts to cry again.

I try moving away, and then getting closer to the door. Click, click, click. Nothing. It's dead.

'Shit, shit,' I say under my breath. I try to think what to do.

My first thought is to ring Joe. But then I realise my phone is in my bag on the driver's seat. Goddamn it!

'It's okay, Toby,' I say. He's crying so hard I can practically see his tonsils. 'It's okay. I'm going to get the door open. I promise.' I press my hand to the glass. He presses his. We are joined there in our mutual despair. I'm going to have to go back in the shop and ask to use her phone. But I can't just leave him here. I have no idea what to do. 'Hello!' I shout towards the window, to try to get her attention. I wave and jump up and down. But she's on the phone again and neither sees nor hears me.

I'm just thinking *Shit, now what*, when out of the blue I hear a voice say, 'What's happening? Can I help?'

When I turn around there's a fit young guy standing beside a black Audi. He has a pleasant face, looks a bit like an approachable professional footballer. Reluctantly, I tell him what's happened.

'I've no idea why it locked on me! I didn't press anything. The key was in my pocket!'

He nods, glances inside at Toby. 'Maybe what happened was you left your hand on the handle a second too long and it auto-locked.' He takes the fob from my hands, tinkers with it. I note the nice three-quarter leather car coat that could only look good on tall slim guys, the black polo sweater and slim jeans. 'I think it's the battery. What year is the car?'

'I have no idea,' I say. I tell him it's my husband's, that I've never actually driven it before.

'Not to worry,' he says, glancing at Toby again. 'Let's just get your kid out of there. I think I've got a solution.'

Your kid. For some reason that touches me in a way that I'm not prepared for, and in that moment I want more than anything in the world for Toby to be my child.

'I've got a similar fob. We can try my battery in yours. If we can get it started, you might be able to drive it. So long as you don't turn the engine off.'

I push hair off my face. There's no way I'm risking driving it and having something crazy like this happen again. The second I get Toby out of his seat I'm calling an Uber X with a car seat. I watch helplessly as he fiddles with his remote, taking out a coin to open the back of it.

'I appreciate this,' I say.

'It's my pleasure.'

I'm just thinking through the logistics. I'll have to tell Joe what happened and he'll have to Uber back with the other fob. What a drama! I turn and do one of my silly acts to try to amuse Toby. Fortunately he smiles.

'Thank you so much!' I say, once the door clicks open.

'What's your name?' he asks Toby, and Toby tells him.

'What's yours?' I say.

He smiles. 'I'm Kevin Westcott.' He digs in his coat pocket and pulls out a card. 'If you ever want to buy a house, I'm in the business.' I glance at the card and see he's CEO of a chain of high street estate agents I recognise. 'Or . . .' He nods to the car. 'If you're ever in need of a mechanic.'

'Let's hope not,' I say, and thank him again.

NINETEEN

When we get home, I try Joe several times but his phone is switched off. Rosamie is held up in traffic getting across London, so the second I hand him over I have to pelt for my connections so as not to be late for my shift.

At some point in the early evening while I'm busy explaining some test results to a patient whose English is very limited, my phone vibrates in my pocket. I ignore it, but a few minutes later it vibrates again.

When I get a chance to check it I see that it's Meredith. I'm just about to call her back when she rings again.

'You locked him in the car? Are you kidding me?' Her fury comes at me like a rogue wave. 'Toby said a man had to come and help you get the door open!'

'Meredith,' I jump in. 'There's no reason to panic. I—'

'No reason to panic?'

'It was two minutes.' I try to keep my voice low. But I've barely got the words out when a consultant walks up to me and gives me the death stare. 'Look, hang on a minute,' I tell her. 'Please don't go away . . .'

The consultant then proceeds to give me a bollocking for not paging him the second some test results were back. I try to tell him that I wasn't aware the results had come back yet as I had been so busy with another patient, but he says, 'Perhaps if you weren't dealing with your social life, you might pay attention to fractionally more important matters.' And then he walks away.

Urgh!

When I come back to Meredith I've no idea if she heard all of that. As if I need to feel any smaller, I say, 'Look . . . Meredith. Toby was completely fine.' I rush out the Coles Notes account of what happened.

'Hang on . . .' she says. 'Back up. Did you leave him in the car when you went into the shop?'

'No. Of course not! He came inside with me. He was with me the whole time.'

'Except when you locked him *in* the car, and you were *out* of the car.'

I try not to let out a sigh of frustration. 'I was right there. Like I said, it was all of a few minutes.'

There's a stiff silence where I can tell she's trying to decide whether to accept this. The consultant is now standing by the nurse's station and sends me a look.

Just when I think this is over, she says, 'What if it had been summer and twenty-five degrees? What would have happened to him then, Lauren? You can't lock a kid in a car. I'm not sure where you've been your entire life in order to miss this fact, but you can go to jail for things like this. It's negligence by any judge's standards. Have you any idea how terrified he would have been?'

I reel at the words *negligence* and *judge*, open my mouth to protest that it wasn't summer and twenty-five degrees and – actually – he wasn't terrified – but the consultant is still glaring at me. I say, 'Look I'm really, really sorry but I have to go. I'm one of only two doctors in the middle of a very busy shift—'

'You're not the only one trying to do a job!' Her tone is cutting. 'I'm at work too. I don't exactly need this either.'

I go to tell her that's not quite what I meant, but she's hung up on me.

I'm just walking back to my station, wondering if I should check in here myself and put a gown on because my nerves feel shot, when my phone vibrates again. Oh, come on! But when I look at the screen, it's not Meredith back for more. It's Joe.

'I'm home. Got your note,' he says. 'That's fine. I'm going to Uber over there and get the car now . . . But just wanted you to know Meredith is pissed off that Toby got locked inside and she's on the war path.'

I tell him I know, we've talked, and that I'm super busy and have to get off the phone. Oddly, now I'm thinking maybe I *did* do something utterly reprehensible, and I'm waiting for him to lay into me too.

But instead he says, 'Ah . . . Sorry about that. It totally wasn't your fault. I've had some issues with that fob for a while now. This morning I was in such a rush I forgot to mention it.'

I'm just about to say, *Okay, well, not to worry*, and hang up when he adds, 'It's a shame Toby told his mother and it's all been blown out of proportion. But I did warn you no secret's safe when there's a four-year-old in on it.'

'Secret?' I say it a little loudly, and one of the interns walks past raising an eyebrow. 'There never was any secret, Joe. I wasn't trying to hide anything. I was trying not to bother anyone with the ins and out of a situation I could manage.'

'I didn't mean it literally,' he says, after a bemused pause.

'Then why say it at all?'

There's a second where he doesn't answer. And then he says, 'Why are you being so touchy?'

'Touchy?' I feel like saying, *I've had a bastard of a day, all because I was trying to help you and Meredith out with your screaming kid. You left me with a dodgy fob. I was almost late for work. Now I'm doing a twelve-hour shift from hell that I'm only going to survive by mainlining caffeine . . . How about we show a little appreciation here?*

But I think of what I identified in the Action portion of the Gibbs reflection cycle and, in an effort to keep it constructive, I tell him, 'I really don't care for your tone. And I didn't care for your wife's either. You both need to rethink how you speak to me.'

There's a hollow silence, then he says, 'What did you just say?'

So I repeat myself. I tell him it sounded like she was giving me some sort of warning.

'Not that. The other thing . . .' When I don't answer he says, 'You just referred to Meredith as my wife.'

Before I can say, *Did I?* he says, 'Jesus, Lauren!' And then he hangs up on me too.

∽

When I arrive home at 7 a.m., I find him in the kitchen, making me breakfast.

'Hi,' he chirps, brightly, as though nothing ever happened. He's at the Wolf stove, in jeans and a clean white T-shirt, a tea towel slung over his shoulder. He steps away and kisses me as I'm shrugging off my jacket. His stubble grazes the side of my mouth, which usually ignites a small flame of desire in me but right now leaves me cold.

'How are you? You look pale.'

'I'm really tired,' I say.

'No wonder! You've had an enormously long day and night. I bet you probably can't even remember where it began.'

'It's been a long shift.'

118

Soon after my phone calls with Joe and Meredith, a man came in bleeding profusely from his mouth. We tried for forty minutes to restart his heart. There was nothing I could have done to save him but for the entire way home all I could think was, *Surely there was something.* Normally I'd share this with Joe. We'd talk about it. He'd say the right thing – the grounding thing – and make me feel better. But all I say now is, 'I'm going to get changed before I eat.'

In our bedroom, I stare at the bed and just want to throw myself down and sleep like Rip Van Winkle. But instead, I take off my clothes, slip into my white fluffy dressing gown and scrutinise my haggard face in the dressing table mirror. There are new shadows under my eyes, like somebody's punched me. And my hair, which was clean this morning, is lank and greasy. I suddenly feel utterly joyless, like the oldest twenty-nine-year-old I know. And more than a little sorry for myself, which I hate.

'Okay?' he asks sheepishly, when I walk back into the kitchen.

'Fine.'

He pours me a coffee, sets down a plate of eggs and I'm blindsided by a flash of gratitude for the way he always tries to take care of me. Maybe I overreacted because I was super busy, crazy stressed, and not thinking straight. I inspect the food. My stomach is queasy. Like you feel after you get off a ten-hour flight in a different time zone, not quite sure if you should be eating breakfast or dinner.

He sits down next to me. 'I'm sorry about what happened with the car and Toby . . . You were trying to help and it all backfired on you, didn't it?'

'I don't want to rehash it.'

'I know. I have no desire to do that either. But I needed to say it. When I'm wrong, I admit it. It was my fault, with the fob. Plus I shouldn't have been so overprotective and should have let you take your own car.'

I nod. I really don't want to get into a heavy-duty conversation, but I find myself saying, 'Sometimes I think she's just waiting for me to screw up.'

He looks askance – like he's misheard. 'That's ridiculous.'

'Is it? I feel like I'm on some sort of probation and she's already decided I'm never going to pass.'

He shakes his head. 'I don't know what to say to that bizarre statement, to be honest . . . She hasn't got it in for you. She's not like that. She's just being a mother. This is what mothers do, Lauren – they fret and they overprotect. She doesn't mean any harm. You don't have to take everything so personally.'

Everything so personally. Do I?

He scrutinises my face, my hair. 'Look, Meredith is not always subtle. Sometimes she speaks first and thinks later. She's had a lot of crap to deal with and it's left her with an inability to sugar-coat life . . . But it doesn't make her a bad – or a vindictive – person.'

This is not the first time he's tried to sell me her good points. I wonder if he ever tries to sell her mine.

I'm inclined to tell him this but he says, 'Don't get me wrong, it's not like she wrote the book on perfect parenting.' He then tells me that she once left Grace outside the airport in Turkey. Got in a taxi with her luggage and forgot about the baby in her stroller in the middle of the street.

'Oh my God!' I try to picture the scene, at the same time feeling something thaw between us. 'What happened?'

'Well, she remembered pretty damned quick, of course. Fortunately some kindly Turkish lady was with Grace and it all ended well.' He smiles, in the way you only can when you've dodged a bullet. 'But it could have been very different. Doesn't bear thinking about, really.'

'Thanks,' I say. 'That does make me feel a little better.'

Then he says, in a somewhat unreadable tone, 'Well, then, I'll have to remember to throw her under the bus more often, if it solves everything.'

It should be a joke. I think it's a joke. But somehow I can't bring myself to smile.

***

Once he's gone off to his meeting, I'm so tired I don't even make it to the bedroom. I must sleep solidly because when I wake the sun is streaming in through the window and I have a terrible crick in my neck from the sofa cushion. Looking at my phone I'm shocked to see it's 3 p.m. – a couple of hours later than I normally sleep after a night shift.

There's a missed text from Sophie.

Yes to dinner at Pig's Ear! Late shifts all wk. Next wk? she says, though I can barely remember what day I proposed, or even what day it is today.

I respond to what now sounds like a bit of a moving target rather than an enthusiastic plan. **Could make Thurs or Friday.**

There's a delay before she replies. **Thurs is better. Friday is generally our 'date' night.** ☺

Hmm . . . For us, Friday is usually change the beds, stock the fridge, plot activities in preparation for the kids' arrival, then flop out – knackered – in front of Netflix.

Thurs it is! I say.

I'm thinking that's it – a plan, finally – when I get another ping. **Oh shoot! Thurs actually won't work! Shame you're not free earlier in week, with having the kids . . . Let's regroup after Easter . . .**

Fine, then. I try not to feel a little miffed that *I* have somehow been painted as the impediment to us getting together.

I get up and let Mozart out on to the patio, still feeling a little battle-scarred from yesterday, and now a little disappointed in my friend as well. I stand there looking at the purple and pink petunias Toby and I planted a few weeks back, the shards of grass thrusting through the join in the stone slabs, thinking about the concept of family and home – and remembering that guy giving me his estate agent's card.

It makes me think of a comment Joe made before we married – a casual remark about how divisible assets were one reason why he thought married couples were better off renting until they felt fairly sure their relationship was going to work for the long haul. And how I'd thought, *But who gets married if they're not sure it'll work?* It seemed uncharacteristically jaded – for Joe. And yet he's never once mentioned us buying a house together – one that might be more appropriate for a family. A place we could fully call ours.

Am I on probation not just with Meredith, but with Joe too?

Once Mozart has had a couple of pees and a few minutes' sniff around, I go back inside and put on a pot of coffee, trying to let these thoughts go. I don't want to poke holes in the fabric of us. Maybe second time around, Joe has a right to be cautious. Also, I think of Joe saying Meredith isn't perfect, she's just a mother, and I try to remember I'm as much of an unknown quantity to her as she is to me. We are both feeling our way around new roles – and each other. It's bound to be tense at times.

I decide to text her, hoping she'll take it as the olive branch it's meant to be.

How is Toby today? I type, before I get cold feet.

The message is delivered. I get a read receipt. I watch for the little moving dots.

Nothing comes.

TWENTY

Over the Easter break, Meredith takes the kids to her father's country home that I'm told is in the Bordeaux region of France.

'Will her father be there?' I ask Joe while we eat our dinner. Her father rose to the heights of banking power and became a Sir, and yet no one ever seems to talk about him. 'Will the kids enjoy spending time with their granddad?' I poke. I can't say I've heard Grace mention him much.

There's a moment where he doesn't seem to want to engage, then he says. 'No. Meredith only goes when he's not there. They don't exactly have the best relationship.'

'So the kids don't see much of him, then?'

'Not really.' Then he adds, 'It's not like he's ever made a tremendous effort to be in their lives either.'

'It's sad,' I say. 'Your folks are in Chicago, Meredith's mother is dead and her father isn't really in the picture . . .'

'The kids often talk on FaceTime with my parents,' he says, defensively.

Often? I've known them do it once.

'So what happened between Meredith and her father, for there to be this discord?'

He sighs. 'It's a long story. He's a rich, attractive, powerful guy who was a bit of a shit to be honest . . . not exactly the most morally upstanding man on the planet.'

I'm reminded of what Sophie and Charlie implied about Joe.

'When Meredith was in her early twenties, he left her mother for a girl Meredith's own age. Some assistant at the bank.' He smirks. 'Bizarre timing. It was exactly one week before he got knighted by the Queen.'

I think about this. 'It's hardly uncommon, though, is it? Successful, attractive man chasing a younger woman.'

Part of me still cringes at Sophie and Charlie implying Joe was some sort of sugar daddy. Despite them knowing I'm an independent feminist on track for the top tax bracket, they still managed to insinuate I was on some mission to become a kept woman. It was bonkers.

'No, it's not uncommon in the ways of the world,' he says. 'But that doesn't make it okay when it's *your* family, *your* father, *your* mother he's fucked over.'

'No,' I say, feeling like we might be on thin ice. I always remember thinking Joe had great family values. His parents have been married forty years. No one in his family has divorced. I remember him saying, 'They're all either the happiest, most compatible people in the world, or they're having affairs left, right and centre and keeping it all under a cloak of dirty secrets.'

'It did a lot of damage to her,' he says. 'To her faith in her father, but her faith in men in general . . .' He meets my eyes. 'There she was, this young, beautiful, supremely intelligent woman embarking on a legal career, and at every turn she was being hit on and propositioned by older, senior barristers. And then she found out her own father was just like the very types she despised.'

'That's awful,' I say. Did he have to call her *beautiful* and *supremely intelligent*?

'Your parents can have a huge impact on how you see the rest of your life, you know. People fuck around and think it's nothing, but the damage lives on . . .' He looks wistful for a moment. 'A father has a massive obligation. Everybody will try to screw you over but you need to be able to count on your dad.'

I study him closely. They hardly sound like the beliefs of someone who is, himself, a cheat.

'Did her mother try to get him back?' I ask.

He shakes his head. 'Meredith always said she died from a broken heart soon after her father walked out on her and tried to screw her financially.'

'Stress cardiomyopathy,' I say. 'When the heart is under such intense emotional or physical stress that it causes the muscle to rapidly weaken.' While it's possible you can die from it, you usually don't. I suspect Meredith's conviction about this was driven less by medical fact and more by her anger and disappointment.

'It made her determined to never be in a relationship with a man unless it was clear that he loved her more than she loved him.' He says it so casually. As though I'm a close confidante, rather than his wife. I doubt he even realises what he's just revealed.

Then he adds, 'Until I met her, she was pretty much a man-hater.'

'I see,' I say.

I'm rather sorry I asked.

The next ten days without the kids are nothing short of paradise.

No one coming to stay. I can wander around the flat on my day off while Joe is at meetings, and not have to speak, not have to make an effort or watch how I tread. These are ten whole days

125

where Joe and I don't so much as talk about the children, let alone see them. It's almost like they don't exist.

We eat, we drink, we slob out. We sleep in on Sunday until eleven o'clock. We have sex like children weren't even invented, and could never be conceived.

And then the holiday is over and they return.

Feeling better about things, I try to approach this as a reset. A fresh start.

On Monday night I say to Joe, 'I thought once I pick up Toby from school, we might meet Grace and go for tea somewhere. You know, given you're not going to be home until late.' Joe is going to a work function. One of those fancy evenings he's told me about where a group of his business associates – all men – hit a pricey steak house and then afterwards some sort of high-end private members' club.

'What a charming idea!' He places a hand on the back of my neck as I stand there in only a bath towel, drops a kiss in the hollow of my neck.

'I have them once in a while.' I feel quite pleased with myself.

As he pulls on one of his crisp white dress shirts, he says, 'Why don't you take them to a hotel for scones and cake?'

For a down-to-earth American guy, Joe has a strange fixation with fancy hotels and English high teas – as I remember all too well. 'Actually, I was thinking of a really cool cake shop near Sloane Square where they make cakes in the shape of cars and buildings and people.' It's near Grace's school, and I have to go to Peter Jones because my mother texted me a list of things she's missing from home that she wants me to send to her. I tell him this.

'Can't she just order them online?'

'She could. But she won't. I think them coming in a box I've had to pack with my own fair hands is part of the charm.'

'Sounds like you've got it all organised then.' He smiles.

Given I don't feel like dealing with central London traffic, I pick Toby up from school and we get an Uber X to Sloane Square where I do a quick scoot around Peter Jones, picking up most of what I need. Grace has grudgingly agreed to meet us outside, at the main entrance, at 4 p.m.

At precisely four, we go outside and wait. And wait. And wait. Double-decker buses and black cabs fly around the central square that houses a charming Grade II listed fountain of Venus and a complex elongated roundabout system, hacking pollution into the late afternoon sunshine. Toby is restless. I hang on to his little hand and voice text Grace. **Where are you?**

She responds immediately. **Here.**

I turn and she's right there.

'Sorry I'm late,' she says, like she actually might indeed be semi-sorry.

'No worries,' I say. I watch her muss the top of Toby's hair. 'Shall we go and eat? I'm sure we're all ready for something.'

But she just stands there, twirling a strand of honey blonde hair. Perhaps because we've stood a while in the shade of the building, it's starting to feel chilly.

'The thing is . . . I sort of badly need a haircut.' She pulls the strand through her fingers, inspects it for split ends. 'Can we do that instead of going for tea? Or maybe do it first then go for tea later?'

I'm hungry as I skipped lunch, but that's not my main concern. 'We could . . .' I say. 'Only I'm not sure there's much in that plan to keep Toby amused.'

When Toby hears his name he says, 'I don't want to go to the hair salon I want to go for tea to eat a car cake!'

127

'It'll only be an hour,' she says. 'It's right there.' She points across the street, sounding petulant.

Since our fight in the kitchen and my text apology – which feels like a long time ago now – she has been unusually low-key, almost a little flat, but oddly cooperative with me. Like she feels bad on some level. I don't want to take one step forward and five back. Plus I'm reminded that Toby does seem to garner the bulk of everyone's attention and she must get sick of that at times. 'Okay,' I say. 'But do you think they're likely to take you as a walk-in?'

'I've already called them. I've got an appointment.' She glances at her phone. 'But I've got to go, like . . . now!'

She starts walking off towards the zebra crossing and I can't help but feel a tiny bit manipulated.

'Okay!' I say, not much choice in the matter now, and we hurry after her. Toby can't keep pace, so I end up picking him up and carrying him.

She strides ahead like a supermodel, through a dark walkway that emerges into filtered sun and a courtyard of beautiful, high-end shops.

'Where's the salon?' I ask.

'There.' She points a finger.

I gaze at the awning, at the name. 'But that's where all the celebrities go!'

'Yup.'

'But . . . Won't it cost a small fortune?'

She flashes me a look that borders on distaste. 'So? It's not like I'm paying for it.'

Last time she said that she nicked a waistcoat. But she can hardly lift a haircut, so I try to tell myself at least I can relax on that front.

'Mummy lets me come here,' she says.

I vividly remember when I first moved down to uni from the north. How I used to go back home every six weeks to get my hair cut simply because it was cheaper.

Mummy bloody would, I think.

I tell her I don't feel like sitting inside with Toby so we'll go walkabout and come back in an hour. She breezes off inside.

Sensing the idea of tea and cake has just gone sideways, I take Toby to a Middle Eastern place on King's Road that does a nice assortment of tasty but healthy snacks. I try to spin out an order of hummus and flatbread and a yogurt drink, followed by a wander around Duke of York Square and a short anecdotal history lesson on the Chelsea Pensioners, which Toby has no interest in, until 5.30, when Grace said she'd be done.

Talking to him about war veterans takes me back to something I don't much care to remember: an outing with Joe's kids soon after we'd become engaged. Remembrance Sunday 2018 – long something I had honoured by attending the Cenotaph, a day that was of the utmost importance to me.

'It might be a nice thing for us to do together!' I said to Joe, who had originally intended for us to go to a hotel for a fancy brunch. 'One hundred years since the end of the First World War.'

'That's all well and good,' he said, 'but I'm not sure there's anything there to interest the kids.'

I knew that Grace was studying the two world wars in history. And that Toby loved his 'Coldstream Guards' – a set of heirloom toy soldiers his grandfather had given him. I suspected Joe might be pleasantly surprised.

I went early and got us a good spot. We found each other after much texting and waving of hands.

'This is boring,' Grace said, straight off the bat.

We waited around some more. The service began – and so did Toby's crying.

After a while, at the end of his patience, Joe said, 'This is bullshit. Come on, let's get out of here and go for brunch.'

'I'd like to stay,' I said, and added that I could just meet them afterwards at the hotel.

'Afterwards?' He frowned. 'By the time this thing's done, we'll have moved on to dinner!'

We went back and forth on it, until he finally said, 'I don't understand. I thought this was supposed to be an outing with the kids? I thought it was about you trying to get to know them better?' He searched my face, as though he wasn't so keen on what he was seeing. He didn't say another word, but the message was clear. By staying, I was showing I was not committed to our relationship; I was being self-centred.

And so we cut a path through the solemn crowd and made our way to a Park Lane hotel where we ordered expensive omelettes and talked about nothing in particular. Just like we could have done on any old Sunday. I was furious. He *knew* how much this day meant to me and yet he'd completely disregarded my feelings. A little voice was saying, *If he's selfish and inflexible in little ways, imagine what he'll be like in the big . . .*

But I didn't listen to it.

Back at the salon, Grace sits in reception on a dark-coloured velvet sofa – looking like a cross between a mushroom and a middle-aged newscaster from the '80s.

'It stinks,' she says, when she sees us come in the door.

I pat some of the poof down with my hand. 'I have admittedly seen better . . . But the cut looks good. That's the main thing, isn't it?'

She rolls her eyes. 'It should do for a hundred quid.'

My jaw gapes. 'What?'

'Cough it up, then.'

I do a double-take. 'Cough what up?'

'Duh! It's not like I carry that sort of change around.' She glares at me as though I'm some sort of sad moron. 'You have a credit card, don't you?'

Hang on . . . I'm paying for this? Does she know I can't even afford to get my own hair cut at a place like this – not on a junior doctor's salary?

Never mind. Dutifully, I hand over my card.

Once we get outside into the sunshine, she snaps a selfie, making sure to get the name of the salon in the shot, and uploads it to Snapchat. 'Oh my God, I can't wait to tell everyone you stiffed them on the tip!' she chuckles.

Lovely.

We leave. None of us seems all that bothered about going for cake now. We hop on the bus instead of calling another Uber.

Given that's all I can now afford.

On our way home, I tell her I want to whizz round Marks & Spencer's food hall. She says she'll go upstairs and look at lingerie, then come find us. I disappear down the escalator. She goes up.

'Can we buy some cake to take home?' Toby asks. 'Because we didn't get any today.'

'We most certainly can if we can find where they are,' I say. I pick up a basket, hanging on to Toby's little hand as we wander around and I get my bearings in an unfamiliar layout.

Then Joe texts, How's tea?

Without taking my eye off Toby, I put the basket down, text back, We didn't go. Grace wanted a haircut. In M&S and then heading home with food. How was meeting?

Bummer, he replies. (Meeting went ok) I was expecting some pictures of delicious cakes!

'Here they are!' Toby says, and hurries off down the aisle. I quickly trot after him.

'What do you fancy?' I say to him. 'I think I know your dad's favourite!' I scan the shelves then find the Victoria sandwich box and take a photo of it. How's this? I text the picture to Joe.

He writes back, Now you're talking! Bring one for me!

I laugh. I pop the cake into my basket. Then I say, 'Okay, little guy! I think we've got dessert covered . . .'

But when I turn around, Toby's not there.

'Toby?' I quickly scan up and down the aisle. 'Toby, where are you?'

He was there literally thirty seconds ago. Where the hell has he gone?

Suddenly my phone vibrates. I ignore it, abandon the basket, and hurry to the end of the aisle to see if he's whizzed around to the other side.

Nothing. Toby is not there either.

'Toby?' My voice is a little louder, panic etched into it.

I do a quick dash around the wine section, my heart kicking up like a tornado. 'Toby?' I dash to the other end of the shop, nearly colliding with an older couple. But it's like he's vaporised.

Oh my God! Where is he? Nerves are shuttling through my body and I feel like I'm going to puke.

'Toby!' My voice cracks.

There is a second where everyone stands still and looks at me.

Then I hear a voice saying, 'What?' with a certain childlike consternation.

When I look down the cake aisle again, Toby is standing there, like he'd never been anywhere else. As though I imagined the whole thing. 'Why are you shouting?' he says. 'I'm right here!'

'Toby!' I fall on my knees and hug him.

While he's trapped in my embrace, my eyes go to the far end of the aisle.

Grace is standing there watching all this.

She smirks.

'Oh my God! It was like a scene from Broadchurch!'

Grace embarks on the 'Lauren lost Toby' story to her dad the instant we are through the door.

'I'm, like, I'm coming down the stairs, and it's like all anyone can hear. "*Toby!!!!!!!!*" She screeches out a terrified, blood-curdling cry. 'It was like, literally, everyone just stopped what they were doing. Just stopped dead in their tracks. There was just this deadly . . . SILENCE . . . Then everybody was like tearing the place apart looking for him!'

I look from Grace to Joe.

'Grace . . .' I say, disbelieving my ears. 'That's not how it happened at all. No one was tearing the place apart looking for him.' I gawk at her as though to say, *Why are you doing this?*

She holds my eyes for a second, then she glances at her dad, throws up her hands. 'Er . . . Okay. Whatever you say . . . I mean . . . I was there!'

'So was I!' I say.

Joe looks at me, bemused. 'What's going on here, Lauren?'

'What's going on?' I hold steady even though I'm pulsating with annoyance. 'Nothing is *going on*, Joe.' *Except your daughter is making up bullshit again!* I'm on the brink of just coming out with it – and saying, *Oh, and, in case you didn't know, she's a thief as well as a liar! Want me to tell you a tale about a shopping trip to Topshop?* But instead I say, calmly, 'Toby wandered off. There was a moment where I panicked – but then he was right there.'

There is an empty pause, a spell of dead air, where my contradiction of Grace's version of events is out there and underscored. Toby fills it by saying, 'I was choosing us a cake! They had so many choices!' But Joe doesn't seem to see or hear him. He is too busy staring daggers at me.

Then his gaze slides to his daughter. 'Is this right? What Lauren just said?'

'What?' I practically spit. Did he really just ask a child to validate my explanation? This can't be happening.

Grace drops her eyes, and for a second I think she's going to own up. Then she says, 'I already told you, didn't I?' She flings her hands in the air, says, 'Not sure why no one ever believes me!' then storms out of the room.

'We need to talk,' I say to him, hours later. We have come to bed. We've barely spoken since dinner. Grace refused to join us and he carried a tray to her room and ate in there with her while I sat at the dining table with Toby. Every time I ventured beyond the kitchen I could hear them talking. The hushed tones. Joe's firm voice. Her wounded, slightly dramatic one.

'Talk, then,' he says, curtly.

I try to keep my composure. 'I can't go on like this,' I say. 'I can't have it always be Grace's word against mine, and you never believing me.'

'Look, Lauren,' he begins, after a moment. 'I know you don't react well to criticism – none of us do. And I know you're trying hard . . . But you can't lie. And you certainly can't call Grace a liar like that, right to her face.'

I almost leap into the air. '*Me* call Grace a liar?' My heart hammers. 'I'm calling her a liar because she is a liar!'

There is another moment where he just looks at me, like he's trying to make sense of my words. And then he says, 'I think you need some time. And I think you need to sort yourself out.'

I digest this, frown. 'Time? What's that supposed to mean? Sort myself out?'

'I don't know,' he says. 'I really don't, to be honest. But I can't have you always at war with my daughter in her own home.'

'At war?' My voice cracks. '*Her* home?'

'She can't seem to say or do anything right! She's tired of it.'

'Because she's *lying*, Joe.'

He flings up a hand. 'There you go again. See what I mean? You. Her. Her. You . . . She's not your adversary, she's not your rival, she's not your competition. She's a kid, for Christ's sake!'

I cannot believe this . . . Adversary! Rival! Competition! It's on the tip of my tongue to tell him about the stealing. Open his eyes. Get the blinders off. But the sad thing is, I have a feeling that if I do, there's not even a chance he'll believe me.

'I'm done!' I say. 'Done with this! I'm leaving.'

I charge towards the door.

And as I do, I'm one hundred per cent certain I'm never coming back.

TWENTY-ONE

'Sorry, I was trying to be quiet.' Charlie misses his footing and slides down the last few stairs.

'Don't worry, I'm not asleep.' I raise my head from my pillow to peer at him. He is dressed for his early shift. I didn't mean to end up here but once I stormed out of the flat I realised I didn't really have anywhere else to go.

'Are you sure about that? This is not you asleep? Because I'm used to people telling me they're not asleep when they're asleep. Sophie does it all the time.'

I struggle to sit up, bring a hand to the back of my head. 'Ow!'

'You drank almost a bottle of wine.' He studies the mess of me. 'No judgement – given I might have had two.'

We did stay up for hours talking. I had no intention of divulging so much, but at the same time, I had to get it out. I have managed to accept that our friendship is being redefined. To tell one is to tell both of them. Sophie and Charlie are enmeshed, we have entered a new era and there's no sense in me mourning what once was, or what may never be again. Still, I gave them an edited version, trying not to focus too heavily on Joe's inability to fight clean. As with everything, there's a chasm between how things are and how they look. I can't quite fully serve up my disillusionment on a platter just yet.

Sophie peeks her head around the wall from the kitchen. 'Fancy a fry-up?'

'Urgh!' I feel green just hearing the word. 'A cup of tea, maybe . . .'

'Get yourself up and have a shower,' Charlie says. 'You'll feel like a new person. We've put fresh towels out and cleaned the bath.'

'Have you?'

'No. But we will next time if you give us a bit of advance warning that you're coming over.'

'Next time?' I pull a face. 'I'm really hoping there won't be a next time.'

'Come on,' Charlie says. 'We can all but bet on it.' He sends Sophie a slightly conspiratorial glance.

'Thanks for the vote of confidence,' I say, too numb to even take offence. I just keep seeing Joe pitting me against his daughter, hearing him essentially call me a liar, feeling this profound sense of loss – of trust, of faith, almost of love.

'For the duration of your marriage, our sofa is your sofa.' He flourishes a hand at the said piece of furniture. 'I've slept on it many a night, when my wife took umbrage and wouldn't allow me in the marital bed. She had the nerve to try to persuade me to spend three grand on a brand new one saying it'll ultimately be for my own comfort, but I've got a sentimental attachment to an eight-year-old sofa from Ikea that countless people have sat on, slept on, shagged on.'

'Thank you for that image,' I say.

Sophie presents me with a china mug that reads *Tea Time. The best time of your life* but Charlie intercepts it before it reaches my hand and takes a drink.

'So what are you going to do for the rest of the day then?' he asks brightly, like I'm on some lovely weekend getaway at a fancy B&B.

I shrug. 'A stroll along the shore. A nap in the afternoon. Fish and chips for dinner.'

He smirks.

'I'm going to go home. Change my clothes. Get into work for 4 p.m.' I don't say, *Hope Joe's out.* I truly can't bear the thought of facing him – could throw up at the idea.

'And what are you going to do about Grace?' he asks.

Charlie's theory was that Grace is gaslighting me – trying to paint a different reality to convince others – her parents – to doubt mine. His solution was that I must always remain confident in my version of events, and, where possible, record all conversations.

'I don't know,' I say. 'Not sure I'll heed your advice, but I do appreciate it.'

'And what about the man you married?'

I look down, briefly. 'Today is a new day,' I say.

'You might make light of it now,' Charlie says. 'But you were very upset last night when you got here and it wasn't all to do with Grace . . .' He sends me a rather caring, concerned look – something I've not seen too often. 'You had a pretty low opinion of Joe. In fact, I don't think Sophie was that down on me when I said I couldn't marry her.'

He glances at his wife, who turns red, like someone finding herself acknowledging an embarrassing truth.

Perhaps I hadn't been as subtle as I'd thought.

'Anyway,' he says, 'I'm sure you'll work it out, but for now I have to go.' He pops the mug on the coffee table, kisses his wife, salutes me, and then we hear the clash of the front door.

He's sure I'll work it out?

I wish I had his confidence.

'Why did Charlie cancel the wedding?' I ask her when we are on to our second cup of tea, both of us curled up at polar ends of the sofa. My private life has been under the spotlight plenty; I don't see why hers should stay in the dark. 'You never really said, just that he's terrified of commitment because not a single marriage in his family has ever worked.'

She nods. 'And that was true.'

'Then how can you have any faith that he won't get fed up one day and just leave, if he's so commitment-phobic?'

She stares, unblinking, at a coaster on top of the table. After a long time, she says, 'If you knew something about Joe – something he didn't want anyone else knowing – would you tell your best friend? I mean, even if you knew the secret would stay with them?'

For a moment I think we have time-travelled back to last night and are three bottles of wine down and this is just some rather odd continuation of our heart-to-heart.

'God,' I say. 'No. If he asked me not to tell anyone, I wouldn't tell them.' Ironic; I don't even know if Joe has ever confided any-thing in me that would merit that level of secrecy.

'What if you personally thought this secret of theirs really didn't need to be a secret at all? That it mattered to *them* but would hardly matter to the rest of the world? Would that give it less sanc-tity? Would it make you change your mind?'

I think about this. *What the hell has he done?* But I comfort myself with the idea that, sadly, Charlie's a little too straight to have done anything truly terrible. 'If people want to keep things private, that's their right,' I say. 'It's not really for me to play judge and jury. So no, I wouldn't tell anyone.' And then I add, 'Not even you.'

'Well, then . . .' she says, a little enigmatically. 'You might have some idea of the position I'm in.'

Intriguing, I think.

TWENTY-TWO

Joe is thankfully out when I get back, so I nap, to make sure I'm fit for my late shift, then shower, change and head into work. When I come home early the next morning, he has left me breakfast and a note. *Had to rush out. Dinner tonight at Alfonso's? 8pm? Meet me there. I reserved.*

I go into our bedroom after I've eaten and I lie there for ages staring out of the window instead of sleeping.

Alfonso's. My mind can't help going back to the first time he took me there, a couple of months after we'd begun dating. It was June. My twenty-ninth birthday.

Joe showed up with a bulky package under his arm. 'Yours, I believe.' He placed it in front of me.

'What is it?' I asked. It wasn't a wrapped gift. In fact, it was still in its shipping packaging, and had his name and address on the label.

He just smiled.

Its origin was France.

I peeled my gaze away from his, tore into the parcel. There was a moment where I didn't believe my eyes. 'Oh my God! My bag!'

He was watching me like he was fixing every beat of this in his mind. 'Of course. What else?'

Just a few weeks earlier I'd been mugged walking from work. Aside from the fact that I could have been hurt, and my credit card was stolen, what I was most upset about was losing the beautiful bag I'd bought in the south of France, from one of those charming little establishments that sells fabric and leather and jewellery.

'How did you ever pull this off?' I asked him. I couldn't have even told him the name of the tiny little shop where I'd bought it, because I didn't remember it.

I could see he was trying not to look too pleased with himself. 'There aren't that many artisan gift shops in Èze. It wasn't that hard.'

Turned out he'd done some research into the town, then rung the shop and described it to the owner. As soon as he'd said jade green they knew exactly which one it was, and had an identical one custom-made and shipped over.

'I truly can't believe it!' Tears filled my eyes. 'That's the nicest thing anyone's ever done for me! So damned thoughtful!'

'I'm a damned thoughtful kind of guy,' he said, and it was cute how he seemed to bask in the compliment. 'At least . . . I hope I am!'

'Seriously. This makes me very happy!'

He smiled a big smile. 'That's good. Because the truth is . . . your happiness is all that matters to me.'

His words, the promise in them, just kept writing themselves in my mind.

'That's a powerful statement,' I said.

He shrugged. 'Just a true one.'

After our meal was finished I asked him, 'What are we doing, Joe?' There had been lengthy spells between eating where we had just sat there and stared at each other.

'I know what I'm doing,' he said. 'I'm falling in love.' He looked rather affected by his admission. 'I think I felt it from the first words you ever spoke to me.'

'What were the first words I ever spoke to you, by the way?' I asked.

'I think they were piss off.'

'I would never, ever say that.'

'You did. With your eyes at least. But it didn't stop me. It was never going to stop me.'

'But we have to be sensible.'

'Do we? I vote we be anything but sensible.'

'I thought you said you were a patient guy.'

'I was. I am. And I still will be, if you tell me this is all too much too soon.'

I opened my mouth to tell him that it really had been no time at all, but then he said, 'The thing is, Lauren . . . I don't want to rush anything, but I don't want to waste your time either . . .'

A change came over him. I wanted to stop him right here, have him not say anything that might ruin this moment.

He looked at me with serious eyes. 'I'm more than aware that I can't offer you what someone who's never been married or had a family can. I've walked down the aisle already, bought my first house, seen my first kid born . . . All those special firsts, those special, priceless events that couples long to share. I've done them all with somebody else.'

Were we really tiptoeing around a life together? Already? I was almost delirious. 'I don't need to walk down an aisle,' I said. 'Marriage is about a life together, not just a day.'

I might have assumed I'd get married in a church, but I'd never whiled away the hours planning my wedding. It wasn't my idea of the most romantic day of my life.

This was possibly the most romantic day of my life.

'I don't even need to have children!' I said. 'I'd be fine if we never had them.'

Was it true? I'd definitely assumed I'd have kids – rather than actively longed for them.

It felt true when I said it.

He looked at me tenderly, almost gratefully. But then he said, 'Lauren, I think what I'm trying to say is that I'm in a compartment here with you, a bubble really . . . And fantastic though it is, it's not my real life. It's not the real me. And you'll see that the moment you see me with my kids – you'll see who I really am.' Then he added, 'In a way, I'm two people. I'm who I am with you, and I'm the product of all my other choices to date.'

I thought about this – the two Joes. Weren't we all a product of our choices? Didn't we all compartmentalise, to a certain degree? Offer up certain aspects of ourselves to certain people, and keep others hidden? Especially in the beginning.

Whatever it was he was saying, whatever reality he was putting forward, I had the strongest sense I was going to deny it anyway.

'Call me crazy but I actually think this *is* the real you!' I said, almost panicked that this was his roundabout way of saying he didn't think we were a good idea anymore. Perhaps the wonderful gesture of the bag had been some sort of goodbye gift rather than a birthday one. I was flooded with emotion, a giddy sense of recognising that you don't know how much you want something until you're faced with its possible unattainability. 'I *like* the real you. I really, really like him . . . and I would welcome every challenge that lay ahead.' Then I added, 'If we have an ahead.'

I can still hear the sound of my voice when I said that. My own intrepid faith. Also, that little voice of reason saying, *How can you be so sure you'd welcome a life you know nothing about?*

I watched him watch me, the tenderness in his eyes. I could almost see – almost feel – his longing to believe it too.

Eventually he spoke, and I dreaded what was coming. 'Lauren, I love that you're saying all this . . . I love your conviction and your fearlessness . . . I'm just not convinced it'll be as easy as you're being gracious enough to think it will be.' He looked sad suddenly. A little uncharacteristically defeated.

Everything was hanging in the balance. As much as I needed to believe in the romantic illusion of us, he needed to believe in the reality.

'I'll take my chances,' I said.

As my Uber cuts through busy London traffic, every second of that conversation is still parked in my head and I can't dislodge it.

Your happiness is all that matters to me.

How could it be? He had kids.

How could I not have seen that?

When I walk in, he's sitting at a table – not the table where we sat that first time, though I can't help but glance at it, as though to frequent, even just mentally, a happier time.

His head is down. He's tinkering on his phone.

'Hello,' I say, and he looks momentarily startled out of deep concentration, then he stands and kisses me, his hand alighting briefly on my shoulder.

'Our table was taken.' He nods over towards the couple who are sitting where we sat that night.

I want to smile at his nostalgia, but all I feel is a little circumspect.

I sit and we exchange an update on one another's day. Eventually, once we've been served our drinks, I say, 'Why here, of all places?'

He sets down his vodka soda, his gaze lingering on the glass. 'I don't know,' he says, then he looks at me. 'Hoping to breathe the rarefied air?' He glances again in the couple's direction. 'I suppose what I'm saying is, it's a heavy burden for you. All this . . .' He briefly upturns his hands. 'And I knew it would be. I *knew*. The fact of the matter is, I was so busy focusing on how you would handle it all – my pre-existing family – that I didn't really think much about how *I* would.' He frowns slightly. 'And I'm not doing the best job of it, I don't think.' Then he adds, 'Clearly.'

I don't exactly rush to contradict him. And then I say, 'I'm struggling with the situation at times, yes . . . I don't always know where I stand with you. And that's a very odd feeling for me to have about the man I'm married to.'

'I realise,' he says, as though he's disinclined to admit it. 'I get it.' He hangs his head a little.

'I sometimes get the impression you don't trust me on some level.'

He continues to stare at the table, nods. 'I know. I mean, I know why you feel like that. And it's me . . . I'm not always the best communicator.'

I wait for him to expand on that, to open some sort of door, but the waiter comes over and asks if we'd like to order dinner. When he leaves, Joe says, 'I'm going to try to do better, make more of an effort.' He brings his eyes to meet mine. 'I never – ever – want to have to live through another evening where my wife walks out of our home.' He looks deeply disturbed by his own words. 'I suppose, in bringing you here, I'd like you to try to remember that you did once have a lot of faith in me – in us. And I'm going to hope you'll be able to feel that again.'

It occurs to me that instead of being informed by age and experience, Joe is the one sounding idealistic now.

I stare at his hands crossed on top of the table, his wedding ring, feel myself searching for this new-found faith he's talking about. But my brain is a bit like sonar in a black ocean.

He cocks his head in a slightly cajoling manner. 'What do you say? Can we try to do better?'

We?

TWENTY-THREE

'Mummy got a fined ticket off the policeman because I was in the front seat and not in my booster seat!' Toby rugby tackles me the instant I walk in the door.

He's waving some sort of – 'What is that?' I say, staring at the long white gadget in his hand. Then, 'Oh my gosh! Where did you get that?' Somehow he's found Joe's electric toothbrush. He's ripped the head off, exposing the sharp metal shaft. I snatch it from his fingers as he's about to fence me with it. 'That's really dangerous. You could impale yourself!'

'What's a pale myself?'

I smile and gaze into his earnest little eyes. 'You could hurt yourself, is what I mean. That's not a toy.'

He chuckles.

'Oh, he loves those things.' Grace walks into the hallway and leans against the wall. I am intrigued by how every day is like a new slate for her – events of previous ones wiped clean. 'He once tried to shove one in a wall socket and nearly electrocuted himself.'

'Yikes!' I say, and he mimics me – 'Yi . . . kes!' He flings his arms around my legs, and I almost lose my balance from the exuberance of his hug.

Joe comes out of the bedroom, his phone pressed to his ear; a business call, I can tell, by his terse tone, the hardness in his eyes. He stares unseeingly at the object in my hand. 'Well, let's circle back later today,' I hear him say, and then he clicks off.

Toby tells him the same thing he just told me, about the ticket.

'What do you mean, Tobes?' Joe asks. We follow him into the kitchen where he goes to the pantry and pulls out a bag of coffee beans.

'The policeman said I was in the wrong seat and Mummy said we're in a hurry and we only live around the corner and the policeman said she had to calm down from swearing because unless she was calmed down from swearing she couldn't drive home and he gave her a fined ticket anyway!'

Joe shakes his head. 'Why were you not in the proper seat in the first place, Toby?'

'Because I didn't want to sit in it and Mummy tried to make me and then she finally said I could ride in the front if only I shut my trap and so I did.'

In lieu of the toothbrush, Toby has found one of my flip-flops and is tugging at the rubber joint.

'Well, next time you've got to do as you're told!' Joe wags a finger at him. 'And hey, don't do that to Lauren's shoes.' He takes the flip-flop away. 'You're going to trash them.'

I smile. But I can't help thinking that if it had been me who'd let him sit in the front seat and not his booster seat no one would see the amusing side.

'I should probably get on my way,' I say, going into our bedroom to find the shoes I'm actually going to wear. I've agreed to meet Sophie and Charlie at our pub off the King's Road.

Joe follows close behind. 'We were wondering . . . How about for today you don't meet your friends and you come with us to brunch? I really hate this Sunday policy of you going off . . .'

I turn to face him. The way he says it almost implies that the motive behind my Sunday gesture of self-erasure has been a selfish one.

'Can you?' he says. 'Grace is going to meet her friend for an hour and I thought we could take Toby for a swim at the lido then head out around one.'

I'm suddenly aware that Grace is hanging by the door, taking all this in. Then Joe notices her, and says, 'Grace. Why don't you tell Lauren you'd love it if she'd ditch her friends and come for brunch with us?' For some odd reason it takes me back to the day at the Cenotaph; that sense of being strong-armed.

Grace gawks at him for a second as though to say, *You have got to be kidding me!* Then, when his expression remains stoic, she says, 'Okay. Yeah . . . Lauren, why don't you come with us for brunch today? That would be great.'

Joe's face is full of so much expectation that I find myself reluctantly saying, 'Sure. I can call them and tell them I'm not coming.' I suppose I did just see them recently, and, besides, the one positive of Sophie and Charlie being joined at the hip is at least they'll have each other to eat with.

'Great,' he says. And then he adds, 'It's just as well I took the liberty of making a reservation at Kenwood House. For four.'

I am off Thursday and Friday. Joe has to go on a business trip to Edinburgh so he suggests I go with him. He has a function with some of his clients on Wednesday night, then on Thursday he has meetings all day.

After we check in and he dresses to go off to his dinner, I order room service, have a bath, then pull out my Kindle. He doesn't come back until late, and smells of Scotch and cigars. He's buzzed and looks handsome. Flushed but sexy, the top two buttons of his white dress shirt undone. We have sex. Then he swiftly falls asleep.

Next morning, I watch him get ready for his meetings. The perfect application of shirt, cufflinks, suit and shiny shoes. We arrange to meet back at the hotel around five with him promising to text me should plans change.

I start out with a list of things I'd like to do and see – a host of great intentions – but the second he leaves I stretch out in a patch of sunshine on the bed and am still there three hours later. Eventually, when the hunger pangs kick in, I order room service coffee and croissants, devour three of them, then FaceTime my parents. Since they moved to Spain I've tried not to focus on this nagging sense of abandonment that follows me around. Perhaps Only Child Syndrome brought on a more pronounced reaction to them giving up England in favour of permanent sunshine and sangria. Retiring to a better life is their right, of course. But I sometimes inwardly baulk at this idea they seem to have – that because I'm on a good career path and I'm married now, I'm 'all right', that I don't need to feel I'm their priority any longer, that I don't require the comfort of knowing that, if all else fails, my folks will always be firmly planted in my corner.

I tune out for some of the call: my dad's latest rant about Brexit, the stories about their vibrant social calendar, their ever-increasing circle of ex-pat friends who have moved to their complex. Some upsetting incident about a dog drowning in a swimming pool and my dad harping on about how everyone should just be grateful it wasn't a kid. When, finally, they get around to asking how I am, it feels like a bit of an afterthought, so I say the usual, 'I'm fine,' tell them a bit about work, then make some excuse about how my phone is almost dying.

After I shower and dress, I take myself for a wander down Princes Street. It's a beautiful day, and I discard my jacket and mostly settle for staring into shop windows. In the late afternoon, I find a beer garden down a back street and have half a lager and a ploughman's lunch. I'm just trying to decide whether it's worth attempting to visit the castle when Joe texts.

Wrapping up early. See u back in room at 4?

Perfect, I reply.

When I return to the hotel, housekeeping has been and I throw myself on top of the freshly made bed. The sun has shifted but the room is pleasantly warm. I open a window, and the white noise of a nearby generator sends me into a short but satisfying sleep.

When Joe gets back, he's in one of his very buoyant moods.

His meetings went well. He reels off his key achievements. Then, as I'm wandering towards the wardrobe, he grabs me by the hand and pulls me close, kissing me with the some of the raw hunger he exhibited last night. He's on top of me, trying to wriggle off my knickers, when he suddenly stops. 'You are still taking your pill, aren't you?'

'Yes,' I say. He goes to kiss me again but I press a hand into his chest. 'Why would you think I wasn't?'

He seems a little puzzled by my question. 'I don't think that. I just . . . maybe with travelling. I just wondered if you'd remembered to bring them.'

His hands go to my underwear again but I slither out from beneath him. 'You didn't seem to care last night.'

He sighs, rolls over into a sitting position. 'Look, last night, I'd had a few to drink . . . I didn't think. But it just occurred to me . . .'

'So if I said no, actually, I forgot to bring them . . . ?'

He sighs, climbs off the bed. 'Forget it,' he says.

∞

150

Later, we shower, I put on a nice dress, then we go out for dinner. Joe acts like the weirdness in the bedroom never happened.

'We really need to get time to ourselves more often,' he says brightly, as we walk hand in hand back to the hotel after a nightcap in a bar that sells more varieties of Scotch than I knew existed.

'Yes,' I say. 'That would be nice.' I picture some revised life. One in which we somehow manage to successfully negotiate all the hurdles that we haven't done a very good job of negotiating up to now.

'Maybe a few days or a weekend away every month?' He glances at me fondly, eyes blazing with optimism.

Between my crazy shift work and his custody arrangement, the obvious question is *How would that actually play out?* But I don't feel like asking it.

'That would be fantastic,' I say instead. I catch myself calculating that Grace might well be off to uni in four more years. But Toby not for fourteen. And what if we have children of our own? Where do they fit in?

But I think I already know the answer to that.

Back in the room he pulls me to him the moment we're in the door. 'Can we finish what we started earlier?'

His apology, I think.

'Sure,' I say.

But when his kiss travels down my neck, I don't feel myself responding to it in quite the same way.

Back in Hampstead the fridge is looking a little bare and the kids will soon be here, so the first thing we do is make a trip to WholeFoods. Joe loves grocery shopping, loves selecting what we're going to eat. I've never seen anyone get so excited about pushing a trolley up and down the aisles.

We are wandering over to the salad bar when I hear a voice call out, 'Joe!'

We turn, almost in sync, and right behind us is someone I almost immediately recognise. The woman from the yoga class.

'Luce!' he says.

There's an instant where her eyes slide from Joe to me and she looks confused. They exchange a few protracted pleasantries and then Joe seems to remember I'm here. He places his hand in the small of my back. 'Luce, I'd like you to meet Lauren.'

'We've met!' she says, and tells him about the class.

'Wow.' Joe glances at me. 'Small world.'

There are a stiff few seconds but then his phone rings. 'Sorry,' he says. 'Actually . . . I have to take this.' He strides off to a less populated corner of the shop, placing a hand over his other ear to block out the background noise.

Lucy and I are left looking at each other. 'Well,' she says, after a beat. 'I suppose he didn't waste much time! Good for him.' She inspects me with fresh interest. 'So how long have you guys been going out? We never did go for that coffee . . .'

I clear my throat, feel my cheeks heat up. 'Actually, we're not exactly going out . . . we're married.'

There is an instant where she appears thoroughly dumb-founded. 'Oh! Okay . . .' And then she adds, 'Well, for what it's worth I was never Meredith's number one fan.' She whips me up and down with her gaze again. 'And it doesn't surprise me that Joe has an eye for the younger pretty ladies . . . I mean, don't get me wrong, I'm not judging . . . Life's short. We owe it to ourselves to find happiness.' She stares in Joe's direction, a certain wistful look on her face. 'Well, anyway . . . tell him it was nice to see him again, will you?' And then she pushes her trolley towards the tills.

I have a very strange feeling that we'll never go for that coffee.

∾

'Why did you introduce me as Lauren and not your wife?'

We are sitting up in bed. His eyes move away from his laptop and he looks across at me. 'What?'

'Lucy. You introduced me as Lauren.'

He appears to think, then he says, 'No reason. It wasn't conscious . . . I suppose maybe because I haven't seen her in ages. I had no idea what she already knew.'

I contemplate that. Sounds plausible, I suppose. 'So how do you know her?' I ask.

There's a slightly awkward hesitation then he says, 'She's sort of an old friend. Her husband worked with Meredith. He was a barrister. The four of us were friends. He died of pancreatic cancer. Very sudden.'

'Oh.' I vaguely recall Lucy saying something about beginning to date again after never really imagining she'd have to. 'So you didn't stay friends with her after her husband died?'

Something changes in his eyes. A wall seems to go up. 'Not really. People drift away sometimes, don't they?'

Would you drift from a bereaved friend? 'So Meredith isn't still in touch with her then? She clearly didn't know you were divorced.'

He sends me a look. 'God, no.'

Hmm . . . I study him out of the corner of my eye, weighing the uncharacteristic note of drama in his reaction.

Clearly thinking I'm done with my questions, he goes back to his work. I stare at his hand resting by his laptop, the curl of his fingers as he reads something on his screen.

'She said it doesn't surprise her that you've got an eye for the younger, pretty women.'

He moves sharply, almost like a reflex – or a hit nerve – and his laptop tips so he has to steady it. 'What? She said that?'

'She said that!'

There is a moment where he looks a little annoyed. Then he says, 'Well, who cares what Lucy thinks . . . For the record, there's only one woman I've got an eye for, and the fact that she's younger and pretty is arguably just a bonus.' He smiles, then returns his attention to his laptop.

TWENTY-FOUR

Joe is agitated when I climb in the car. He has Meredith on speakerphone. When she must hear me greet him, she says, 'Joe, are you still there?' And then, when he doesn't instantly reply, 'Look, are you too busy for this now?'

'Hang on,' he says to her, then takes her off speakerphone. 'Sorry.' He casts me a glance, switches off the engine. 'Just give me a minute.' Next he is out of the car, mobile in hand, and pacing up and down the path.

I sit there and watch him, wondering why he'd rather walk around jacketless in the rain than have me overhear his conversation.

After what feels like an unreasonable amount of time, he returns to the car.

'Plan's changed.' He reaches over to kiss my cheek as though it's only now that I've become properly visible. 'I'm going to have to take you home, then I'm heading straight over to Meredith's.'

'What's happened?'

He pulls out of the parking space. 'Grace's head teacher wants to meet with us in the morning. Grace has been accused of stealing a girl's AirPods Pro and then vlogging about them.' He presses on the brake a little hard and I pitch forward. 'It's obviously a huge mistake . . . Or some sort of vendetta. I mean, of all the things Grace might be, she's certainly not a thief.'

My brain scrambles to make its way around this information. Then I say, 'Have you actually seen the vlog?'

'No.' He sends me a frown. 'Would I need to?'

I sit there contemplating this, then pull out my phone and log on to Grace's YouTube. Within a moment or two her face fills my screen. She's got her silky hair pulled back in a ponytail and I can see the little wireless devices sticking out her ears. I turn up the volume and we hear her chattering away about silicone buds and active noise cancellation, like she has a PhD in the subject.

'Aren't those things pretty expensive?' I'd considered buying myself some a while back until I made a trip to the Apple store and blanched.

'She's hardly strapped for cash.'

Hmm. True.

'It'll all blow over but it's damned annoying. I've had to get out of a meeting, which took a bit of manoeuvring . . . Meredith says they've no evidence. It's this girl's word against Grace's.'

I stare at my kneecaps peeping out below the hem of my skirt, wondering what I should say or do. 'I don't really feel like going home,' I tell him. 'Why don't you just drop me off at the pub and I can have a glass of wine and wait for you? You'll need to eat at some point. Even if it's later.'

He shakes his head. 'I've no idea how long this is going to take. I tried tracking Grace down but she isn't answering her phone. I'll probably just get something at Meredith's. No sense in you waiting around.' He sends me a plaintive, but vaguely dismissive, glance.

I have a mental picture of them sitting sharing one of Rosamie's home-cooked lasagnes over a bottle of wine while they wait for their daughter to come home, the alcohol perhaps loosening Joe's

tongue. Meredith asking him, 'So how is newly married life, then?'
And Joe prefacing his reply with a sigh and the word, *Well* . . .

'I'm sorry,' he says. 'I'll make it up to you.'

He drops me off at our door.

When his white Lexus pulls up in front of the flat hours later, I am sitting on the sofa by the window, reading my Kindle. Mozart alerts me to the fact that Joe is here by leaping out of his bed and running to the door. I watch Joe walk the short distance up our path, none of the usual spring in his step.

'God. What a day!' he says the instant he sees me. 'Do we have anything to eat? I'm ravenous.' He plonks himself down in the armchair, arms and legs splayed, like someone just shot him.

'I thought you said you'd get something at Meredith's.'

'Did I?' he says, tiredly. 'I don't even really remember.' His eyes go to the pizza box sitting on the coffee table next to the half-empty wine bottle.

'Sorry. I ate the whole thing. There wasn't much else for me to do but stuff my face with pizza . . . If only you'd texted.'

'Was it good?' he asks. 'You can at least let me imagine.'

'Awful. That's why I ate all of it.'

He smiles, like the sight of me has suddenly brightened his day.

I smile back, recognising that his arrival home is actually a bright spot in mine. 'So how are things? If I dare ask.'

'Oh . . . it's fine. This other girl – Sara – isn't the most reliable person, I don't think.' He gets up, goes over to the drinks cabinet and pours himself a Scotch. 'Maybe she was jealous. Or maybe she lost the earbuds, didn't want to tell her parents and just looked for someone to blame.'

'Wouldn't there be an email receipt from the store? To prove Grace bought them?'

His hand with the Scotch bottle in it turns still. He meets my eyes. 'The onus isn't on Grace to prove she bought them. It's on her accuser to prove she didn't.'

I contemplate him. 'But surely if Grace just presented her receipt, then that makes it all so much simpler, doesn't it? Don't you just want it dealt with?'

'It will be dealt with,' he says coldly, almost disapprovingly. 'Tomorrow. When the girl admits she tried to frame Grace.' He puts the bottle back in the cabinet.

Accuser. Frame. Perhaps that's the language you pick up if you live for many years with a barrister but it all seems a little over the top to me.

He walks back to the armchair, sits, takes a sip of his drink. 'Anyway, if you really want to know, she doesn't have the receipt – I asked. She said she empties her inbox regularly and would never keep something like that.'

I try to see if anything about his expression indicates he's thinking, *Convenient!*

'I am sure the store would have a copy.'

'What's this about?' he says sharply. 'How is there time to be going to the store now? We're meeting with the school at eight-thirty in the morning.'

'I was just trying to be helpful.'

He sips in silence, stares across the room. I watch him: the contemplative Joe who is here in body but not fully in mind. Then he says, 'Meredith expects the girl's going to deeply regret bringing an allegation like this, when she has zero proof.' He stares through his glass at the amber liquid. 'And my guess is that once Meredith is done with her, she'll wish she'd never been born.'

It bothers me all night. Joe and Meredith don't know if Grace stole them, but either way, they're not prepared to consider that she might have. I'm not sure what this teaches Grace – or what it says about my husband, whom I've always thought of as having practically written the book on integrity. But something else bothers me, too. By not telling them what I know about Grace's shoplifting I feel complicit. And yet I can't exactly put forward something for which I have no proof. Grace may have stolen the waistcoat, and other things, but that doesn't mean she definitely took the earbuds.

'There's something you should know,' I say to his back when I struggle out of bed, wander into the kitchen and find him making breakfast.

He glances over his shoulder, his hand freezing momentarily on the frying pan handle. 'What's up?'

The sun streaming in the kitchen window casts him in an attractive light, and for a moment I want to hold on to our cosy domesticity and keep this other reality of our lives at bay.

I hitch myself on to a stool at the breakfast bar. 'Grace stole a waistcoat from Topshop. The one she was wearing when she was doing her Brian May act. And it's not the first time she's shoplifted either.'

'What?' He gives a single snort of laughter.

'It's true. I'm not making it up.'

He pulls the towel from his shoulder and wipes his hands. 'I'm confused,' he says, cautiously. 'How do you know this?'

I tell him about our conversation.

'A magnet?' He throws me a doubting, almost defensive look. That fissure is there. The disaffection that makes itself apparent when he's preparing for something he doesn't want to hear. 'You can't seriously expect me . . . This is bullshit.' He quickly seems to remember his pan, and turns around to pull it off the gas. 'She must have been messing with you. I mean . . . how would she even know how to do something like remove security tags with giant magnets?'

'YouTube? It's not like she's exactly a stranger to the medium.'

It occurs to me that the magnet might be in her room. But I can hardly go on a digging mission to incriminate her and wave it under his nose – *Ta-dah!* 'Apparently she's been shoplifting for years – it seems to have started around the time Meredith fell pregnant with Toby.' I try to ignore the look of vexation in his eyes when I say this. 'Only now it seems to have got more serious . . . She thinks she's a brand ambassador. That vlogging about brands gives her the right to take things for free.'

'Don't be ridiculous!' He throws it back as though the problem is not the information – but me. 'If this is true, why wouldn't you have said anything to me before?'

'Because – obviously – it put me in a very odd position. I didn't think that snitching on her would exactly help our relationship and I thought that if we had a gentle talk about consequences, she might think twice about doing it again.'

His brows knit together. He wipes a palm across his mouth. 'You didn't think maybe it was up to me or Meredith to talk to Grace about *consequences*? Since when was that your job?' The expression on his face is colder than his words and it takes me a second or two to recover.

'What exactly *is* my job, Joe?' I throw up my hands. 'Because I really wonder sometimes!'

We lock eyes. He give me a hard, diagnostic stare and I do my best to return it. Finally he says, a mite less rattled, 'Why would she admit it to you? It doesn't make sense.'

'Maybe because I caught her. I don't know,' I say, watching him pour himself some water at the sink then gulp it down. 'Maybe because she actually wants someone to know. She'd rather get into shit than feel ignored.'

'That's crazy! Grace isn't starved of attention!'

'Maybe not. But you have to admit her life changed when a new baby came along, after a decade of being an only child. And it's changed again. Her parents get divorced. Her dad remarries. She's got two homes. And now there's . . . me. Another draw on your attention. Maybe she just wants someone to ask her how she's feeling about all this.'

It suddenly just hits me. I don't know why now – or how I didn't see this before. But suddenly it all makes sense.

'Oh my God . . . Does Grace know for sure you began seeing me *after* you and her mother split up?'

He looks puzzled by my question at first, and yet I can see a light going on. 'Yes,' he says. 'I mean . . . I assume. It's not like we've ever had the conversation.'

'Well, maybe you should have,' I say. 'Because I've a feeling she might be under the impression that I broke up your marriage. And maybe that's why she's having a very hard time with my presence in her life.'

Maybe this is what she meant when she told Toby that her mum and dad split up because he was having an affair!

I'm the affair!

'My God,' he says, after seeming to ruminate on this. 'You really missed your vocation. You should have gone into psychiatry.'

There is no ignoring the sarcastic tone. It's a nasty dig, and one I'd least expect from him. For some odd reason, I think of the day we met. How genuinely impressed he was that I was studying to be a doctor. And now he's putting me down for it.

How far we have fallen.

'You know what?' I say, jumping to my feet. 'Screw you.'

His jaw drops. Then he says, 'What did you say?'

161

'I said screw you. You're threatened by any opinion you don't share, aren't you?' My heart hammers. 'Maybe it was because I'm twelve years younger than you that made you feel so secure with me, Joe. Because I couldn't challenge or threaten your ego, or your parenting skills . . . Well, fuck this bullshit!'

I don't think I've ever sworn at him. He just stares at me, astonishment blazing in his eyes.

'You're right,' I say, with a little less vitriol. 'She's your daughter. Get on with parenting her. Don't listen to a thing I've got to say. What would I know? Because you know everything. And, I mean, Grace – clearly – has been the beneficiary of that!'

I walk to our bedroom, go in and slam the door.

TWENTY-FIVE

For some inexplicable reason, I have patients who feel like old friends or family, and those who are mere faces, bodies, problems to solve. I can be remarkably detached from their conditions, or they can trouble me for days.

I've been on shift about two hours when they come in. A young guy clutching his wife's hands. His big thumb caressing her wrist.

'Everybody just keeps telling her to give it time,' he speaks on her behalf. 'But it's gone on way too long. Nobody seems to be taking this seriously.'

Twenty-six-year-old Renata Nicols can't keep anything down, not even liquids. She has lost twenty pounds in three weeks. X-rays of her stomach and bowel taken during her last visit to A&E eight days ago all came back normal, as did her blood work. She is pale and despondent but quietly enduring. Her husband is clearly worried sick.

'You definitely shouldn't still be vomiting like this if it was just food poisoning,' I say when she talks me through all her symptoms. 'And I'm very sorry you've felt no one is taking you seriously.' I address both of them. 'I can promise you I'm going to get to the bottom of this if it's the last thing I do.'

They thank me profusely, and there's a moment where I look at both their faces and catch a simultaneous welling in their eyes.

'I see you've an appointment with a gastroenterologist, but it's three months away. Obviously you can't wait that long or there'll be nothing left of you, will there?' I try to sound upbeat. She attempts to smile. 'So what I'm going to do is get a scope down to take a look at your oesophagus – today. It might mean waiting around a while, but give me an hour or so and let me see what I can come up with.'

They thank me profusely again.

I pull my gaze away from their joined hands and try to tamp down an unexpected surge of envy at how wrapped up in themselves they are. They don't have kids, ex-wives, friends who don't understand them. They are the centre of each other's universe, cocooned in their newly married bubble. And no one would expect it to be any other way.

I walk back to my station and am just about to page the duty gastroenterologist when my mobile rings.

'Grace denied it,' Joe says – almost like he's serving a ball for me to hit back. 'She said there was never any stealing of any waistcoat, never any conversation about it with you . . . She had no idea what I was talking about, in fact.' There's a pause and then he says, 'Why would you say that about her if it wasn't true?'

The blood rushes to my face, pounds in my ears. Once again I find myself walking to the less populated end of the unit – to take a damned personal call.

'I don't know, Joe!' I fire back, under my breath. 'Think about it. Why would I . . . ? Don't you think that perhaps Grace's reasons for lying are greater than mine?'

'I don't know what to believe, to be honest,' he says, after a protracted silence. 'I'm starting to think I have no idea what's really going on in our home or . . .'

In our marriage? Because neither do I!

I take a deep breath. 'This is horrible timing for me. You can't bother me at work with this stuff.'

'I'm sorry,' he says, sounding one part guilty and two parts offended. 'We can talk about this later.'

I feel like saying, *Why don't you talk to your damned daughter?*

But then he adds, 'Anyway, it's gone away. The earbuds thing. Sara withdrew her accusation. Meredith gave her the money to buy a replacement pair.'

Because she knows Grace stole them! She paid the girl off! I want to scream *Doesn't that say it all? Is everybody burying their heads in the sand?* But as though he knows exactly what I'm thinking, he says, 'It just seemed easier than the whole business of one girl's word against the other.'

Easier to believe a lie if it's your daughter's lie. Of course.

'You know, Joe . . .' I say. 'I thought you had more integrity than that.' And then I hang up.

I go back to my station to try to remember exactly what I was doing but I cannot pluck that conversation out of my head. I can just picture that distasteful little scenario. *Sara, you're a liar. You've accused my daughter of being a thief and risked getting her expelled, but here's a pair of expensive earbuds anyway. Just because, you know, we're generous people.*

Urgh! The wrongness, and his attitude, beat away at me like a stick. Then I try to remember what this is really all about. Grace is acting out. She thinks I broke up her parents' marriage. She thinks she's losing Joe.

And right this minute I have to say I know how she feels.

TWENTY-SIX

Dear everyone. Things have deteriorated rapidly! SD is a thief and both parents are in denial.
BM just used her money and power to make an
annoying little problem go away, and what's
shocking is DH seemed fine with it. SD made
up lies to her mother about me. DH doesn't
know who to believe. I am trying really hard to
hope a wand can be waved and all will come
good, but a horrible part of me feels my marriage was a mistake.

Miserable (No kidding!)

I post it before I've a chance to talk myself out of it.

When I check back half an hour later, I've got five replies. One
of them is a nonsensical tirade about something entirely unrelated.
Another, from Disillusioned, says:

There's no such thing as a blended family.
Blended implies you throw a lot of stuff in the
mix but it all comes out smooth. The fact is

there are always these lumps that stick in your craw.

WickedWitch:

Welcome to the club! If I could do it all over, I'd never do it over! OH will always, ALWAYS take the side of his kids. It's the biological wiring of a father. You're a second wife but the real second is where you fall in relation to his children. My advice? Get out before you have kids of your own with him. There are plenty of amazing single men who don't have baggage!!!

DoginKennel:

A relationship is only worth saving if you're on the same page, if you bring out the good in each other, if you're able to share concerns, if his actions and words match – and, if you feel he values and respects you even in times of conflict. In my case, DH did. Ultimately that kept us together. Wishing you luck.

Odd One Out says:

Just remember there are also lots of single men who are fuck-ups too! All relationships have their challenges. Have you considered couples therapy? Might be worth a try!

I like Odd One Out's input generally.

But – seriously – five months married and already in therapy?

I try to swallow a ball of sadness but it won't go down.

It's as warm as any summer's evening so, as Joe is at a client dinner, I decide to go out for a walk. I make my way to the Heath and head towards Parliament Hill, one of my favourite routes, which takes me just over an hour. At the top of the hill I stare out across London – to Canary Wharf and the Gherkin in the distance, the Shard gleaming in the end-of-day light.

I try to get my head around what I'm feeling but am somehow deprived of my normal range of emotions. Then I realise that everything feels difficult because it *is* difficult. But difficult isn't the issue. I can handle difficult.

It's Joe. I can't help but wonder if I like him anymore, let alone love him.

As I walk back through the village, I don't think I've ever felt more disheartened. I'm rounding a corner that has a popular pub on it, one Joe and I have never ventured into because he's not crazy about the young crowd. The place is bustling with people my age. I slow down and gaze at them through the window, some sort of vicarious longing running wild in me. The cadence of elevated voices. Wide smiles, sleek hair, short shirt sleeves on fit male arms. Their collective laughter, an echo of my own from before all this – before Joe – so faint I can barely hear it. The me I used to be. Next I'm pushing the door open, going inside.

I have to inch my way through the bodies standing with drinks in their hands. It used to be so commonplace – a night after classes, at a pub. A lot of us camped out at a big table in a beer garden in summer. A rite of passage I never even thought about until now.

The bar is less crowded than I'm expecting. Less of a tussle to get a drink. The barman sees me right away and asks what I want, and I order a gin and tonic.

As I stand there and take my first sip, I could not feel more like a fish out of water, and not because I'm the only person who appears to be on their own. Then three lads take pity on me.

One of them, the cheeky redhead, says, 'What you doing standing here like Nellie-no-mates?'

Despite myself, I smile. Then I tell them I'm actually waiting for a friend, and she's just walking up from the Tube. And for a moment I think, *God, I wish I was! Back in those carefree days!*

To give me something to do I decide to log back on to the forum to reread some of the responses. But as I do, I see I have a personal message from Odd One Out.

Dear Miserable,

Hope I haven't been too much of a pot-stirrer on your thread. It can be a negative place in there – although nuggets of wisdom do emerge. Our situations actually sound eerily similar. Like you, there are days when I really wonder what I've done. Life was fairly simple before I married. I don't regret it, for the most part, but sometimes I wish it was just a normal marriage with normal problems. Anyway, I'm not massively comfortable with my presence in the forum. If you ever need a more private vent, I am here probably feeling much the same as you. Hope that's not too forward! By the way, my real name is Mel.

She sounds so nice. I'm excited to have a new friend! I quickly reply:

> Thank you for getting in touch, Mel! Not forward at all! It will be great to connect with one person rather than a sea of strangers! And my real name is Lauren. What's your situation? I am curious . . . Personally, I'm struggling at the moment with my choices. No sense of my husband and me being a team right now. No real idea where I belong. Seems to be a world of pressure on us as stepmothers, and very few people can relate to that. It's great to feel someone out there understands. I look forward to being in touch! Best wishes, Lauren.

'Big texter, your mate, is she?' Redhead asks, swooping in to peer over my shoulder as my thumbs work the keyboard.

'Which Tube stop was she at?' his friend says. 'Piccadilly Circus?'

'Ha, ha, ha.' I move my phone so Redhead can't see it. 'You don't believe she's coming, do you?' I tease them back.

'Seriously?' he says. 'Nah! But you know what? If you're a Nellie-no-mates, there's no shame in admitting it. We all have our crosses to bear.' He double-nudges my arm.

I'm just smiling when another message pops up from Mel.

> Okay Lauren! Nice to properly meet you! I will look forward to further chats. And yes, you are right – tremendous pressure that few understand. You got married and found yourself in the thick of someone else's family. You're not

the kids' parent, but you'll still feature in their lives and memories and will help shape their perception of themselves. It's a huge responsibility! Finding your way and your role is hard. Anyway, big topic! Don't want to hog your evening! Nice to get to know you.

Mel.

She's so right! Says it so well!

'What's the story this time then?' Redhead asks. 'Let me guess . . . she stood you up. Or . . . she met someone else on the way over here.'

'Why should I tell you anything?' I say. 'You guys have all the answers!' I grin. A few years ago I'd have given these lads a wide berth. But it's been so long since I had a bit of frivolous banter with anyone – even if it's inane – that I find it blissfully refreshing.

I type another quick note to Mel. Agree with everything you say. More to come!

Then I slug back my drink and tell my fan club I'm leaving to a chorus of 'Argh!'s. Then I begin the rather underwhelming walk home, pleased – at least – that it seems like I've got a little ally in Mel.

When I walk in, Joe is sitting on the sofa in the dark, listening to opera. It's only when I switch on the wall sconces that he notices me.

'Oh, you're back,' he says. 'I was worried you were never coming home. You didn't text.'

I drop my bag into the armchair, slide off my jacket. 'I thought you were out with clients. I just went to the pub for a quick glass of wine with a couple of the nurses,' I lie, and stroke the dog.

'So you've eaten?'

'All I want, yes.' I walk into the kitchen to pour a glass of water. He follows. 'I talked to Grace.'

I feel myself bracing for this conversation. I turn, meet his eyes.

'I met her for tea after school. We had a talk. And she admitted she may have taken one or two things without paying for them. In the past. But she doesn't do that anymore.'

One or two things. 'The earbuds?'

He stares at his feet like a shamed altar boy.

'So is anyone going to apologise to Sara for not believing her?'

He looks at me like I've got two heads. 'What? No. That's over now.'

'And what are you going to do with Grace? About this stealing problem? You're saying she took one or two things in the past, but it's hardly in the past if she stole from a friend just a few days ago.'

'It's not a problem,' he says. 'It's a few isolated events.' Then he adds, 'Meredith and I can sort that out. It's not really for you to worry about.'

'No,' I say, an edge in my voice. 'Of course not.' It wouldn't be.

I wait for him to say, *I'm sorry. You were right. I really regret doubting you.* Instead he just looks lost in his own private world again.

Then after a while he says, 'I'm going to try to spend more time with her. Maybe Monday nights I meet her after school and we have an early dinner, just the two of us.' Then he glances my way. 'I think she probably did suspect you and I had an affair. I brought it up. She didn't exactly correct me.'

I wait for more, but clearly that's all I'm getting. The bare minimum of an account. He is telling me what I need to know. But *only* that.

He goes back to the sofa. I follow him this time. 'Have you considered getting her some therapy?' I ask.

'Therapy?' he says, like it's a dirty word.

'Maybe we could use some too.'

Disappointment writes itself all over his face. And then he says, 'If *you* think we need therapy then maybe *you* should go and get some. But, believe me, you're on your own with that.'

TWENTY-SEVEN

I have two messages from Mel when I next check.

> Dear Lauren,
>
> Sorry, I think you asked me a question before and I didn't answer. I have been married for almost a year. Archie is twelve and Olivia is seven. OH had acrimonious divorce and doesn't like to relinquish control – in general, but also as a parent. They are great kids – if only OH would let them breathe! I am not a quitter though. Things are a bit better now than before. My advice, not that you're asking, would be to give it a year – that's what I plan to do – and then reassess.
>
> Mel.

The next one says,

PS: Where do you live? We are in London, Clapham area. Renting right now because I'm just on a teacher's salary, and my partner is paying spousal maintenance and child support. Would love to own a house one day, maybe somewhere quieter. Anyway, hope you're doing well. Mel.

I read these with glee. She sounds so nice. Like a kindred spirit. I respond:

Mel, thanks for the info. We are in north London but I work in south. Actually, I pass through Clapham on the train almost every day! Maybe we should have coffee some time!

Lauren.

She replies a few minutes later.

Small world! Sure, if you ever feel like getting off the train someday (the literal one, not the metaphorical one! Haha) I'd be happy to meet for coffee. Here is my mobile. Drop me a text.

Mel.

This is great! I swiftly pop her number into my phone.

TWENTY-EIGHT

Since the therapy word was outed, the silence between us is deafening and after a week or so of it I start finding other things to do with my evenings, rather than head straight home.

On Wednesday night I go to a Pilates class – first scanning the room to make sure Lucy isn't in it. On Thursday, I meet Sophie at the Pig's Ear for a glass of wine and a Scotch egg. Out of the blue, she texted and suggested it. For the first time ever – and perhaps because it's blissfully just the two of us – I tell her honestly about how things are between Joe and me, how there are days when I almost regret marrying him.

'It's like, when we first met – from the very moment, actually – he made me feel so *seen*. And yet a few months into marriage and, at times, I think I'm invisible.'

I tell her I don't mean it in the sexual sense. It's the rest of me – my thoughts, ideas, my feelings, that are being ignored.

She says, 'Well, your marriage is tested, on some level, by Joe's kids. Ours is tested by the lack of them.'

I sense it's taken two large reds and Charlie's absence to get us here.

She meets my eyes and then surprises me by saying, 'Charlie and I can't have children.' Before I can react, she says, 'It's him, not me. It's why he decided he couldn't go through with the wedding. He said he didn't see the point of being married if we can't have kids.'

'So *that's* the big secret?' I can't help but feel horribly underwhelmed.

'It's big to him, let's just say that. He's struggled with it. Sometimes he gets depressed.' She looks a little tight-lipped suddenly. I don't press her for details. If she wants to tell me, she will.

'I tried to make him see that it doesn't matter to me.'

I scour her face. 'Doesn't it?'

'Not enough to dump him. Maybe some people would say it's odd – a paediatrician who doesn't actually care if she has kids . . .'

Kids are not something Sophie and I have ever talked about. And yet I suppose there was always an assumption that we would both end up having them.

'Some might say he was prepared to walk away from me, to stay single and play the field rather than have a life with me . . .' She briefly lowers her eyes. 'Maybe they'd be right. But he said that had nothing to do with it. He was just worried it would eventually come between us . . .' She shrugs. 'It definitely would have been a great opportunity for me to say, "Okay, let's just part ways . . ."'

'But instead you ended up changing his mind and marrying anyway.'

'Yes,' she says. 'I think I put his mind at rest, more than changed it. I told him it would never, ever come between us. That I'd be fine with it being just us . . . I think deep down he fears being alone, fears ending up with no one who would properly love him – like family.'

This makes me wonder if Grace and Toby would one day properly love me, or if I would always be left with a sense that I never quite belonged. 'Is this why he always seems to go with you everywhere you go? Because he hates to be alone?' I'm glad I've finally got this out.

She doesn't flinch, or seem surprised. 'No,' she says. 'Or . . . well, maybe a bit. He doesn't like to be . . . passed over, or feel he's not included. He's just that personality type, I suppose. Seems confident and blustery but deep down he's a bit insecure and needy . . .'

It strikes me that she seems to have him all figured out. If only I knew Joe that well.

'And maybe there's part of me that enjoys that, you know. Maybe I secretly love being needed. Maybe it gives me a sense of purpose.'

I think about that. I had never really thought that anyone who was so driven in their professional life would consider themselves in need of a purpose.

And then I say, 'Well, on some level I can relate.'

I have never told her about my conversation with Joe on the topic of kids. The one that came shortly before he proposed, and – interestingly – soon after my strange pub night with Meredith. It would have been one more black mark against his character, and another excuse for Sophie and Charlie to tell me, again, why they thought Joe was wrong for me. But as we've ventured into this, I say, 'Joe doesn't want any more children.'

She looks stunned, then says, 'Seriously?' And then, 'I don't understand . . .'

'I never actually found a way to talk about it. Maybe for the same reasons you didn't.'

'Tell me,' she says.

And so I do.

I picture it so vividly, like it happened only days ago.

Joe sitting on the sofa, his left arm extended along the back, right ankle on his opposite knee. I could sense immediately that a serious conversation was coming. And that's when he brought up my birthday night at the restaurant, when he'd given me my bag. When we had danced around the idea of a future together, and I literally would have said anything to convince both him and myself that we were on the same page – and I almost did.

'You know what we touched on? Well, I actually lose sleep over it, you know,' he said.

Apprehension crept up my spine. I was in love. I only wanted happy conversations, not ones that kept people awake at night.

He didn't immediately go on. I felt the impact of it, the concept of there being something that wasn't going to go away just because I'd decided to pay it no mind.

'Lauren . . .' he finally said. He patted the seat beside him. When I sat down he took my hands, stroked the knuckles with his thumbs. 'You're a young, beautiful woman and it's only natural that one day you're going to want children.'

He had articulated it. I was stunned by what might be coming next.

'And you don't,' I pre-empted.

He shook his head. 'No, I didn't say that . . . I didn't exactly say I don't want them, but I do think we need to talk about timing.'

He was trying to be tactful. That's how I knew this was big.

'What I'm trying to say is, you've got another foundation year to complete, then another *three* before you become a family doctor. I think we have to be realistic . . . I can't imagine it would be ideal for you to have a baby in the middle of all that.' He fixed me with a level stare. 'You're not going to want to interrupt your studies to become a mother, are you?'

It was true. I'd never really thought about it consciously or with such calculation, but now he put it this way, I couldn't deny it. Having a baby before I was established in my career would not be the best timing. I shook my head. 'You're right.'

'So, then . . .' He had let go of my hands and, with the gesture, I felt something way more than just a physical parting of skin. 'If you wait until you've been a family doctor for, say, a year or so, then you'll still only be in your mid-thirties, which is fine for you.' There was a loaded pause. 'But it's not fine for me.'

'What?' I said. I was genuinely not following.

'I don't want to be an old dad.' The way he said it was final. Like there was no room for movement.

I suddenly felt like I'd been lifted to an extraordinary height and then dropped on to concrete.

'Old dad?' Nothing about Joe was old or ever would be.

I told him this.

He didn't look flattered. He was on a mission.

'Think about it from my perspective,' he said. 'By the time it was born, I'd be forty-seven/forty-eight. I'd be in my mid-to-late sixties when it was going off to college!' I could tell he was searching my face, desperate for me to understand.

All I could hear was him calling a baby we might have *it*.

I couldn't look at him. Was there a possibility I'd misheard? Got the wrong end of the stick?

Part of me longed to just rush headlong and fall in line with his wishes, to say, *It's fine! Really! I can have a baby sooner than that. Now. Tomorrow. In fact . . . just tell me when it's convenient for you.* Anything that would make this – obstacle, if that's what it was – go away. But I was aware that, unlike on other occasions, that compliant pleaser in me was hanging back. Perhaps it was shock.

'I'm sorry,' he said finally, as the silence between us grew and grew. 'I'm only saying this because I care about you and I feel it's my responsibility to be honest with you, and put my selfish interests aside.' He took hold of my hands again. 'I once told you all that mattered to me was your happiness, and it does . . . I want to give you the life you deserve. But I can't give you something I don't have in me to give. And the very last thing I could ever stand knowing is that for some reason you didn't end up having a family of your own, you were deprived of being a mother, because of me.'

I wondered if the timing thing was a bit of a red herring, because this almost sounded like he was saying he didn't really want any more kids *at all*. Tears swelled in my eyes. I tried not to blink so they wouldn't fall.

He was studying me closely. I felt his eyes combing over my face, my hair. After a long spell, he said, 'I don't want to lose you. But I think you need to think through what a future with me would look like, given what I've said and where I stand.'

I didn't press for clarification, like I should have done, perhaps out of fear of losing him. I told him I'd think it over.

When I've finished, Sophie says, 'That's terrible! It seems so selfish. Where does it leave you, Lauren?'

I think of Scotland and the birth control reaction. 'I'm not sure,' I say. 'I married him knowing how he felt. I told him I was probably okay if we didn't have kids of our own.'

I remember I was so caught up in our romance that I would have signed away every last right to be with him; I would have sacrificed pretty much everything and convinced myself it was no sacrifice at all. I pretended it didn't matter simply because I didn't want to confront it.

She searches my face. 'Can't you talk to him? Change his mind? I mean, he's got two already, what's one more?'

'I don't know that it's fair to accept something big like this and then try to change somebody's mind about it. Love isn't about trying to take what someone can't give.'

'Can't is different from won't.'

I nod. But something occurs to me: as we've just been talking about male insecurity, I wonder if it's got nothing to do with being an old dad. Is Joe worried that if our marriage doesn't work, he could end up with *two* broken families? I think of the buying versus renting comment. His recent remark in the restaurant: *I never – ever – want to have to live through another evening where my wife walks out of our home . . .*

Despite his behaviour sometimes indicating otherwise, is Joe terrified of losing me?

∽

It must be confession time. Or perhaps it's catching. Because when I get home, Joe is sitting up in bed working. He promptly closes his laptop.

'I want to tell you something,' he says. 'It's been on my mind for a while.'

For some utterly inane reason, I'm thinking he's going to say he's changed his mind about having a baby.

But then, as I perch on the end of the bed, he says, 'You asked me a long time ago about why Meredith and I divorced.'

My mind drifts back. 'I did,' I say.

His gaze coasts over my face, my shoulders, drops down to my hand resting on the duvet. 'You were right. It was more than just about us feeling like we were ships that passed in the night.' He looks pensive suddenly. 'Meredith cheated.'

It takes me a moment to think straight. 'Meredith did?'

'Yes,' he says. 'And not once, but twice.' And then he adds, 'Well, as good as . . .'

TWENTY-NINE

'She had an affair with Alistair – you met his wife, Lucy.'

Lucy? After a shocked pause, I say, 'The guy who died?'

'Yes.'

I rush to try to make sense of this, remembering how she insinuated she didn't like Meredith. 'So Lucy knew about it?'

'Yes.' He stares off in the direction of the window. 'Apparently on his deathbed he got some urge to come clean, so he told his wife.'

'What?' I must look aghast. 'Why would he do that?'

'Don't ask me. Maybe he thought clearing his conscience would serve him better in the afterlife. Who knows?'

I contemplate this. 'That's utterly . . . horrible!'

He studies my reaction. 'If he'd never said anything, Meredith would never have told me, I don't imagine . . . It was only because she didn't want me hearing it second-hand.'

'My God,' I say.

'It happened a long time ago, apparently. It didn't really mean anything. At least that's what she told me.'

I frown. There's something I'm not grasping. 'So why did Lucy imply you were the one with the wandering eye?'

'I don't know,' he says. 'It may have something to do with the fact that she once came on to me at a party years ago. I turned her down. Maybe she took the rejection personally and this was her way of getting back at me. I don't know what would motivate her to say something like that, to be honest . . .'

'Wow . . . So did Meredith know about her coming on to you?'

He shakes his head. 'God, no. That would have only put a match to petrol. Anyway . . . it was nothing. No huge big deal. I put it right out of my head.'

'This is crazy,' I say. 'So how did you feel when she told you?'

'Fantastic, of course,' he says sarcastically. 'I was angry, naturally. Angry she'd done it, and angry I had to find out, in a way.'

'You'd have preferred not to have known?'

'Of course,' he says, a little awkwardly. 'I'd always thought of her as loyal.' He looks off across the room again. 'She can be a contradiction at times; she's inherently loyal in some respects, yet she can be *dis*loyal in ways she doesn't think are important . . . But I didn't think it applied to something like this.'

It strikes me that this is perhaps the biggest thing he's ever revealed to me. 'So is this why you divorced?' Something about this is confusing me but I can't pinpoint it.

He shakes his head. 'I didn't divorce her for this exactly. No.'

I must look incredulous because he says, 'I had Grace and Toby to think about, didn't I? If there had only been the two of us . . . Toby was a baby! I had to put them first. Besides, it's not like the affair was ever going to start up again – Alistair was dead. It was in the past. So I just decided to let it stay there.' Then he adds, 'It was purely for my kids.'

I think of what he told me a while back. *Everybody will try to fuck you over but you need to be able to count on your dad.*

We sit through a spell of silence. Finally I say, 'Why didn't you tell me before? Why was it such a big secret?'

He stares at a spot on the duvet. 'It's not a topic I like to revisit, to be honest. It was all very painful at the time. It made me question my judgement, made me doubt myself – how could I not have known she'd do something like this? Why did I not suspect at the time? Plus, Alistair was supposed to be . . . a friend.' He looks away. 'Besides, it's not exactly the best reflection on me, is it? When your wife cheats. Not something a guy probably wants to go around advertising.'

Go around advertising? It's astonishing how he can sometimes make me feel so insignificant. But I don't have the energy to take issue with it.

'But I know you had some unanswered questions around this . . . I accept your right to know.'

So this is Joe's way of letting me in, of bringing me closer? I have a lot of questions, but only one is pressing. 'You said she cheated twice – or as good as. So what happened the second time?'

THIRTY

He says, 'I need a drink,' and then he gets up and goes through to the living room.

I follow, like a puppy, and watch him pour a couple of Scotches, dropping a single oversized ice cube in each glass.

'Meredith assaulted a colleague. A twenty-six-year-old pupil in her chambers.'

'Assaulted?' I picture her getting annoyed and clonking someone on the nose.

'They were at the pub celebrating a big win. She had a few too many to drink and made a pass at him . . .' He frowns, as though the memory pains him. 'He wasn't up for it. I suppose to him she was just this older woman – and his boss, to boot!' He takes a sip as though he's not even really tasting it. 'It's possible it could have all died there, but when the time came for him to apply for tenancy – after his apprenticeship was completed – she didn't keep him on.' He briefly meets my eyes. 'She told him he wasn't compatible with the set . . . I imagine nobody knows for sure if the two were connected, but clearly, he felt they were.'

'He reported her?' I try to picture her hitting some guy up when she'd had a few too many drinks, remembering that evening in the bar – how she'd been checking out the young, fit barman.

He shakes his head. 'No, he didn't exactly report her. Not in the way you mean. Not to the Bar Standards Board . . . I suppose he could have. But it's a tricky thing to file that type of complaint against someone, isn't it? And it's probably almost always the woman filing against the man – not the other way around. Maybe he was worried that if he went down that route, the allegation would stick to him throughout his career, influence his job potential – which we all know it might. We've seen it happen to women plenty of times.' He takes a sip of his Scotch again. 'The thing is – the really unfortunate twist to the story for Meredith – was that she had no idea this kid's aunt was actually Chief Justice and OBE, Pamela Carlton – the chair of the QC appointments panel. So, when Meredith came to apply for QC, she didn't get accepted.'

I almost slap a hand to my mouth. 'But I thought she was a QC! Didn't you tell me ages ago that she was?'

'No. I think I mentioned that she applied . . . I was actually going to tell you the whole story but then, well, I thought maybe it was best not to bother.'

'My God,' I say, cringing as I recall my gaffe when I met her at the pub that time – when I congratulated her on her recent appointment. 'So this young lawyer . . . she never knew about his aunt?'

'No,' he says. 'But I get it. The guy probably wanted to succeed on his own merit. I'd have probably kept it quiet too. In fact, I absolutely would have.'

I nod. I could totally see Joe decrying any form of nepotism.

'Like I said, Meredith is a bit of a contradiction. She can have so much integrity on the one hand – she's devoted her career to fighting for the underdog, she sits on boards that champion women lawyers' rights . . . All her career she's taken a firm stand against the sexual misconduct that's rampant in the legal profession, and then she goes and does the very thing herself.'

'This is astonishing!' And more than a little hypocritical. 'Maybe she thought she was getting even on men . . . after being so badly let down by even her own father's behaviour.'

'Who knows . . . Meredith is always in battle. But I've often suspected her greatest fight is really with herself.'

With all this new information, I can barely keep up. 'So how did you find this out? Did she just admit this, too?'

'No, I don't think she had any intention of breathing a word. But there were rumours aplenty when she got denied Silk, and some of them found their way back to me . . .' He tilts his head benignly. 'So there it is. Everything you wanted to know about my ex-wife but felt it was pointless asking.'

I study him, oddly grateful for this breakthrough. 'You forgave her the first time for the sake of your kids. Why not the second?'

He frowns. 'Come on! Enough is enough.'

THIRTY-ONE

I'm on the platform at Victoria waiting for the train to East Croydon, and someone pops into my head.

I pull up her number and type a text.

Hi Mel. Just wanted to say hello. Still hoping to have coffee sometime – just been so busy with work and a few other things. How are things with you?

She replies almost instantly.

Hello Lauren. Hope all is well. Busy here too. OH away for a week on business so I'm holding the fort. In some ways it's actually easier (!!!) but zero time to come up for air. Great to hear from you!

I respond. Well, let's definitely try to make coffee happen!

She replies after a moment: Let's stay in touch, see what opens up, time-wise, in the next week or so.

Perfect! I say.

On Saturday morning, Joe picks up Toby and Grace from their mother's. I make pancakes, and then we take Toby to the lido and Grace goes off to meet a friend. I sit on a bench in the sunshine while Joe tries to teach Toby how to hold his breath under water for five to ten seconds, and coordinate the movement of his arms with his legs. I snap photos of their frivolity, Toby thrashing and splashing, Joe intermittently ducking and disappearing, then popping up and surprising him. In the afternoon Toby has a birthday party to go to, and his mother is going to take him, so Joe drops off Toby at Meredith's and then takes Grace to the Apple store to sort out an issue with her new iPhone. Joe asks if I want to join them but a friend from my home town is in London for the day and I promised to meet her for drinks.

On Sunday the weather could not be more beautiful again, so we take the kids to Hyde Park. Joe makes a reservation for brunch at The Ivy on High Street Kensington. Mealtimes are a big thing to my husband, I am learning. The food, yes. But also the act of four people sitting around a table, no matter how discordant. They might say success is the journey, not the destination, but Joe would not subscribe to this; Joe is all about destination.

Grace sleeps in until after ten and only surfaces because her dad gives her very little option. Joe and I share a second espresso, then we pile into the Lexus and drive across town, where we park down a random back street in Mayfair. We cross the Park Lane underpass – Joe carrying Toby until we are on the other side – emerging at the entrance to Hyde Park, back into fresh air. We watch the horses on the bridle path and then wander down to the Serpentine. As we pass the cafe, Toby sees people walking out with ice creams, so, of course, Toby wants an ice cream.

'After brunch, buddy, I told you that.' Joe rumples his son's hair.

Toby is not fond of this idea of after lunch. 'I want one now!' he chants, over and over.

'Lots of things we want we don't get, little guy!' Joe tries to take hold of his hand because Toby refuses to walk now, but he snaps them behind his back. 'I said I want one now!' He starts to wail. 'Now, now, now, now, now!'

When Joe says no again, Toby stamps his feet and starts to bawl. A family coming out of the cafe throw us a dirty look.

'For fuck's sake, this is driving me insane!' Grace says. 'Can't you just get him one to shut him up?'

'Grace!' Joe looks stunned. 'Will you watch your language, please!'

'What about a really small one?' I say. 'It's a pretty long walk. By the time we get there he'll have more than worked up an appetite again.'

'Lauren's right!' Grace sends me a look of support and despair. 'Just let him have one. Please!'

Joe ignores us. 'Let's go!' He scoops Toby up and runs with him, scattering the pigeons and seagulls in his path. Toby squeals – something between a cry and a laugh. I'm exhausted just watching Joe, with his extraordinary patience and show of stamina that could rival those of a guy half his age. But there's a moment where his point about not wanting to be doing all this when he's approaching fifty rings true.

'Toby, look at the swans!' I point to the half-dozen circling the water in a choreographic arc. 'Aren't they beautiful?'

But right now Toby couldn't give a flying banana about the swans. 'Ice cream. Ice cream. I want ice cream.'

I dig in his bag and pull out Godfrey the Giraffe and try to do the ventriloquist act I was teaching him this morning, when he'd tried to copy my silliness and ended up in peals of laughter.

He watches me clowning around and lets out a humungous scream.

'Come on, buddy,' Joe says, irritated now. He suddenly looks thoroughly worn out.

'Look, can I just meet you guys at the restaurant?' Grace gawks at her brother like he's an alien life form. 'I might duck into H&M. It's right across the street.'

'Why don't you do that?' I say, momentarily dreading the idea of her popping into a clothes shop. Although a week or two ago I caught myself entering her room and having a quick scan of her wardrobe to see if there were any suspicious new arrivals. There weren't.

'If I get to the restaurant first, I'll see if I can get us a table in the gazebo.' Grace smiles at me, then mouths, 'Thank you.'

Joe looks a little peeved. 'Anyone else want to leave while we're at it?' My husband is clearly determined to make us an episode of *The Waltons*.

Grace tuts, but before she strides off Joe says, 'Here. If you're going to a shop, take this.'

He hands her three crisp twenty-pound notes.

'Thanks,' she says, and off she goes. I watch her long slim legs in her denim mini skirt and gold Converse. Her confident, lengthy stride, her hair a sleek and shiny wave down her back.

Toby eventually wears himself out. The walk ends up being slow but pleasant. We take a few diversions, pass the Princess Diana memorial, Round Pond, then exit on to Palace Gate. There's some royal movement about to happen at the side of the palace, judging by the convoy of motorcycles and Range Rovers idling inside the gated grounds. 'I wonder who's coming out!' I say. 'Look, Toby . . . do you think Prince George might be going to church today?'

'I don't know!' Toby says. 'But if he is, will he be going on a motorbike?' He looks up at me, his green eyes huge from the magnification of his glasses.

I laugh. 'I don't think so! I doubt he'll be getting his licence for quite a few years!'

Joe and I smile.

'But if he's royal can't he go on a motorbike if he wants to?'

'Life doesn't quite work like that, buddy. Not even royal life.' Joe's face is full of fatherly adoration.

'I want to see Prince George now,' he says, his attention on the cars, rapt.

We stand and watch for a while. Joe holds Toby's hand and I sneak glances at them. Father and son. Their interlocking grasps. Toby's long slim fingers that look so much like his dad's. Joe's amazing hair. The Ray-Bans and worn black leather jacket; he looks effortlessly sexy.

And then, quite out of the blue, Toby's little hand reaches for mine. I stare at it, feel our palms pressing together, and I am overcome with the most disarming sense of togetherness. As the three of us stand here, I think, *He could be mine*. This could be my son, with Joe. A child we created.

When I glance up, Joe is watching me, something charmed and introspective in his eyes. We smile again. And I can't help but wonder if right this minute he might be thinking the same thing.

THIRTY-TWO

Grace is in the gazebo when we arrive. She looks up, grins.

'What did you buy?' I sit opposite her.

'Just some white jeans and a mock-croc belt. I might go back later though. They had some really nice tank tops but I didn't have time to try them and I've still got twenty quid left.' Then, after a brief hesitation, she says, 'Would you like to come with me? They've got some cool summer stuff in . . .'

'Yes,' I tell her. 'That would be great.'

Joe gives me a little cock of his eyebrow. I don't know if he's trying to say, *That's great you guys are getting along!* Or, *Thank God she clearly didn't nick anything.*

Either way, it feels good.

We peruse the menu. I order the salmon fishcake with the poached eggs and arugula, Toby and Grace want French toast and Joe orders a steak with eggs, and we mock him for his very American choice. Grace is chatty, and I notice that my attempts to join in aren't met with her usual apathy or eye rolls. We order a bottle of Prosecco and Grace starts telling us about a concert she wants to go to in Reading.

'Look, hang on. I'm going to find it.' She picks up her phone and starts googling.

The waiter brings over our drinks.

'Urgh! I can't believe this damned phone . . . It's doing the same thing again!' She glances up, drops her jaw in exasperation and looks at her dad.

'What? I thought they fixed it!' he says.

'I thought so too! This is ridiculous!' She tinkers on with it then finally throws it on the table. 'Can I borrow yours?'

I realise she means mine. 'Of course.' I enter my password and hand it over.

I watch her long slim fingers with the blue-varnished nails, the thumbs flying over the keyboard. 'My God, don't you ever close your apps? There's loads open! They really drain your battery. Look . . .' She flashes the screen around so I can quickly see it, double-clicks the Home button, flicks her index finger upwards and a multitude of screens go by.

'Yikes,' I grimace. 'That explains a lot of things.'

'God, you've got millions . . .'

I watch her messing about with my phone, oddly uncomfortable with how she's suddenly taken possession of it. 'Can I have it back now?' I hold out my hand.

'Just a second . . .'

As I wait, I am aware of her index finger stilling, her eyes narrowing as she focuses on the screen.

'Grace?' I say.

But she's not listening. And then her brows knit and her face turns beetroot red.

And then she glares at me and says, 'Oh. My. God.'

THIRTY-THREE

'Biological Mother was never there?' Meredith comes stalking down our hall towards me the instant I get the front door open. At first it's so disorientating to see her here – in my home – that I cannot even drum up a reaction.

'Telltale, troublemaker. Sullen, silent, ANGRY . . .'

She moves in on me, her words hitting me like bullets. My eyes slide past her to Joe standing stiff as a board in the background.

'Meredith . . .' She is about two feet away and I hold up my hands. 'Please stop. I can explain if you calm down and let me.'

'How could you say all that?' She comes within an inch or two of my face. 'About the kids. About me!'

I'm puzzled.

'How do I know all this?' She seems to mind-read. 'Because I logged on to your forum with a fake account under a fake name. Any experience of that, Lauren?' She glares at me with contempt. 'I read everything that *Miserable* wrote and the replies of all your pathetic little cohorts . . . I mean, my God, I'm glad we all know how you feel. How arduous your plight has been. All – what? – five months of it!' She throws up her hands, laughs.

'Look.' Joe finally speaks. 'This is not helping. Can we all maybe sit down?'

I am held prisoner by her gaze for a moment, then I manage to slip past her and walk into the living room. Grace is sitting on the sofa staring at the ground, cheeks blazing.

Meredith stalks after me. 'Don't just walk away! I want an explanation.'

I turn around. We are face to face again, in the middle of the room.

'You go on a forum and tell the world you hate my children? Can you tell me what sort of person would do that? Oh, and what did you say about me? *Wouldn't want to be on her wrong side.* Well, honey, I promise you you're on it now!'

She takes a long breath and lets it out slowly, like she's trying to get a grip of herself – or reload.

'I don't know what to say,' I say finally. I look from Meredith, to Joe, to Grace, who is still staring hard at the floor. 'What you saw was personal. What you've done is a complete invasion of my privacy.'

'Whose privacy? *Your* privacy?' she mocks, then casts Joe an exasperated glance. 'Do you believe this woman? You go online and assassinate me and my family and you think you're the one whose privacy has been violated?'

The ground seems to be moving and for a second I think it's an earthquake, then I realise it's me. I am shaking. My mind whips through the very little I know about the law, thinking of words like, *defamation, slander* . . . Have I done something legally wrong? Is she going to go after me?

I head to the nearest chair and sit down. As I do, I feel Grace monitoring all this. We meet eyes, something breaking in the hardness of her gaze, giving way to utter bewilderment and betrayal.

Then she jumps to her feet. 'I'm sitting nowhere near her!' She storms across the room, almost tripping over the dog, her voice breaking. 'I'm going home. To my *real* home!'

Joe calls after her, 'Grace, darling!'

But it's too late. The door clashes behind her.

There is an interlude where her departure settles on us, where the tension eases a fraction.

'Do you know why I was never there when they were growing up, Lauren?' Meredith turns those sad, soulful eyes back to me. Her voice is firm, but calmer. 'Because I was working. Because I am a woman, and no one is cutting me any slack. Unlike my male counterparts, I am still expected to run a home and raise my children, and to do that while trying to rise to the top in a male-dominated world where not one of those males has the same expectations placed on him. Not one of them . . .' She breaks off, a little breathless from indignation, looks me up and down witheringly. 'My God, you're an educated woman yourself. A doctor. Of all the people, I would have thought *you* would understand.' She shakes her head, like I am some disappointing enigma to society at large. 'Have you just gone through your entire life walking between raindrops? Can you really be that out of touch with the world?'

I swallow hard. They are both waiting for me to speak, and yet I cannot find a response. Joe has relocated to the chair and is leaning forward, elbows on knees. Under his breath I hear him groan, 'Jesus.'

'I'm not out of touch,' I say, when I think I can talk without breaking down. 'You know nothing about me.'

'Then tell me. Tell me what sort of person would go on to a forum and say all that horrible shit about someone else's kids? The children of someone you purport to love?'

My heart pounds. The tears build, and I just think, *Oh God, please don't let me cry!* She is staring at me hard, waiting for my answer.

'I'm sorry,' I say. 'I was feeling very, very down and there was literally no one I could talk to.' I throw an accusatory glance at Joe, sitting there on the fence – his favourite perch. 'No one,' I repeat.

'So you chose a bunch of sad strangers who are disillusioned with their lives. Because you're a sad person yourself, Lauren.'

Tears roll down my face. I quickly push them away, try to take a breath.

'Are you going to say anything?' she asks.

'Are *you* going to say anything?' I say to Joe. 'Or are you just going to sit there, mute?'

He frowns, seems bamboozled by this. After a spell he says, 'What do you want me to say, Lauren? That all this was a great, admirable, mature way of dealing with the situation? That I approve?'

And perhaps because of Joe's inability to defend me on any level, even for appearance's sake, to make this fractionally less terrible for me, I suddenly think, *This bullshit ends here!* I find my spine straightening. 'Is Meredith going to leave right now, or am I?' We hold eyes. 'Because once I'm out of that door, believe me, I am *not* coming back.'

He opens his mouth, but it's Meredith who speaks. 'You don't have to leave,' she says, less inflamed. 'I've said all I intend to. I need to go home and be with my daughter.' Her gaze coasts over my hot face and I am held there in her wake of her scorn. 'I think, once you've calmed down, you might want to consider apologising to Grace.' And then she adds, 'And we can only hope my daughter will be a bigger person than you've been.'

And with that, she leaves.

THIRTY-FOUR

'*Miserable?*' He perches on the end of the bed, where I'm lying with my back to him in a foetal ball.

'I'd like to be alone.' I pull the duvet over my head and squeeze my eyes shut.

'You said I'm in denial about her, that I never know who to believe, that your marriage was a *mistake!*' I hear the pain and disenchantment in his voice. 'You painted me as some sort of irrational, unreasonable monster! It doesn't even seem like something you'd do – go online, on to a *forum*.' And then he almost spits, 'What's wrong with you?'

I finally sit up and look at him. 'Wrong with *me?*'

'What gives you the right to talk about me like that, about our marriage, on a public forum?'

I've never really heard Joe raise his voice, except when he's lost it occasionally with one of his business partners.

'Would you rather I'd told friends? People who – like me – thought I was marrying someone very different to the person I clearly did marry? People you'd have to look in the eye at some point?'

'I thought I was your friend,' he says.

The comment sits there. I suddenly fill with regret.

'We could have talked,' he says, more levelly.

'I tried talking.'

'You could have tried harder. You *should* have tried harder. And kept it . . . in-house.'

I attempt to take a breath, and then I say, 'And what trying have *you* ever done in this marriage, Joe? Because for all your fancy words about how you were going to do better, not a single thing has changed.'

He glares at me. He doesn't correct me. Because he knows he can't.

THIRTY-FIVE

Joe works late for the next few nights. I have a long chat with Sophie on the phone and tell her the gist of what happened. The kids arrive at the weekend. I set it up so that Joe takes Toby out to the lido and I can speak to Grace alone. She stands there staring at her feet while I tell her I'm sorry, that I needed to vent, needed an outlet. At the time I was writing it, I felt I meant it, but the reality is, it was just my anger. I tell her that just like the time before when I offended her, I hope we can put this past us.

She continues to stare at her feet, a faint bloom of pink across her nose. Then she says an overly chirpy, 'Okay!' and flits off to her room – looking a bit like someone just told her she won the lottery, rather than reminded her of something she'd rather forget.

On Sunday, reverting back to old practices, I meet Sophie and Charlie for a pub lunch. Despite my intention to insist we don't talk about it, it's almost all we talk about.

'It could have been worse.' Charlie takes a sip of his pint and sets it on the table.

I frown. 'How?'

He shakes his head. 'I don't know. That's the part I'm trying to think about . . . The one thing in life you can always rely on is that whatever shit happens to you, it truly could have always been worse.'

Sophie's face turns serious. 'I feel really bad for you. You seem really low, Lauren. I don't think I've seen you like this before. Do you think you and Joe are going to be okay?'

I want to say, *Yes, of course.* That despite everything that's happened, underneath all this, I do still love him even though he's not perfect, and that's all that truly matters. Instead I say, 'I don't know. I'm not sure how much more of this I can take.'

'Look . . .' Charlie stares me bluntly in the eyes. 'I know you're furious with Joe and everything, but come on . . . you went online and you maligned his little fuckers. Okay, that's not entirely unforgivable, but he's hardly going to give you a medal and send you to a spa for a week!' He shakes his head in despair. 'Just give him some time. He'll come around. People always do.' Then he adds, 'Or they don't. And they end up splitting up. But even if that happens, then you can be guaranteed there will be some other path in store for you. That's another one of life's truisms. As one door closes, another always opens.'

'Wait,' I say, something about his earlier comment troubling me. 'I never said I maligned any little fuckers.' All I told Sophie was I said a few things about Joe and Meredith that they hadn't liked and Grace found the link.

He rolls his eyes. 'Duh!'

He seems to be waiting for some sort of penny to drop.

When it doesn't, he says, 'If Manifesto Meredith can go online and set up a fake account, we can't have her outdo us.'

I swallow a big chunk of lamb without chewing. 'What?' I glance from Charlie to Sophie, who blushes and lowers her gaze.

'I'm sorry,' she says, after a hollow silence. There's an instant where she looks like she might actually cry. 'It wasn't my idea.'

'Oh, my God.' The realisation fully lands on me.

203

'We just wanted to have a clear picture, if we were going to be helpful,' he says. 'You can't really tell us half the story.'

My mouth drops open, the words slow to line up. I cannot believe what I'm understanding. 'Don't you have enough to do to just focus on your own shit?' I glare at Sophie, making sure to include her too. 'Why is my life so enthralling to you and so ripe for ridicule? What's *wrong* with you two?'

I'm dying to tell him what I know about him, to burst his pathetic little bubble. But I can't bring myself to.

'You two deserve each other,' I say instead. I dig in my bag, find a wad of fivers and throw them on the table.

'Lauren?' Sophie calls after me as I stride across the room.

But I don't look back.

❀

As I am walking to the Tube, at a brisk pace, desperate to put some distance between me and what just happened, my phone pings. I think it might be Sophie texting, but then I see the name.

Hello Lauren,

Been a while since we wrote. Just thought I'd check in and see how you are.

Mel! I had virtually forgotten about her. I latch on like a lifeline, start dictating a reply as I walk. Mel! Your timing could not be better! Been a very bizarre time lately! We never did have that coffee! I am off at three tomorrow, how about then?

Oddly – and sadly – I feel closer to a stranger than I do to one of my best friends. It seems surreal. I try to push that very upsetting thought out of my mind.

She texts back. Sorry to hear things are rough. I can't make tomorrow. My dad is having chemo and I need to drive him. Maybe the week after next? Generally, with teaching, I'm free weekdays after 3 p.m.

I text back that I'm sorry to hear about her father, and that I'll be in touch the week after next.

On Monday, after school, I take Toby to the park. Before we arrive at the swings, we come across a wounded young crow on the ground near some bushes. Some other crows kick up a fuss when I try to pick up the bird and examine its drooping wing. 'We had better leave him with his family,' I tell Toby, doing a quick google search to see what we should do. 'He might just be learning how to fly.' Toby peers over my shoulder and tries to read from my phone, which I think is cute. 'If he's still here tomorrow we'll consider taking him to a wildlife rescue place,' I say after we sit for a while on the ground beside him – at Toby's request – 'To keep him company'.

'But won't he be hungry if he can't get his food?'

'His mummy will feed him. Crows are very clever.' I tell him some things I've heard they can do. He listens, intrigued. 'Maybe when we get home we'll see what else we can find out about crows on the internet.'

'Let's go now then!'

'You don't want to play on the swings?'

'No.' He stands and waves for me to do the same. 'I want to read about crows.'

The next day when we come back, the bird is still there. We've brought a box with us which Toby has lined with one of his T-shirts.

'He recognises us!' Toby stares at the bird with adorable tenderness. 'Can I hold him?'

'Remember what it said online? The parents won't like it if we handle him too much.'

'Why not?' he says, looking up at me with innocent eyes.

'Because his mother is protective. She might not know we're trying to help him. It might upset her and she might not like us.'

'Oh, okay,' he says.

I manage to get the bird in the box.

'I hope they're not going to attack us,' Toby says, shrinking when he hears the other birds squawking.

'I'll protect you!' I say brightly.

'You will?'

I smile down at him. 'Always!'

He beams. 'Okay then.'

The next day, Wednesday, is my thirtieth birthday. With falling out with my friends weighing heavily on my mind, and the stiffness in the air between me and Joe, I'm not exactly brimming with celebratory spirit. It's technically my day off but I even contemplate calling in to see if there's a shift I might be needed to cover.

I'm just lying spreadeagled on my bed when Joe texts. R U awake?

He generally tries his best not to phone in case I'm still sleeping. Just I reply.

A few moments later, my phone rings.

'Well, good morning and happy birthday!' His voice is very much that of the old Joe. No hint of coolness. He's almost flirty.

I take this to mean I'm forgiven. The one thing I'd say he's good at is not holding grudges. And it seems I'm good at it too.

'I left you breakfast. Had to rush. Didn't want to wake you.'

I vaguely remember the brush of his kiss goodbye.

'Thank you,' I tell him. 'I haven't emerged from under the covers yet.'

'It's going to be a very long day for me, and I'm afraid the reason I'm phoning now, while I've a minute, is it's going to go on longer.'

'That's fine,' I say, still a little too indifferent to be disappointed. 'I'm really not all that bothered about going out. We can always do it another night.'

'No way,' he says, chirpily. 'We're absolutely still going! Reservation's not till eight. But the problem is Meredith can't pick up Toby from school as she had to fly up to Manchester for a court case and won't be back until evening, and Rosamie is with her sick daughter again . . .' He sighs. 'I was wondering if you could pick him up and take him to ours for a bit. Grace will come back too; maybe you can order a pizza for them? Then I'll drop them off before we go out.'

'Of course,' I tell him, wondering why Grace wouldn't just want to go straight home. 'I can easily make some pasta or something for dinner.'

'That's fantastic!' He sounds happy. Then he says he's got to dash.

When I go into the kitchen, I find a plate with a triangle of frittata on it. Beside it is a half-bottle of champagne, some orange juice and a bouquet of gardenias, my favourite flowers. He has left a card, and inside it has written, *I love you. Always. Look forward to celebrating with you tonight.*

'How is Russell?' Toby's first words when he sees me at the school gate.

We googled crow names and this was the best we could come up with.

'Let's go home and we can phone the wildlife rescue centre. See how he is!'

'Okay!' he says, and his little hand slides into mine.

We arrive at the crossing. Our car is about half a block down and on the other side of the street. 'What do we do when we want to cross the road, Toby?' I hang on to him extra tightly.

'I don't know, Lauren. What do we do?' Then he quickly adds, 'We look both ways and we listen for cars and if we can't see any cars we cross!'

'Exactly!'

We can't see any cars so we cross.

'Arrive alive!' we say, once our feet land on the other side.

Grace is sitting on the sofa when we come in. Toby darts to the cupboard to bring out his Lego.

'Happy birthday,' she says, rather flatly. Other than FaceTiming with my parents and calls from a few friends – Sophie and Charlie's being conspicuously absent – I'd almost forgotten it's my birthday.

I tell her thanks. 'How was school?'

She shrugs. 'Was okay.'

'Toby,' I say. 'Let's make our phone call!' I briefly tell Grace about the bird. She listens, doesn't say much, then flits off to her room.

I phone the wildlife centre while Toby stands there with expectant eyes. 'Sorry, buddy,' I tell him. 'We'll have to call back tomorrow. Doctor has to do his rounds!'

Toby looks glum for a second, then goes back to playing with his Lego.

I go over to the kitchen to have a look in the fridge for a snack to give him before dinner.

Grace emerges a moment or two later. 'For you.' She places an envelope in front of me on the breakfast bar with a flourish. 'I didn't really have time to do the gift thing. I stink at buying presents for other people.'

I stare at the neat cursive writing of my name. 'Well . . . thanks!' I pick it up and tear into it. 'That was thoughtful of you.'

It's a simple message. Chunky black type on a white background:

AND SHE GAVE NO FUCKS.
NOT A SINGLE ONE.
AND SHE LIVED HAPPILY EVER AFTER.
THE END.

Inside she has written *Happy Birthday from Grace*.

'That's . . . Erm . . .' I meet two eyes that are monitoring me closely. 'Extremely poetic. I like it. Very much.'

She beams. And then we chuckle.

'I've got an idea,' I tell her. 'How about if we have a small glass of champagne? Your dad got me a bottle. It seems like the right time of day to crack into it.'

She gives me her *What? Are you serious?* face. Then she says, 'Oh . . . Well . . . Okay.'

'Where is Dad taking you anyway?' she asks when I pull out the flutes, pop the cork and pass her half a glass. 'You're supposed to go somewhere posh for your thirtieth, aren't you?'

'We're going for a steak. That new place in Shoreditch. The meat-lover's paradise.'

'Gross!' She wrinkles her nose. 'What's he buying you?'

'I don't know. I don't need a gift.'

209

She gives me a wide-eyed, disbelieving look. So I add, 'But if I get one, I won't exactly make him take it back.'

She beams again.

Before I put the pan on, I tell her I'm going to pop into my room to figure out what I'm going to wear.

'Can I come too?'

'Of course,' I say, thrilled with this transformation.

Toby is talking to his imaginary friends while he builds his Lego. Grace and I take our drinks into my room where she throws herself on to the bed and watches me as I make a couple of trips to and from the walk-in. Black satin cigarette pants. A little fitted bolero jacket. Two pairs of shoes that go well with the ankle-length hem of the pants – an open-toe wedge and a strappy stiletto. Ordinarily I'd opt for the wedge but I have a memory of Joe lifting my foot and kissing my ankle, then all the way up my leg, when I wore them last time, and telling me that, in case it wasn't obvious, he really liked high heels.

'I love the trousers but I don't love the jacket,' Grace says, after she's had me model everything for her. 'It's very dated. Like it belongs in the '80s. A bit square-shouldered.'

I study myself in the mirror. 'Damn. You're right!'

She jumps off the bed. 'Let me see what else you've got.' She disappears into the walk-in, humming a tune, and I hear her ripping through the rack.

'I love this.' She emerges with a silk, long-sleeved pewter grey blouse I'd almost forgotten I own.

'Really?'

'Put it on.'

I dutifully whip my T-shirt off and slip into the blouse, leaving the bow hanging long and loose. 'Nah!' she frowns, then ties it in a classic knot. 'Much better! It would look great with those jeans you had on.'

'Seriously?' I put them back on. She tells me to tuck the shirt in tight.

'*Voila!*' She grips my shoulders and turns me to face the mirror. 'It rocks.' She dusts her hands off – task accomplished. 'Now for the shoes.'

Back in the kitchen, once my outfit has been sorted, I take the pesto I made a couple of days ago from the fridge, add a little more olive oil to slacken it up and give it a brisk stir until it returns to its proper healthy green colour. Then I grate some fresh parmesan, pinching a few shavings and popping them into my mouth as I put a pan of water on to boil, placing it safely on the back burner out of instinct.

From across the room I can hear Toby doing his ventriloquist act with Godfrey the Giraffe for his sister. 'Wewo Gwace!'

Grace chuckles. 'You're insane!'

'Ow wis whe weather?'

'Ha ha! Stop it!'

I smile, slice a French stick into rounds and butter them.

Joe texts. All good? Kids home?

All fine. And me too! I snap a close-up of the champagne flute. Perfect! Enjoy!

I send him a thumbs-up.

He sends a red heart.

I reach into the cupboard for pasta bowls, set them on the table with the cutlery.

'Small portion for me,' Grace shouts over. 'I'm not that hungry.'

I dig in the cupboard to find the strainer. 'Okay!'

'Can we phone and find out how Russell is?' Toby is now standing by the breakfast bar, trying to perch Godfrey on the end of it.

'We just did! They won't have any more news yet. We'll have to leave it until tomorrow.'

'Will Russell come home with us while he gets better?'

'Maybe.' I smile. 'We'll have to wait until they tell us what to do.'

I'm just lifting the pan from the gas with the oven glove and switching the knob to OFF when I hear him say, with great excitement, 'I really want Russell to come and stay with us! Can we, please?' And then without even a hint of a warning, he runs up behind me and throws his arms around my legs, right as I'm turning.

There's a horrific moment, immediately before it happens, where I see it coming.

My hand wobbles.

The pan slips.

Toby screams.

THIRTY-SIX

'Oh my God!' I hear Grace saying. 'Oh my God!'

Toby's scream – more chilling than anything I've ever heard before – hits me like a gut punch.

Somehow my brain kicks into gear and I quickly scoop him up. He is saturated from his shoulders to his little bare feet and stiff as a board. A bubble of saliva gurgles from the corner of his mouth.

I tell Grace, as calmly as I can, to dial 999. But she stands there, stunned, inert.

'Do it,' I roar, as I hurry past her. Toby is squealing, thrashing about in my arms. 'Put me on speakerphone so I can talk to them.'

'Okay!' She finally comes to her senses, as I rush him into the bathroom.

I set him on the toilet seat while I fiddle with the bathtub taps until the water coming from the mixer is lukewarm. 'I know, Toby. I'm so sorry. I'm going to make you feel better. Okay? Come on, baby.' I lift him. He squirms, squeals and thrashes again. 'This is for your own good. This is going to help you.' I try to hold him under the running water. He resists with every ounce of his will. 'Please, Toby,' I say. 'Please let me do this.' I can't hold him at this awkward angle, so I've no choice but to climb in with him. My flip-flops meet the bathmat, almost suctioning, my knees going down, the weight of water in my tracksuit bottoms almost pulling them off me. 'Shshshsh . . .' I try to soothe him. 'Please stay still. I know, I know . . .'

Grace hovers in the doorway as the call handler comes on the line. I try to hold him so there's a continuous flow of water on his scalded skin and to recount to this woman precisely what's happened. I inform her I'm a doctor and I want to bring him in as an emergency. My voice is serrated from the struggle of trying to keep him under the taps.

It feels like the longest twenty minutes of my life, but finally help arrives. I've managed to dry him off, wrap him carefully in a fresh towel. In no time at all, we are off to hospital in the ambulance. I try to hold on to his good hand; his tiny fingers are curled into a fist, his knuckles pressed into my palm. His other hand and arm have been mummified in cling film like a piece of raw meat to keep his body from losing heat, an IV delivering a painkiller. Grace sits on the seat immediately behind me. She is still too shocked to say much. Toby's pupils are dilated, eyes slightly unrecognising.

Eventually, when we're about halfway there, his cries lose their ferocity and plateau to a long, low whimper. I try to tenderly cajole him but it's like I'm a stranger. 'Mummy. Mummy. Mummy,' he keeps saying, over and over. I press a hand to my mouth. The sound of him longing for the comfort of his mother's arms almost breaks my heart.

'It's Dad,' Grace croaks, her voice full of nerves and dread. She holds out my mobile. At first I'm confused, but then I remember I tried to ring him and he wasn't picking up.

'Hi.' I clutch the phone with a sweating hand, tell him there's been an accident.

I'm aware of a drawn-out silence. Then he says, 'Accident? Who?'

I stare at the scalded child before me, this little boy who had finally learned to trust me, even though he never actually knew it was a journey he had to take.

'Toby,' I tell him. I explain how it happened.

'Jesus Christ!' His tone is riddled with accusation as much as alarm.

I tell him the name of the hospital and that the paramedics have everything under control.

'Right then,' he says, and then, 'I'm on my way.'

I am no stranger to hospitals. But not from the perspective of hard plastic seats outside a room where Grace and I have been instructed to sit, like we are dispossessed. 'The doctor will want to examine him alone,' the nurse said. Code for: we need the physical evidence to corroborate your story. In situations like these, no doctor goes looking for cause to be suspicious, but it's there – part of the training – the need to rule out intentional harm. Grace's tears are a soft slur. We wait what feels like a cruel amount of time.

So this is what it's like on the other side, I think.

And then the double doors groan open, and through them walk my husband and his ex-wife. Is it symbolic that, while they've hailed from opposite ends of London, they've arrived together? Just the very sight of Meredith makes my stomach flip. She spots me before Joe, her eyes dropping to my hand laid over her daughter's.

And then she says, 'My God, what have you done now?'

On seeing her dad, Grace jumps to her feet and throws herself into his outstretched arms.

For the first time in my life, I recognise the utter inadequacy of words.

She trusted me with her child. Toby got scalded on my watch. It wasn't his mum he bulldozed into. Wasn't his mum he knocked off balance. Wasn't his mum whose hand slipped. It was me. It was mine.

Tears spring to my eyes. A sudden rush of realisation that in years to come, Toby might not remember much about his early years, but he will remember today.

Joe is still holding his daughter. I register their solidarity – the three of them standing there, on the other side of some invisible barrier that has been re-erected, that will probably always be there, no matter how I try to break it down.

We are saved by the arrival of the doctor.

He appears from around the corner, in pale green scrubs and a soft cotton shirt with sleeves pushed halfway up his arms. A uniform I'm used to. A stance I recognise. An expression of utter exhaustion in his eyes that I have also felt. Only I don't know this doctor. This is not my hospital.

'Are you Toby's parents?' he asks, meeting no one's eyes in particular.

'Yes,' Joe and Meredith say together.

'Would you both please come this way?'

By the gravity of his tone, and the slight flex of the muscles of his neck, I have a feeling it's going to be worse than I thought.

THIRTY-SEVEN

I take an Uber home alone, in a blur. The driver is chatty. I barely hear a word. Eventually he gives up and I stare out of the window, not realising we've even arrived at my door until he says, 'Er . . . Lauren. This is it, right?'

When I get inside I stare at the pan on the kitchen floor, the pool of water, a few remaining pasta bows that the dog didn't eat. Then I march straight to the toilet, and throw up.

Once I've retched until there's nothing left, I go back into the kitchen. I should mop up, but all I can do is sink on to a stool and relive what just happened.

Arrive alive! Toby's little hand in mine. *Can we find out how Russell is doing?* His excitement, the utter trust, as he threw himself at me.

Could I have reacted faster? Managed to at least get the pan out of the way somehow?

Reaction time. Humanly impossible to be faster than between 150 and 300 milliseconds. In the instant my brain processed what was happening, it was already too late. I couldn't stop time or control a different outcome.

I drop my forehead on to the island and I cry.

After what feels like a fair amount of time has passed, and I've cleaned up the kitchen and sat on the patio while the dog sniffed around and peed, I realise I need to find out what's going on. I try Joe's phone but it's off. Meredith's too.

I text Grace. What's happening? How is Toby?

I see the message is read, the three little moving dots that appear soon after.

Not sure. Mum made me Uber home.

Hmmm. You're at home now? On your own? Would you rather come here?

There's a longer wait for a reply this time. And then it arrives. It's okay.

Finally, a long time later, after I've walked Mozart around the block, mainly for distraction, and then attempted to eat a piece of dry toast, Joe walks through the door.

He slumps into the chair, unable to be bothered to even stroke the dog, who nudges his limp hand.

'How is he?' I ask.

'He's fine. They're going to keep him in for a night. He's in some pain still.' After a pause he says, 'The doctor said something about possible second- and third-degree burns to his right hand.' His voice is tired and flat. 'They won't know if he'll need a skin graft for a while – until it starts to heal, I think. Meredith insisted they transfer him to the burns unit for a more specialised opinion. She didn't seem to think the doctor knew what he was talking about.'

Suddenly the reality of this hits me. Toby may be scarred. Toby may have impaired use of his right hand. An injury for life. 'What did the doctor say exactly? About his injuries?'

He shakes his head. 'To be honest, I don't entirely remember. Pretty much just what I told you, I think.'

I press my fingers to my lips and gasp. He watches me, his eyes holding steady on my face.

Then he says, 'Can you explain it to me again? How it happened. I just need to have a clearer picture.'

I don't know what I can add that's any different from what I've already said, so I just repeat it. There is a moment or two when he doesn't comment. And then he says, 'So he was running around? I've told you he's not allowed to run in the flat. Do you know how many accidents happen that way with kids?'

'He wasn't running around!' I have a vague memory of us talking about the bird, of him standing there by the breakfast bar, doing something with Godfrey. I think. 'He was with Grace and then he came over to where I was, in the kitchen.'

'But if he threw himself into you, like he does sometimes . . . I'm confused. I just need clarity on the details.'

The harder I try to remember, the more muddy my memory becomes. 'Joe, I . . .'

'Your hand slipped.'

'Yes,' I say. 'He took me a little off balance.' I can vividly recall the feeling of the pan in my hand, my struggle to keep it steady, the water spilling.

I try to look away from the distressing memory. He is staring at me, measuring me.

'What is it?' I ask.

There's a long pause, and then he says, 'Well, the thing is . . . Meredith told the doctor she didn't believe it was an accident.'

THIRTY-EIGHT

His words circle the air, unable to land. 'What?'

'She's talking about reporting you to Social Services, to the General Medical Council and possibly even suing you for negligence.'

'Suing me?' I almost bolt off the chair. I can't be hearing straight. 'But it *was* an accident!' The words come out emphatically but I almost sound like I'm beseeching him to believe me. 'She thinks I threw water on him deliberately? Boiling water? Is this some sort of joke? You can't be serious!'

When he just drops his gaze to the floor, I say, 'Grace was there. Didn't anyone ask her?'

'She said she was on the sofa. She wasn't paying attention. All she heard was his screaming.'

It's true. She wasn't exactly *right there*.

'Oh my God.' My legs are about to give out. I have to sit down again. 'She's going to report me to Social Services . . .' I try to visualise what this means. 'How can she – or anyone – think I'd want to hurt a child?'

'Lauren,' he says, matter-of-factly, coldly. 'You went on a public forum. You pretty much admitted you hate them.'

I cannot believe my ears. 'She's going to use that against me? What I said on a *forum*? She's going to attempt to destroy my career with this? My *life*?' Adrenaline is blazing. The blood pounding in my head.

I search his face for some sign of sympathy, or outrage. But there is nothing. Instead, he studies me for a while, then he says, 'She believes the environment was . . . unsafe. You had a duty of care towards him, and she thinks you failed in that regard.'

'And what do you think?' I ask.

His lack of an immediate response is pretty much all the answer I need.

'Wow,' I say. 'You actually agree with her. You think I deliberately tried to hurt him . . .' My voice breaks. I look at him properly now but there is something impassive and shut down in his expression. I can't gain entry.

'I don't think you deliberately tried to hurt him. Of course I don't . . . But you can't be handling pans of boiling water when there's a four-year-old darting around the place! I mean . . . for God's sake, Lauren! How can you not know that?'

'But he wasn't darting . . . !'

'It's a basic . . . Such a *basic* thing. You don't have to be a parent, you don't have to be anything . . . It's something anyone would intuitively know!' He sounds so mystified, like he just can't fathom the degree of my incompetence. 'How could you put him in harm's way like that?'

Harm's way?

I suck in air, but I cannot let the breath back out. It's all just trapped, locked there. When I can recover a part of myself, I say, 'I need air. I have to get out of here.'

I don't even wait for another word from him, cannot face hearing another single accusation. I bolt from the sofa, grab my keys, and rush out of the door.

THIRTY-NINE

I am sitting in my car watching the rain roll down the windscreen. None of this feels real. My mind tries to play it all back but it's all scrambled.

I'm startled by the loud ping of a text notification. I glance at my phone sitting on the passenger seat. Sophie.

I click on her message. So sorry it's late in the day! HAPPY BIRTHDAY!!! Hope you're having an amazing day! Can we talk?

I stare at the words HAPPY BIRTHDAY. All the exclamation marks. It's an olive branch and my eyes well up. Once I can gather myself, I dial her number. But the second I hear the comforting familiarity of her voice, I burst into tears. It takes me a while to be able to compose myself enough to tell her what's gone on.

'What are you doing right this second?' she asks, in that no-nonsense way of hers.

'Sitting in my car, a few streets away from my flat,' I tell her.

'You need to drive over to our place. Right now.' And then she says, 'In fact, don't drive. Get an Uber.' When she senses I'm dithering she says, 'Lauren. Get yourself over here right now. Or, alternatively, tell me precisely where you are and I'll come and get you.'

'I'll get an Uber,' I tell her.

Over a curry I can barely stomach looking at, let alone eating, and a beer that feels like it's just sitting in a fizzy puddle in my oesophagus, we try to get our heads around what happened and where I stand.

If Meredith goes ahead with her complaint, I know from my knowledge of hospital procedure the first step will be a formal report. Then Social Services will get involved. If the allegation seems substantial then maybe the police will also feature. Then . . . it either comes to nothing, or the worst-case scenario happens and I am charged. That would lead to a hearing, a possible conviction, a sentence, a criminal record. I would no longer be able to practise medicine. My life would be ruined.

I can barely come out from hiding my head in my hands.

'Yes, yes, yes,' Charlie says, as I repeat all this. 'We know all this is *possible*, but whether it's *likely* is a whole other ball of wax. You didn't do anything wrong. If it was this easy to break the law, we'd all be in prison!' He sounds furious on my behalf and I find myself hanging on to his logic, trying to believe it for the sake of my sanity. 'Even if she's the best barrister on the planet, she's got to have some sort of proof. And some daft shit you wrote in a forum is hardly going to stand up in court!' He cracks open another beer and passes it to me.

'I'm sure you're right. But even if there's no criminal case . . .' I can't believe I've just uttered the word criminal in the context of myself. 'If she sues me in civil court she could ruin me financially.' I'd done a quick google while they were ordering the food. 'You think uni debt is bad! I could be stuck paying legal fees, damages . . . I could be in debt for the rest of my life!'

Oh my God, this is a nightmare. I jump up and pace the floor. I have to calm down or I'm going to combust.

'I seriously cannot imagine she's going to go to that extreme, Lauren!' Sophie says. 'You have to remember she's furious right now. She suffered a terrible shock. I'm sure once she's calmed down she'll see sense.'

I gaze from one face to the other. 'I hope you're both right. I don't see her as a person to make idle threats, but maybe I'm wrong. And she's never liked me from day one. Not *really* . . . Maybe she's been waiting for an opportunity like this . . .' I remember the day she told me about the case she was working on – malicious mother syndrome. It seems more than a little ironic that I'm sitting here wondering if Meredith might be a malicious mother herself.

'Look, keep a level head. Getting freaked out about it isn't going to help,' Charlie says. 'It was an accident that could have happened to anyone. You did nothing wrong in the eyes of the law or the GMC! Or in the eyes of anybody else! End of.'

End of?

I want to be optimistic but I can't help thinking this is just the beginning of.

FORTY

When I get back to the flat the next morning after crashing on Sophie and Charlie's sofa, Joe is finishing up a business call. When he hangs up, he doesn't ask where I've been all night, just looks at me tiredly – like he doesn't much care.

'How is Toby?' I ask. 'And Grace? Is she okay?' I think of how frozen she was, how terrified. Grace may not be the most openly demonstrative big sister, but she was grief-stricken to see her little brother hurt, and I feel so awful about that.

He sighs, sends a hand through his hair. 'Grace is fine. I talked to her earlier. She's going into school because there's nothing to be gained by staying at home . . . I'm going in to see Toby now actually. Meredith has to get to court.'

'Can I come?' I ask. And before he can protest, I add, 'I'd obviously like to see with my own eyes how he's doing.'

I'm almost one hundred per cent certain he'll say that's really not a good idea.

But instead he says, 'Sure.'

Toby is sitting up in bed in his private room while a young nurse has a bit of banter with him. My heart sinks at the sight of his lower arm and hand swaddled in bandages.

'Daddy!' he says, surprisingly cheery. 'Where's Mummy?'

Joe goes over and kisses him. 'Mummy had to go to court today so she's going to come and see you later.'

His gaze slides past his dad's head – to me – and I wonder if the sight of me is going to make him cry, but instead he says an upbeat, 'Lauren!'

The nurse tells us she'll be back in a bit, and leaves the room.

'Godfrey says hi!' I wave the leg of his favourite toy at him.

'How is Russell Crowe?' he asks, as I set Godfrey down beside him.

'Who's Russell Crowe?' Joe sounds puzzled.

Toby rushes out the story.

'Wow!' Joe sends me a brief look. 'Interesting what you two get up to when I'm not around!' But it's fake joviality, put on for Toby's benefit. His eyes are devoid of any affection when they look my way.

'Russell is actually doing well!' I say. 'I bet he's going to be back with his family in no time! Maybe we can check up on him again when you come home.'

He turns a little downcast. 'When can I go home? I don't want to be here anymore.'

'Soon, little man.' Joe tickles his cheek. 'Keep your happy face on, buddy.'

Toby peppers him with questions about how long his bandages will have to be on. Meanwhile I find my eyes being drawn to the foot of Toby's bed, to his medical chart, and my hand instinctively reaches for it.

I first scan the results of the bloodwork, then the scribbled notes: *partial thickness, superficial, irregular margins, non-uniform depth . . . non-intentional injury.* Then I go back and reread, process it better.

'Can we go to the park when I come home so we can see if Russell's family is still waiting for him?'

I distantly hear him ask me a question, but I just keep staring at the page before me.

'Lauren . . .'

It takes me a moment to snap back. 'Yes, Toby!' I plaster on a big smile, put the notes back where they came from. 'I'm sure we can do that when you come home.'

'Oh, okay,' Toby says, his left arm drawing Godfrey in for a hug.

I sneak a glance at Joe, noting the tender way he gazes at his son. He is sitting in the chair next to him, his index finger stroking Toby's bare knee. I am deeply moved by the sight of them – and troubled at the same time.

Toby is sent home. His injuries – mercifully – won't be any worse than blistering and discomfort. For the next few days Joe drives over there in the afternoon to take him to get his dressing changed when Meredith has to be in court. I put in a couple of long shifts at the hospital, still utterly cheerless in the wake of all this, dragging it all around with me.

Joe and I don't say much about the accident. There are no sharp words or remonstrances. But when we go to bed he doesn't hold me. When he speaks he looks several inches past my head.

On my last night shift we are insanely busy, which fortunately keeps my mind away from my marriage, my mistakes and other troubling things I know. But as I take an old man's HR, temperature, BP and SATS, as I remove a chest drain from a middle-aged

227

manual worker, insert nasal packing in a teenager and review the gastroscopy of a patient with oesophageal cancer, I don't feel my normal confidence and connection to the tasks at hand.

On the Tube home at 8 a.m., as the train flashes through the tunnel, I don't know if I'm too exhausted to feel overwrought anymore, but one comforting thought does occur to me. If Meredith was going to report me, I'd probably have heard something by now. Silence can only be a good sign.

Buoyed by that thought, I walk out of the lift at the underground, when my phone rings and I see it's Joe.

'I'm just coming out of the station right now,' I tell him. 'Almost home . . .'

There's a brief pause, and then he says an uneasy, 'Okay . . . Good.'

'Do we need any groceries? I can pop to the shop.' I vaguely recall us being low on milk.

'No,' he says. 'Don't pop to the shop. Come straight home.'

There is something in his tone that unnerves me. 'Is everything all right?'

Silence again. And then, 'Not exactly.'

My walking slows to a halt.

'What's wrong?' I ask.

I hear a slight sigh. And then he says, 'There are some people here. From Social Services. They'd like to talk to you.'

FORTY-ONE

When I walk into the flat, everything is quiet. At first I think, *That's odd! Maybe they've gone.* But as I close the door behind me, something in the hollow of silence, in the subdued way the dog comes to greet me, tells me otherwise.

And then I hear the low rumbling of Joe's voice – and others. A steady, serious quality to their tone.

'Lauren.' Joe gets to his feet the moment he sees me. Sitting on the sofa, side by side, are a lanky young man in a severe grey suit and an older woman in an olive-green pencil dress.

The woman stands first and tells me she's Audrey Richardson from Children's Services. The young man follows her lead, less confidently, tells me he's Trevor somebody – I don't catch the last name. He doesn't meet my eyes.

Joe asks me if I'd like some water.

The woman says a perky, 'Or a cup of tea?'

'No,' I say. 'I think I'm okay.'

Audrey asks me to sit down. As I do, she adds, 'I'm sure that as a doctor you must get tired of being on your feet.'

I tell her she's right. The dog comes and lays his chin on my lap, and when I happen to glance at this Trevor person, he is watching

Mozart like someone who isn't particularly a pet-lover but needs somewhere to put his eyes.

Audrey gets down to business. She tells me there's been a report to their department – concern for the welfare of my stepson, raised by the child's biological mother. She goes on to give me a few more details, setting it all out, most of which I don't hear except for a few key terms.

Accident.

Toby's well-being.

Child endangerment.

As I swallow and try to unclench my clasped fingers from the backs of my hands, she asks if I can explain to her exactly what happened in the kitchen when Toby was scalded.

And so I do. I tell her everything I am sure I've recounted half a dozen times before.

She doesn't speak when I finish. Trevor addresses me instead. 'You were celebrating your birthday, were you not?' He glances up from his notes, looks like he's trying really hard to not appear as uncomfortable as he's feeling. Instead of meeting my eye, his gaze settles an inch or two to the right of me. 'I believe you had a bottle of champagne. You served some to your fourteen-year-old stepdaughter apparently. Is that right?'

'To Grace,' I say. 'Yes. A small glass.' I glance at Audrey, who is looking at me with an expression that borders on sympathetic.

There is a suspenseful silence, then Joe fills it. 'Sorry . . . I'm not sure what the point of this question is – or how it's relevant. It's not a crime to give a minor a glass of bubbly in your own home, is it.' There is no question, no uncertainty in his tone.

'Not a crime,' Trevor says. 'No.' He returns his attention to his notes. 'So your stepdaughter was on the sofa here with Toby while you were cooking, is that right?'

'She was, yes. She and Toby were playing a ventriloquist game.'

230

Audrey smiles.

'And when did Toby start running around the kitchen exactly?' Trevor asks.

'He didn't,' I tell him. 'He came and stood by the breakfast bar at some point. He wasn't running, though. He was playing with his Godfrey the Giraffe.'

He looks unconvinced. My heart flares.

He then asks me some other questions about our family's practices. Whether I am regularly alone with the children, if I generally prepare all the meals for them, take them to and from school or to extra-curricular activities . . . how I discipline them. I realise he's not as green or as awkward as he first looked. He almost looks like he's enjoying himself now.

'Discipline?' I frown, the word conjuring school mistresses and corporal punishment, a cane cutting the air, landing on the palm of a hand. 'I wouldn't say I ever *discipline* them, as you put it. That's not really my role.'

Joe says, 'What my wife means is that we haven't been married all that long. Lauren tries very hard to have a positive relationship with my children. And while there really hasn't been any incident where she would have been required to correct their behaviour, she would likely not feel comfortable doing so at this stage, I don't think.' He looks at me. 'Right?'

'That's right.' I send him a flicker of a smile.

The young man, who is getting into his stride now, says, 'So your relationship with your stepchildren could be described as positive, could it?' He finally – properly – meets my eyes and I have a sneaky feeling he's setting some sort of trap.

My mind immediately goes to the forum. What Meredith – or Grace – might have told them. 'Positive might be a stretch,' I say, and I give Joe a look that says, *Sorry. I have to be honest.* Then, directing my comment to Audrey, perhaps for no other reason than she's a woman, I add, 'It hasn't always been easy. Grace and I don't always get along. But we are trying – all of us.'

She gives a short nod. 'Tell me about it, love! I've got teenagers and I hardly ever get along with them these days. Most of the time I can't say a right word.'

I smile, feeling a degree of relief.

The guy asks if they can take a quick look around the flat. I realise that since I moved on from wringing my hands, I've been clutching handfuls of my skirt just to stop my hands sweating.

Audrey says, 'Perhaps Lauren could show us where Toby sleeps.'

So we walk down the hall to Toby's room. I hang back while they have a little look around – briefly glancing in his wardrobe, taking in his vast collection of toys on the small window seat and his train set on the desk.

'He's the little boy who's got everything, isn't he?' Audrey catches my eye.

'He doesn't want for toys,' I say, 'nor for love and attention.'

She studies me a moment, then skims through a pile of his books – his vintage Ladybird collection that I bought for him shortly after the book debacle in the hotel.

'Bedtime reading,' I tell her.

'These are almost collector's items!' She seems nostalgic.

'I know. I found them online. They were a big part of my growing-up. I thought it might be nice if they were part of Toby's.'

She regards me with kindness. 'Do you read to him or does his dad?'

'Both of us,' I say. 'But I suppose mostly me . . . Joe says Toby finds a female voice soothing.'

She nods, seems to like this.

'Soothing or not, they don't always put him to sleep.' I try a smile.

'And what about you? Do you like reading to him?'

I suddenly feel desolate, a sense of all that being past tense now. 'Actually, yes. I love it. I didn't really grow up around younger kids. It's been my favourite thing about being a stepmum.'

Audrey smiles, glances at his toys again, and then we leave the room.

I go back into the living room while the two of them chat in low voices at the end of the hall. After a while, Audrey pops her head around the half-closed door.

'Thank you for answering our questions.'

'Just one more thing,' Trevor says. 'Before we go . . . Were you at a petrol station a few weeks back, and did you happen to lock Toby in the car?'

My heart skips a beat.

Joe says, 'That's not strictly accurate. She didn't lock him in the car. Her key fob failed.'

'But the upshot was he got locked in and you couldn't get the door open, right?'

I can't believe Meredith would have told them this! Now I wonder, did she also bring up the fact that he fell on the slide? That Grace said there was practically a man-hunt for him in Marks & Spencer?

'It was minutes,' I say.

'Minutes. But you had to wait for help.'

I shake my head. 'There was a man there. It was sorted quickly.'

'Thank you.' Audrey is the one to bring the interrogation to a close. On their way out she adds, 'If we need anything else we'll be in touch.'

FORTY-TWO

'I'll talk to Meredith again,' Joe says, shortly after they've gone. 'Try to get her to see sense.'

Their questions, their implications, cling to me like some sort of vile contamination.

'I'm going to see what I can do,' he says, but I wish he sounded more infuriated, more impassioned, on my behalf.

In the night I can't sleep, and decide there's no point in just lying here, wide awake, blinking at the ceiling. I drag my feet into the kitchen and sit at the breakfast bar with my laptop. I find myself doing random google searches, combing through websites for the Met police, Citizens Advice, the NSPCC . . . I read about child protection law, what happens if you get charged with child neglect, as well as countless personal cases – horror stories, more like – in the *Guardian*, *Daily Mail* and *Mirror* – which leave me more panicked than ever.

Joe wanders into the kitchen, places a hand on my shoulder. I nearly jump out of my skin.

'I want to see her,' I say, after he's made coffee, poured me a mug and sat down. I'm not convinced he's going to make a good enough case for me to get her to back off. I peer at the time at the top of my computer. Only 5 a.m. 'First thing. I want you to call her and tell her I'm coming over. We need to have this out.'

'That's fine,' he says, rather disengaged. 'I'll call her in an hour or so when she'll be up.'

He doesn't say, *I'm coming with you.*

Her house is an elegant, white stucco-fronted, Grade II-listed, mid-terrace on a quiet, leafy avenue a short walk from the charming, understated, picture-perfect Primrose Hill village. Joe said they paid two million pounds for it fifteen years ago, and while it's worth more than double that now, Meredith preferred to buy Joe out and stay in the low-key, celebrity enclave she'd come to love, while he moved a couple of miles up the road – close enough for shipping the kids back and forth, but far enough away to not be running into each other in the coffee shop.

Now that I'm here, my stomach pitches with dread. It's hard for me to think this was once Joe's home too. That he walked these streets, ate at that cafe in the village, lived a life behind that royal blue front door. A life that might never have changed if Meredith hadn't cheated. I have never stopped to wonder if he compares and contrasts his marriages. If, cheating aside, he would rather have still been with her than with me.

I understand I have about twenty minutes before she has to get into work.

I intend to have a rational, unemotional conversation, but the second we come face to face my resolve crumples, and my blood boils. 'You called Social Services on me!' I try not to sound border-line hysterical. 'You reported me for child endangerment?'

I don't know what I'm expecting. To appeal to her humanity? For her to regret – even for a millisecond – taking us down this path?

But those big soulful brown eyes hold mine, their expression quickly turning into a look that could sever bone. 'You're not fit,' she says.

In the background – down a long narrow hallway with blank cream walls and dark, imperfect wooded floorboards – I see Grace lurking in the shadows.

Indignation pulses in me. 'It was an accident, Meredith! An accident. It could have happened to anyone. You or Joe could equally have been in my situation. Only you weren't, were you? Because neither of you were there.' I point a finger into my own chest. '*I* was there.'

She looks me up and down again, two spots of colour blooming on her cheeks. I'm still conscious of Grace watching, taking it all in.

And then I hear Grace say, 'Lauren is right, Mummy. It really was an accident.' She walks down the hallway in her pyjamas and stands beside her mother.

Meredith throws her a look. 'Grace, you need to stay out of this.'

She directs her attention to me again. 'Lauren, we make judgement calls every day. Risk assessments. Most of them are subconscious. Many are basic common sense. Even if I put your feelings for my children aside, what does this say about your judgement? In fact – let's face it – what does any of your behaviour to date say about it?'

She holds my gaze. I can't look away from this horrible picture she's just painted of me. Before I can say anything in my own defence, she presses on. 'You're so damned untrustworthy! I don't know if it's your age, or your lack of life experience, or just the fact

236

that these are not your children so you don't really care, because even if you actually liked them, you don't *love* them . . . You can't love them like a mother.' She pauses, draws breath. Her gaze is unflinching. Her tone has gone from mildly sympathetic to indignant again. 'You are honestly not cut out for the position you've found yourself in, and the thing is, I think you know it.'

All I can focus on is her saying that even if I liked them, I can't love them like a mother. This unbearable feeling of inadequacy and exclusion, of staying a course that gets us nowhere in the end.

'I'm sorry,' she says. 'I suspected it from day one. I never thought you were cut out for this. And that's got *nothing* to do with your age, or any feelings about Joe remarrying on my part . . . It was just a sense I got from you. And I'm sorry to say you proved me right.'

I listen to this character assassination, my brain scrambling back over it. Grace is staring at the ground, her face ablaze with colour. She will not meet my eye.

'That's very unfair,' I manage to say levelly, though it takes a degree of self-control I never knew I possessed. 'You have no idea what I think or don't think, or what I feel.'

She doesn't even blink. 'Be that as it may, that's not really the issue here. This isn't about you. It's about my children. And the reality is – like I said – you are not fit to be responsible for them. Or anyone's children. And I cannot allow mine to be left in your care anymore.'

Grace says, 'Mummy!'

'I'm sorry . . .' Meredith adds. 'We tried . . . We really did. But we can't trust you.'

I have no idea who the *we* is. Her and Joe?

A tear rolls down my face.

Grace says, 'I just told you, Lauren didn't do anything wrong! Toby wasn't anywhere near her. He was with me. I was playing with

237

him.' She glances from me to her mother, her eyes full of questions. 'How are we going to be able to go to Dad's, if you don't want Lauren around?'

'Grace,' Meredith says. 'Toby was in Lauren's care, not yours, and she was the one who failed to adequately supervise him.'

The veiled threat sits there. It would almost be better if I could see some satisfaction in her face; then I could somehow convince myself that this were just a vindictive strike on her part. But nothing here suggests 'malicious mother' motivation. She almost comes across as – paradoxically – decent.

I wipe the tear off my cheek. 'So suing me, ruining me . . . that will make you feel better, will it? That's the only solution?' It comes out as a small plea.

I'm aware of Grace standing as still as a statue, hanging on to her mother's words.

'Lauren, it's not about suing, ruining. Tell me . . . What am I supposed to do?' She flings up her hands. 'Wait around to see what the next one's going to be? What other "*Oops! I didn't mean it, it just happened!*" screw-up is going to come along? Hope and pray that whatever it is it'll be minor?' She glares at me. 'This child is four! He's a baby.'

She scans my face as though I'm incomprehensible to her. 'Tell me,' she says. 'If he was yours, if you were in my shoes – what would *you* do as his mother?'

FORTY-THREE

I try to get to grips with what I can control, and what I can't.

'Before I can become a fully registered doctor, before I can even begin Foundation Year 2, I've got to declare if there are any current or future proceedings that could lead to my licence being suspended or removed.'

I am FaceTiming in my lunch break with Sophie and Charlie from a bench in the courtyard. It's not cold but my teeth are chattering, the breath almost trapped in my chest.

This is beyond a nightmare now. All I can try to do is minimise the damage.

'I think I need to write them a letter,' I tell them. 'So they don't hear it first from Meredith. Unless they already have. But let's hope they haven't.'

Charlie is exasperated. 'They're not going to deny you your licence, Lauren! You were questioned by an old hag and a young upstart from Social Services. Nothing more. You need to leave it alone! Don't go suggesting things to them. The second you identify something as an issue, it becomes one!'

I appreciate this, but I say, 'Yes, but you're supposed to bring it to their attention if there are possible issues that might affect people's perception of you as a doctor. You know, like if someone told Social Services you threw boiling water at a kid!'

'Oh God,' Sophie says, briefly covering her face with her hands. 'Can you stop saying that? It's so awful!'

We go back and forth on it some more. What I think I should do versus what they both think. They manage to talk me off the ledge. 'Okay,' I say, 'you've convinced me. I'll do nothing. For now.'

I thank them for finding time in their day to listen to me go on about all this. I am suddenly highly grateful for them – both of them. But as I ring off, I can't help but feel it should have been Joe's shoulder I was crying on, not theirs.

Days come and go. None of this leaves my head even for a second. I text Grace: Thank you for sticking up for me. That was big of you, and took some guts.

She quickly replies. Didn't make a difference though.

We will work it out, I say.

As I trudge to East Croydon station from work – an early shift that ended at 2 p.m. – I feel like the walking dead. And yet I don't want to go home, have to creep around Joe who seems to retreat into himself when I am in the room, and be on my best behaviour.

I'm just trying to decide what on earth I should do when I get a text.

Hi Lauren!

I haven't heard from you in such a long time! Hope all is well? We never did have that coffee. All is okay here. Gearing up for a family holiday next week and trying to find the will to live! 😊 Just wanted to say Hi!

Mel.

It's more than a little bizarre that this woman always seems to message me when I'm in the depths of despair. I stand against a wall and type what I intend to be a short reply, putting her in the picture, but it ends up being not very short at all. I delete it and start over.

Mel! Actually, I'm at East Croydon station right now, on my way home from work! I could get off at Clapham, meet you at Costa's on the high street if you happen to be up for a coffee? No worries if too short notice! I really hope your dad's treatment is going well and that he is okay. Lx

Two seconds later she replies: I am free right now as it happens!

This perks me up no end. Want to switch to glass of wine instead of coffee?

Sure! she says, after a moment. Meet me at the Silver Shilling.

She attaches a Google map.

The Silver Shilling is one of those mainstay watering holes that has long been a London institution, and today is a leaner, sleeker version of its former shabby self: all bleached floorboards, pine dining tables, linen napkins and Farrow & Ball paintwork. As I walk in they're playing the catchy little Jon Boden song, 'How Long Will I Love You?'

I glance around – she doesn't seem to be here yet. I plump for a table by the window, sitting so that I am facing out and will see her when she comes in. I send a quick text to Joe telling him I'm just having a drink with a friend. He responds, Stay as long as you like.

As I'm trying to read it for tone, he adds, Try to have a nice time.

241

A young waitress ambles over and tells me that if I'm here for food, they don't put out their daily sheet for another hour, but she hands me their snacks menu instead.

Because my shift started at 6 a.m. I ate a quick sandwich at eleven, so I am a little peckish and could probably handle some buttered Cornish crab on home-made English muffins.

I'm just scanning the menu to see what else they have when I hear a voice say, 'You're not Lauren by any chance, are you?'

I look up to see a devastatingly handsome young guy standing there. He has a thatch of prematurely grey hair, twinkly brown eyes and a short beard. And he is smiling somewhat sheepishly.

FORTY-FOUR

At first I think, *Ah! Mel couldn't make it and this is the husband.*

But then he says, 'Sorry. I know this is probably a shock.'

Probably a shock? I can't speak. It takes a moment or two before my brain can signal to my body what to do.

And then I stand. 'Oh my God!' The chair scrapes loudly along the floor.

I'm just reaching for my bag when he puts out a hand that doesn't quite make contact with my arm. 'Please . . . Lauren . . . I know how this looks, but would you please give me two minutes to explain myself?'

We are standing a couple of feet apart. My blood feels like it's barrelling through my veins. His gaze, an imploring quality in it, hangs on mine.

For reasons I will never know, I find myself saying, 'Two minutes.'

'Thank you,' he says, looking genuinely relieved. Then he indicates the chair opposite the one I'd occupied. 'Is it okay if I sit down?'

I cross my arms and pointedly look off to the side. 'For now.'

He sits, and I follow suit.

'My God, I bet you're not even a teacher, are you – *Mel*?' My brain darts back over all our conversations, searching for other signs of deception.

'I am!' He brings his hand to his heart and my eyes are drawn to his fit arms and broad chest in his white short-sleeved shirt. I vow not to look there again. 'God's honest. I can give you the name of my school and references if you want . . . I teach maths.' He tells me where and for how long. And then, perhaps because I haven't bolted yet, he says, 'I realise the name thing is misleading, and I know you won't see it this way, but I never set out to be dishonest.'

'But nor did you exactly make full disclosure your priority, either.'

We lock eyes. He tells me his name is Mel Thompson. That Mel isn't short for anything; it's what his mother had him baptized. He tells me he's from Manchester. That he was a rugby player until a shoulder injury ended his career. That he's twenty-seven, and has been teaching for five years.

'Thanks for all this,' I say, somewhat sarcastically. 'Particularly the bit about how Mel isn't short for anything. You know . . . Like *Melanie*.'

The waitress appears and asks what we'd like to drink. I quickly tell her we need a moment. She glances at Mel a little reactively and then says, 'No probs,' and walks away.

'Look, answer me this,' he says. 'Would you have continued to talk to me if I'd said I was a man? You know, a bloke in a forum for stepmothers?'

I tut. 'No. Which leads me to the obvious question . . .'

'I know,' he says. 'I've definitely got some explaining to do. But the truth is I joined for the same reason you did. I felt alone, frustrated. I've got lots of mates but none of them are in my situation and there's no use talking to them because they just can't relate. My parents thought it was a bad idea to get hooked up with Siobhan in the first place, so I didn't exactly feel like alerting them to the fact that it was all falling apart . . .' He stretches out his arms on the table, looks down briefly at his hands. 'Believe it or not, there are no forums, no support groups for men in my situation. Plenty for divorced dads, if I'd been one of those. Just none for stepdads.'

He regards me frankly as he says all this. He seems to be waiting for me to break the silence – let him off the hook. When I don't, he says, 'If you think about it, there's actually nothing I've said to you that's been a lie . . .'

'That's a bit lame,' I say. 'Lies of omission are still lies.'

'The forum is for mums. Once I was in it I could hardly let it out of the bag that I wasn't one.'

I glance away, still miffed. 'You've made me feel like a bit of a mug. Which is not exactly endearing.'

He holds up his hands, looks sincerely humbled. 'Look . . . I'm sorry. I don't know if you noticed, but when you suggested we meet for coffee sometime, I didn't exactly jump at the idea, did I?'

I think about this.

No. He didn't. I drove it, I suppose.

'It's because I knew that once you saw me you were going to jump to the natural conclusion that I was either a weirdo, or an opportunist on the make.'

'I jumped.'

'I know.' He briefly hangs his head. 'And I'm sorry.' There's a guilty pause and then he says, 'I should have told you, but then it got harder the more we went on chatting.' When I'm a little lost for a response he says, 'Anyway, if you take away the fact that I'm a man, everything else stays the same. Same issues. Same not knowing what to do about them . . . Can we just maybe resume from there?'

The waitress ventures back over. 'Any decisions yet?'

I tell her I'll have a gin and tonic.

Mel's eyes don't leave my face. 'So then . . . are you fine if we make it two?'

FORTY-FIVE

Joe is on the sofa when I come in, feeling a little lighter in my stride. I have never seen him sitting around as much as he's been doing lately.

He truly does look worn out. There are dark crescents under his eyes, aging him by a decade.

'How was Toby today?' I say, slipping off my jacket.

'Better.' He sounds so flat. 'I took him to the health centre to get his dressing changed again. He seems to be getting used to the drill and he didn't even cry this time.' He smiles; a sorrowful smile. 'He's got a big crush on one of the nurses. She makes a lot of him. I took him for ice cream after.' He finally meets my eyes. 'He's really got a thing for that bird. He was asking again today when he's going to be able to see Russell Crowe.'

I'm about to say, *Well, whenever he's next over here I can take him to the wildlife centre*, but I clam up for fear of what his reaction might be. 'I'm glad he's feeling a lot better,' I say instead.

His face doesn't change. And then he says, 'Meredith is talking about wanting to change the custody arrangement.'

'What?' I collapse into the nearest chair. 'You mean for her to have sole custody?'

'Something like that, yes. It's going to be very rough on the kids. I can't imagine what this is going to do to them, in fact.'

I think of what she said about her client that day, how parental wrangling and malicious legal action was harshest of all on the children. 'This is utterly horrible! Can she even do that? What a hypocrite she's being! Would she even have grounds?'

Mild annoyance flares in his eyes. 'I don't think name-calling really gets anyone anywhere, does it? But yes, she seems to think she's got a good case. We haven't gotten into the details yet . . .' He briefly looks at the floor and all I can do is sit here and be flabbergasted – he's *still* defending her, even after all this! 'Something about my no longer being able to provide a suitable environment . . .'

My heart hammers as the realisation hits home. 'Because of me.'

He nods.

After I try to process the scope of this, I say, 'What are you going to do about it?'

He eventually shrugs. 'I don't know. I'll have to see my lawyer. There's going to be a court battle, of course . . . And they'll be wanting to subpoena you.'

The blood rushes to my face. 'Me?'

'Of course. What did you think?'

I swallow hard. I have no idea what he means by that, or what I was thinking.

'I'm going to bed,' I say.

He looks bewildered. 'Bed? At this time? I thought we were having a conversation.'

'We're not,' I say, firmly.

As I walk down the hall, my phone pings. A text.

It was great to meet you. I enjoyed chatting. Hope there's no lingering weirdness between us after you learned she was a he.

Anyway, would love to meet up again – as friends. But if that is too awkward for you, I understand. Mel.

My head feels like it's spinning. I can't accommodate this now. I shut my phone down.

I have to drag myself into work for the next few days for 8 a.m. starts, struggle to even find the will to get up out of bed when my alarm goes off. I'm standing on the platform at Victoria, waiting for the train to East Croydon, when I get a phone call.

Audrey Richardson, from Social Services.

She tells me that she just wanted me to know that they were satisfied with the outcome of our meeting and they will not be pursuing the matter any further.

When I thank her for letting me know, she says a rather loaded, 'Good luck,' before she rings off.

On the train I try to feel happier. So that's gone away. Thank God! But what about Meredith threatening to sue me for negligence? The custody battle? My name being dragged through the courts? I try to envision what all this will look like for Joe, as well as for myself: the very possibility that he could lose his children – a situation he would not even be in if it weren't for me. Where's that going to leave our relationship?

At work I can't focus on anything I'm doing. Then in the afternoon I do something I've never done before.

A fifty-four-year-old woman comes in with chest pain, shortness of breath and wheezing after a Zumba class. The class instructor accompanies her, concerned she's suffered a heart attack. I examine the patient, ask her detailed questions about her medical history and then perform a lung function test. 'I think what you have is exercise-induced bronchoconstriction,' I tell her after some consultation, and suggest we prescribe her an inhaled medication – Flomax – to open her lungs, after which we'll repeat the lung function test and compare results to see whether the bronchodilator improved her airflow. If I'm right, then she can be given a short-acting beta agonist – an inhaler – which she'll take before her next class.

When I've finished explaining all this and writing up her script, preparing it for a senior doctor to sign, her face bursts into a smile.

'What?' I ask.

Her face flushes. 'Oh . . . sorry . . .' She chuckles. 'It's just that, well, my husband takes that. You know . . . Flomax. For his enlarged prostate.'

There is a moment where my heart gives a single skip. All I can do is stare at her and play back what she's just said. But then, miraculously, I am saved by a spot of quick thinking. '*Vol*max,' I say, as though obviously it was she who misheard. 'It's an inhaler, essentially, for asthma.' I smile, the confident professional that I am. 'Don't worry!' I try a little laugh. 'I can assure you I would never – ever – prescribe you prostate medication!'

By the time I finish my twelve-hour shift and walk to the train, I'm still shaken by what I nearly did. Maybe everybody is right and I am incompetent and not to be trusted. Maybe I need to find some other line of work where I can't be a threat to anyone, can't almost mis-prescribe medication. Maybe I need to be single so I can't mess up anybody's kid, or even one of my own.

Or maybe I don't.

Maybe I need to pull out the only weapon in my arsenal.

FORTY-SIX

This time, she is a little less self-assured when she answers the door.

As she stands there, not two feet away from me, I catch Rosamie having a nosy peek, and then she disappears into a room, emerging moments later with her coat on to leave, and scurries past us.

'You'd better come in.' Meredith shows me into a high-ceilinged, well-lit reception room with almond-white walls and three matching cream sofas arranged around a fireplace. On one of the sofas their cat Fishcake is curled into a ginger-and-white ball. On another there's a scattering of files and loose papers and an open MacBook, a coffee mug on the table beside it.

I imagine this is just how the place would have looked when Joe lived here, and find myself trying to transplant him into this life. Right now it's actually easier to imagine him in this one than in mine.

She invites me to sit. At first I think I'd rather say this standing, but I perch on the sofa beside the cat and she sits on the one opposite. My eyes go to a simple watercolour of sailing boats on a slash of blue sea above the mantelpiece, flanked by two funky light sconces that look a bit like drones.

'So . . .' she says.

I'm aware of the hair tied back in a messy, low ponytail, the face that is devoid of make-up, the pale grey, unironed V-necked T-shirt and skinny jeans. Her feet are bare, slightly tanned, and her red toenails sink into the wool of the cream rug.

A doubt that I'm going to do this starts to worm its way in, but I try not to focus on it. Instead, I meet her eyes.

'So I've come here, really, to say just one thing,' I begin. 'I've come to tell you that you need to back off. You need to rethink any idea you might still have about suing me, or reporting me to the GMC. And you need to rethink your intention to take Joe to court to change the custody arrangement.'

Her eyes stay fixed on mine, but a surge of colour comes to her cheeks.

'Because if you don't then you're going to leave me with no choice.'

I try to take a discreet, steadying breath. And then I say it.

'I'm going to have to tell Joe that Toby is not his son.'

FORTY-SEVEN

Her mouth gapes open and she stares at me, a little punch-drunk.

Then she says, 'Where on earth did you get that idea from?' It's delivered confidently, but her face tells another story.

'A man who has type AB blood can't father a child who is type O,' I say.

A single deep trench appears between her eyes. Some of the colour drains from her face. 'And you would know Toby's blood type how?'

'From his medical chart.' I clasp my hands in my lap. 'I went to the hospital with Joe and I read it. I wanted to see what the doctor said about Toby's injuries. First-hand.'

'So you've come here to blackmail me with this?' she says, after a spell of shock.

'Yes. If that's what you want to call it. Whatever it takes for you to rethink your actions.'

'With zero regard for the people that will affect.'

'Pretty much. If you think you're going to drag me into court, make me a witness in a custody battle, you have massively underestimated me.'

I swallow, hear the nerves in my voice, the tension rising to choke me.

But I keep on. 'Remember how you said you were surprised I didn't seem to grasp how hard it is for women to be wives and mothers, and rise in their chosen careers, despite me being a professional woman myself? Well, believe me, I know how hard I have had to work to get to where I've got – and how hard I'll have to go on working. But being a doctor is everything I am and everything I have always wanted to be, and I am *good* at it, and *no one* is going to take that away from me.' My heart hammers. '*You* are not taking it away from me.'

The cat wakes up and staggers over, lies across my lap.

'What makes you think Joe doesn't already know?' She looks down at my hand resting on the cat's back.

'He doesn't. I'm pretty sure of it. But if he does, then I imagine you'll encourage me to go right ahead and tell him, won't you?'

We hold eyes.

'Meredith,' I say, as calmly and directly as I can. 'I am broken up about Toby. I have thanked God a thousand times that it wasn't worse. But I cannot change what happened. And I am *not* going to pay for it with my career and with my reputation.'

She redirects her gaze to the coffee mug on the table. 'Fine,' she says, almost under her breath.

I have no idea what that means, so I just sit here, wait.

Then she says, 'You're right. Joe doesn't know. And if you tell him, do you think he's going to thank you for it? Because I can promise you, that will be *it* for you.'

'I can live with that,' I say smoothly.

There is a moment where I can see this has surprised her. And then, after staring off into space for a while, her face changes again. 'He died. Toby's real father . . . I found out I was pregnant exactly a month after I learned he had stage four pancreatic cancer. He died just a few weeks after Toby was born.' Her eyes tear up.

When I'm not sure she's going to add any more, I say, 'I know. You told Joe . . . because you were worried Lucy would get to him first.'

She blanches. The muscles flex in her long neck.

'Good for you,' she says, abrasively. 'I suppose I'm not surprised Joe would have told you.'

It suddenly just comes to me now. The thing that was a bit puzzling about all this. 'You told him it happened a long time ago because you wanted to throw him off the scent of Toby possibly not being his.'

I'm waiting for her to take issue with my remark, but instead she nods. 'If I said Toby was Alistair's, if Joe even suspected, I ran the risk of it all being too much for him, of him not wanting to be a father to him. Of Toby ending up with no father.' Her dark, woeful eyes remain locked on mine.

'Did Alistair know?'

She shakes her head. 'Not that it's any of your business, but no. What would be the point? He'd have probably wanted to see him and that would have been very disruptive.'

I am actually surprised she's being this open. 'Did he suspect, do you think? He must have known you were pregnant.'

She says nothing at first, and then, 'I don't know what he knew. I wasn't in his head. He and I hadn't seen each other in a while. I'd kept my distance . . .'

I don't really know what she means by this, and don't feel like drilling any deeper.

After a time, she says, 'It probably doesn't make a lot of sense to you why I would have an affair with Alistair when I had a great guy like Joe.'

'Was it because Joe had also cheated at some point? Was it revenge?'

She frowns. 'No! Joe never cheated. That's not who he is . . . Joe is a very loyal person. He's intensely loyal to the people he loves.'

If it's meant to be a little dagger, it certainly pierces me like one.

The comment is left to lie there, and then she says, 'If you tell Joe, then he's probably never going to look at Toby the same way again. It will always be there . . .' There is a hard, but slightly vulnerable quality in her eyes, similar to the one I've witnessed in Grace's. 'Is that what you want to do to him? To Toby? An innocent little boy? Run the risk that Joe will somehow love him less?'

My mouth is dry. I could badly use some water but don't feel like asking for it. 'Do you think it's more scrupulous to have Joe go on believing a lie? Get into a bitter custody battle and go through hell for a child that isn't even his?'

'Knowing what you know about Joe, do you really think he'd even want to know?'

I don't know what to say. After a spell of us sitting like this, me contemplating the sudden transparency between us, she says, 'I think we've said all we need to say on this, don't you? I think the decision rests with you. If you tell Joe, then you'll hurt him more profoundly than he's ever been hurt – and change his relationship with an innocent child. And then *you* will have to live with that.'

The way she smoothly regains the high ground reminds me we are not newfound friends, suddenly allied by our divulgences.

'Are you prepared to do that?' she asks. 'Because deep down, for all your confidence in coming here, I don't think you are.'

FORTY-EIGHT

The following night, Sophie and I go out to dinner – alone – although I'm so wrung out I can barely sit upright at the table.

And while I don't tell her about Toby not being Joe's child, I do tell her that I don't know if I now see a future for me and Joe – even if things all magically righted themselves tomorrow – if I can put myself through all this for a man. If *any* man is worth it.

'I was envious of you,' she says, after she has listened to me sounding off. 'I think Charlie and I both were. In fact, I know we were.'

'Why?' I ask, wondering why it's easy for her to admit this now. 'Because you just assumed I was going to go off and make babies with Joe?'

She absently plays with the base of her wine glass. 'Two reasons, really . . . I think it was the way you met and the way he came back into your life. It was storybook.' She blushes, smiles, looks wistful. 'He tracked you down! He married you the second his divorce came through. It was so romantic! You both just . . . you had this tremendous, instant connection, like we all dream of having. And you never doubted it. And neither did he . . .' She drops her gaze. 'And my fella cancelled our wedding a week before the big day.'

I frown, look at her hands on the table, the index fingers making a pyramid around the base of her glass. 'Because of the kids issue, right? He didn't really reject *you*. He did it mainly because he worried the childlessness would later come between you . . .'

The glow has gone from her face. She shrugs. '*Was* that the reason? I mean, that's what he *said*. That's what I chose to *believe* . . . But we can believe a lot of things when we put our mind to it. Sometimes that's just another word for denial.'

I think about this in relation to her saying that maybe she had to feel needed by him to give her purpose. And about denial. How I believed there was nothing about Joe and Joe's life that I couldn't handle. That I'd sacrifice anything – willingly – to fit into his world. How I was so in his thrall when he told me my happiness was all that mattered.

'We were friends before we were lovers and we are friends now – maybe more than we are lovers,' she says. 'We never had that incredibly vital rapport and chemistry like you had. There is a part of me that will always wonder if I was the one he married because I convinced him I'd be fine with his sterility – if we both just . . . *settled*.' She says it like it's the most unpalatable word.

'Don't be silly,' I say. 'I mean, how's that for overthinking it?'

She sniggers. 'Maybe! But in our darkest moments, we can't help how we think.'

I take a sip of my wine. 'What was the other reason for this envy of me, as you put it?'

She blanches, pulls a cheerless smile. 'Obviously . . . the obvious one. You acquired a ready-made family. This stunning young girl – okay, a quirky girl – but you seemed to be taking it all in your stride . . . And that adorable cute little boy! As hard as it was going to be in the beginning, one day it would all gel, they'd grow up . . . Even if you had no kids of your own, you'd have them, and they'd have you. They would think of you as their family . . .' She looks overcome with emotion. 'I once said to you it was a lot to take on – someone else's kids – that I didn't think I could do it.' She gazes far into my eyes and I see a flicker of guilt and regret in hers. 'At the time I was very jealous. I think I just needed to convince myself that your situation was so undesirable . . . The reality is that I'd have happily done it.' Tears roll down her face.

I absorb all this, taken aback by her surprising admission. 'And now?' I ask. 'Knowing all this, are you still envious of me, Sophie?'

She sniffles, wipes at a tear with the back of her hand. 'No,' she says, a fraction brighter. 'Right now, I wouldn't want to be you for all the money in the world.'

FORTY-NINE

'You're not going to believe it,' Joe says, a few days later. He is standing at the end of the hall as I walk through the door, mobile phone in hand. 'This is crazy . . . Good crazy. But still . . .'

I wait for him to actually look at me.

'That was Meredith.' He finally turns his head in my direction, his gaze seeming to take a moment to properly focus on me. 'She's decided she's not going to pursue this business of changing the custody arrangement.'

'Oh,' I say, as I shrug off my jacket. 'Well, that's . . . that's excellent, then.' I could possibly have injected a note of surprise, but he doesn't appear to notice. Actually, though, I am a little surprised. I went there thinking I had the upper hand and left with the ball seemingly back in her court.

'Yes,' he says. 'It is. Really . . . truly.' He wipes a hand across his mouth, shakes his head a little. Mozart walks over to him; he absently extends his fingers. 'She didn't say why. Didn't really give any reason . . . And it's not exactly like her to do a U-turn on *any-thing*.' He smiles. 'It's all a little mysterious, to be honest.' Then he suddenly snaps into action. 'Can I pour us both a drink? It feels like we should be celebrating.'

Later, when I'm taking off my make-up in the bathroom, he appears behind me in the mirror. He is holding up a small box with an open lid. I stare at what's in it.

'It's odd timing, I know . . .' He smiles somewhat joylessly. 'I bought you this for your birthday. Was going to give it to you at the dinner we never got to go to. I've been trying to find the right moment to let you have it ever since, and there really hasn't been one. Not that this is really it . . .'

I turn around, take it from him, inspect it.

'It's bronze and baroque pearl.'

I admire the block-like, architectural-looking pendant, the richness of the metal, inset with what appears to be a warm, roughly cut stone that I wouldn't have immediately identified as a pearl – my traditional birthstone. 'It's beautiful.' He's right – it does feel like odd timing, as though we are now healed because of Meredith's decision and a belated birthday gift. 'So very unique.' I note the delicate nature of the chain. 'Fragile but deceptively strong.'

'That's what I thought, too . . .' His voice takes on a sentimental quality. 'It's a one-off piece made by an up-and-coming designer who got his big break through the Alexander McQueen foundation. The minute I saw it, it just sort of had your name on it.'

'Thank you,' I say, wishing the gesture could undo the all the negativity I will forever associate with turning thirty. 'I like it. It was thoughtful of you.'

On Saturday morning, time seems to either shift back or shift forward. It's like it's all behind us, or it didn't happen at all. Just like any other weekend, Joe walks in with Grace and Toby after picking them up from their mother's.

Toby sees me. His face lights up. 'How is Russell Crowe doing?' He runs over to me and throws his arms around my thighs.

He no longer needs the dressing on his hand. It bears the pink of new skin: a lingering reminder of how bad it all was, but also of how much worse it could have been.

'Russell is great and the wildlife centre returned him to his family!' I say, even though I know from my phone call yesterday that the crow is dead.

He frowns, his bottom lip jutting out. 'I thought we were going to return him together! I thought I was going to see him again.'

I drop on to a knee, make him look at me. 'I have a feeling that when we go back to the park he'll still be around.' I tell him about how crows have great memories, how they always remember faces – especially those of kind people who tried to help them.

He smiles and I pop a kiss on his forehead.

'I do have another idea though,' I say, glancing at Joe, who is fondly observing us. 'I had a word with your dad a few days ago, and, well, we've decided we should get you a budgerigar!'

Joe shoots me a look that says, *Huh?*

Toby's eyes widen. 'A budgerigar! That's so great.' And then he frowns. 'What's a budgerigar?'

Joe and I chuckle.

We take Toby to look at budgies, and then Joe takes him to the lido for a swim. I watch them walk out of the door, hand in hand, Joe having first stopped and crouched to remove Toby's glasses and clean them on the hem of his jumper. While they're gone I run a few errands, conscious as I trot up and down the high street of a lightness to my stride, a loose sense of relief in my bones.

When I get back to the flat it's around six and I'm not expecting anyone to be here, but as I walk in I see Grace's Doc Martens on the front door mat.

And then I hear what sounds like voices coming from down the hall. Wondering if she brought her friend over, I creep towards her room door but quickly realise the voices are actually coming from the bathroom.

And there's really only one of them. Grace's.

She is singing in the bath. My song. The Billie Jo Spears, '(Hey, Won't You Play) Another Somebody Done Somebody Wrong Song'.

You'd be hard-pressed to believe it's not actually Billie Jo herself. She belts out the lyrics with jaunty confidence, hitting all the notes in soulful harmony, and she knows every single word.

She's singing like no one can hear her. I stand there a bit like an interloper, and smile.

FIFTY

A week or so later, Meredith asks to meet me in a coffee shop in Chalk Farm.

She is almost done with her large latte by the time I arrive. And she doesn't say, *Aren't you going to order something?* so I know this is going to be short.

'You might as well sit down,' she says, as I hover by the table. When I perch on the end of the chair she fixes me with a cool, though not entirely hostile, stare. 'Toby's hand is healing very well, according to his doctor. There's not going to be any scarring. I thought you should know.'

I nod – though I'd managed to come to that very conclusion myself. 'I'm glad.'

Her eyes comb over my face and I know that's not all she wanted to tell me. And then she says, 'Look . . . I'm prepared to give all this another try.' She says it with a certain begrudging benevolence. 'Mainly because I don't believe there's any choice, and moving on from all this is probably the best path forward – for all of us.' There is a suspense-filled pause and then she adds, 'I believe I underestimated you.'

'Okay.' I let this settle. There's a loud hissing of steam, the banging of portafilters in the background. I look at the ends of her fair hair hitting the mandarin collar of her white-and-blue striped shirt, the small gold pendant in the shape of a star, with a tiny diamond at its centre, hanging from a fine gold chain. My mind casts around for something more to add, but she fills the gap.

'I once told you that I hoped we wouldn't start out as enemies, or become them, but that may have gone a little to pot somewhere.' She flashes a brief and slightly ghoulish smile. 'Anyway, I firmly believe that we do what we do for our own mixed-up reasons, but somewhere in there we can hope some of the right reasons are fuelling everything.'

I have no idea if she's trying to apologise, but I don't find myself feeling very magnanimous. I go on staring at her, conscious of a certain imbalance correcting itself.

She slides her coffee cup away, her fingers lingering on the saucer. 'What I'm saying is . . . I have given a lot of thought to this and I hope – obviously not any time soon – but maybe with a bit of tolerance on both our parts, we can put this behind us.'

She sits back in her chair, crosses her arms, and waits.

'Thank you, Meredith,' I say eventually, when I can find my voice. 'That may be a bridge too far. But I suppose – for the same reasons as you – I'm willing to give it a try if you are.'

She nods, stands, her chair scraping along the floor. I feel her briefly look down at the top of my head, like she might say something else, but then she walks out.

'I was thinking about August,' Joe says.

Normal life has somehow resumed for about a month now. We have come to one of our favourite restaurants on the high street, the first time we've been out for dinner since before Toby's accident. It's one of those places that does a great job of British food. Big hearty

264

portions. For some odd reason the sight of Joe's plate of English lamb makes me think of a conversation we had in the early days of our courtship. Joe told me all the things he found weird about England when he first moved here. Welsh Rarebit that contained no rabbit, separate taps for hot and cold, almost as many pigeons as people at every tourist monument, and Scotch eggs that he had to eat way too many of before concluding there wasn't a single drop of alcohol in them. How I'd laughed. That was back when every word that came out of his mouth was enthralling to me, when Joe was sitting on a pedestal he never asked to be on – I just put him there, unwittingly setting him up to fall.

'You're going to be done with your first foundation year soon. We should do something to mark the occasion.'

I want to feel excited by this – by the idea of us doing something celebratory to mark this new phase where I become a fully registered doctor.

'What did you have in mind?' I ask, looking briefly at my food.

He chews fast, wipes his mouth on a napkin. 'I was thinking . . . well, to be honest, I was thinking of a trip to *Chicago*.' He lets the idea land for a second or two. 'I would like you to spend some proper time with my parents. It's sad you've never actually met them except through FaceTime.'

As I navigate the last flakes of my Cornish cod, I find myself saying, 'I haven't seen my own parents in months. You've only met them once.' We took a three-day break to Spain before we were married. We stayed in a hotel because Joe didn't really want to be holed up in their small guest room, and met them for dinner, which felt so impersonal, like they could have been anybody.

I wonder if he senses I'm feeling a little ornery because he looks up from his plate. 'I know that . . .' he says, rather open-endedly.

For some reason I am reminded of our scaled-down wedding day. A civil service at Chelsea Town Hall. Not attended by either

265

set of parents. His, perhaps because it was too far to travel for a second go around. Mine, because I suspect it just wasn't 'wedding' enough to be the day my parents had waited for – though it was never acknowledged. And yet I didn't see it as devoid of anything at the time.

'So it would be nice if you could get to know them a bit better, too,' I say.

I wait for him to say, *Then why don't we go to Spain first and then on to Chicago?* And to suggest it like he means it – like the old fix-everything, solve-everything Joe – but instead he says, 'The thing is, you could hop over there for a long weekend any time – we both could. But I can't do that with Chicago. If we go – as a family – we have to go for at least a couple of weeks, or maybe three, to make it worthwhile.'

I believe this is the first time he's referred to the four of us as a *family*. And while I've wanted this, craved this sense of belonging, of – finally – everything falling into place, all I'm feeling right now is disappointed.

When I don't answer, he says, 'The way I saw it panning out . . . maybe we spend a week with my parents, then we leave Grace and Toby there with them, and you and I go off on a little trip.' He smiles. 'I was thinking maybe back to Santa Monica.'

Santa Monica. Instead of flooding with nostalgia, those words fill me with a tremendous sense of loss. The truth is, in the early days of our relationship I'd imagined us going back sometime, perhaps for a landmark anniversary. I'd envisioned what it would be like, caught myself almost stage-directing it in my mind, thrilled with the idea of recreating how we met.

As he holds my eyes, with so much optimism in his face, I want to say *That's a fantastic idea! Let's do it! It would be great for us! Just what we need!* But when I go to put voice to this fiction, there is this huge glottal stop. The vocal cords come together, stop the breath and stop the sound.

'Can we ever go back?' I say instead, and set my cutlery down, suddenly overcome with a horrible heavy heart. 'Because I don't believe we can.'

His face changes; a darkness seems to settle around us.

'Okay,' he says carefully. 'We don't have to go there. We could go somewhere else.'

I try a smile for his sake, for the way he seems to be window-dressing the issue. 'Let's think about it.'

I resume eating, feel him scrutinising me. Then he resumes eating too. After an interval, he says, 'Well, thinking's fine, but we can't think for too long if we're going to be securing four airline tickets at the height of the season.' He says it as though it's only the logistics that are at stake here, not something much bigger.

I look up and we meet eyes.

Then he adds, somewhat potently, 'I'm going to need you to decide soon.'

'Then I will,' I say.

After we get home, I change into my dressing gown and wander back into the living room. He's standing by the patio door, lit by the moon, watching Mozart sniff around the plant pots.

'What's changed?' I say to his back.

He turns around. A brief frown. 'What do you mean?'

Part of me falters. I try to breathe steadily despite a tightening in my throat. 'For months now I've hardly done a thing right. I mean, from virtually the minute I came into this family I seem to have blundered my way through everything . . . had this sense that

267

you're trying to be patient with me, but you're carrying around some feeling that you backed the wrong horse.'

'The wrong horse?' He almost laughs. 'What?'

'Joe, just a few weeks ago you said I was highly irresponsible, that I put Toby in harm's way—' Repeating his expression stings. I try not to exhume the awfulness of all that.

'Oh my God,' he says. 'We're not going back to that, are we? I thought we were over all that business?'

'Not to that, specifically, no. We're not going back to it. But like I say, I want to know what's shifted in your mind – about me? Why the vote of confidence in me – in us – now?'

He shakes his head in bewilderment, perches on the end of the sofa. 'There's no sudden vote of confidence. I never lost confidence in the first place . . . The accident . . . Toby . . . It turned out fine.' He says it as though none of this should be any mystery. 'It all ended up being okay, didn't it?'

'Did it?' I say. 'If he hadn't been fine, would we still be here, Joe? Discussing a family trip to Chicago? Because somehow I feel we wouldn't.'

I sit down and he angles himself to better look at me.

'If Meredith had sued me, if I'd had my career ruined, would we have weathered that, do you think? Would you have supported me through it?' I don't let him answer. 'In fact, have you ever fully supported me, in either your actions or your words?'

He looks utterly bruised by this, throws me a hard, uncomprehending stare. 'Why are you saying all this, Lauren? What are you getting at? Do you really think anyone else in our shoes would have found it easier? Are you that unrealistic?'

'No,' I say. 'Probably not. But I'm also wondering if anyone else had been in my situation and had been made to feel as you've made me feel at times . . . would they still be around? Would they not feel they deserved *so* much more? Someone who treated them with so much more consideration?'

He blinks and then he looks at the floor.

'Maybe I am overly sensitive, but you lost faith in us – in me. You might deny it, but I know you did. Well, the thing is, I lost it in you too. And I don't really ever see me getting it back.'

He looks up, stares at me with a slight vacancy. I can almost see his brain trying to negotiate all this. But he doesn't say anything. He doesn't make a case for how I am so very wrong.

'There's one more thing, too,' I say. 'A couple of months ago, I stopped taking the pill. Right after we came back from Edinburgh, actually.'

'What?' His jaw drops briefly. 'And now you're pregnant?'

'No,' I say. 'You needn't panic. I'm not pregnant, because I don't want to be pregnant right now, so I've been careful.' I clear my throat. 'But nor do I want to be on the pill because someone else insists on it. I'm not going to be held to an agreement we had before we married with the understanding that I am not allowed to change my mind about something as huge as this. I'm not going to be checked up on before you touch me.'

He regards me in disbelief, like someone desperately searching for a way to protest.

He goes to speak but I hold up my hand. 'You made it known how you felt about the timing before I married you – that you didn't want to be an old dad. You said all you cared about was my happiness, like you were being honest for my own good. But the only good you're interested in is your own, Joe. The only person whose happiness you are truly invested in is yours.'

'That's not true,' he says. 'That is so not true! It's actually the farthest—'

'What if I'd insisted I wanted to have kids *after* I became a qualified GP, would you have still married me?'

There is a moment where all he can do is look at me. His mouth opens, but any answer he might offer is a little too late out of the gate.

'You wouldn't have,' I finish for him. 'It would have been a deal-breaker.' I hang my head, wondering how I could have been so naive.

When I look up his face is a picture of sadness and regret.

But he still hasn't spoken.

He still hasn't contradicted me.

'So that's why I'm going to do what I'm going to do,' I say.

FIFTY-ONE

For the next two weeks, the kids are in France with their mother. My days consist of several back-to-back night shifts, sleeping spottily during the day while Joe makes himself scarce at meetings, and in the waking hours where our paths manage not to intersect, trying to get my head around the exhausting logistics of moving out.

On Tuesday I go to see a few flats that Sophie helped me find. One in particular – a studio in a four-storey townhouse off High Street Kensington – could fit the bill, but it's two hundred pounds a month over my budget. I need to think about it.

On Thursday, when I return home after dragging myself around the block with the dog, I think Joe isn't home, but our bedroom door opens and he wanders out, looking uncharacteristically dishevelled, unshaven, tired, and still in yesterday's shirt.

'Can we talk?' he asks, lifelessly.

I walk into the living room and sit down. Mozart trots to his water bowl and I listen to the loud rhythm of him lapping.

'I don't want you to leave.' He sits down beside me. 'Please . . .' He reaches for my hands that are folded in my lap, takes them in his own and slowly rubs my knuckles with his thumb. 'It's agonising, this . . . I can't bear the idea that I'm going to lose you . . . Please let's find a way around this.'

I can't look in his eyes. I gaze, instead, at the way my hands lie inert in his.

'I love you, Lauren. If this is about the baby thing . . . I'm prepared to think about it.'

I want to say *I don't love you*, but I can't say it.

I take my hands away and fold my arms. 'Joe . . . I am so wrung out from talking and thinking about this. I don't want you to rethink anything. As much as you might believe I do, I actually don't want you to live a life that's some massive compromise to you – just for me.'

As I say it, I am never more certain that it's true. It's like someone said in the forum – if we don't want the same things, what hope is there?

'But neither am I going to convince myself I'm happy. Or that because I'm in this – because we're married and I've made some huge commitment to you – I can't change my situation, I can't leave.'

He leans forward, elbows on his outspread knees, places his head in his hands. I watch his fingers, the way they crook, hear his soft, distressed sigh. After a moment or two, he says, 'You can change anything you want to. Obviously. No one's keeping you here . . . What I'm asking . . . is that you don't.'

It's the closest I have ever heard Joe come to putting his heart on the line since the day we became husband and wife. But I am not dissuaded.

'I went to see a flat this week.' I stare at a mid-point on the floor. 'And this afternoon I signed a six-month lease.'

'What?' He looks up, uncomprehendingly. When he can recover, he says, 'It's fine. Just because you've signed a lease doesn't mean you have to leave . . . We can make the payments . . . You could keep it, use it if you needed a break. Or we could sublet it.' A flicker of optimism appears in his eyes. 'A lease isn't the end of the world.' He says it as though we're both aware I've made a huge mistake, and he's just righted it for us. Joe, who is ever-practical, who always finds a way to guide you out of the maze. *I will miss this about him*, I think.

'I didn't lease it to keep it as some sort of occasional escape hatch.'

'Then live in it,' he says, less victoriously. 'If that's what you want to do. Take the time you need.'

'To what? Think? Joe . . .' I throw up my hands. 'I'm not leaving to go away and think about coming back. It's not some stopgap. Don't you get it?'

Finally he looks at me as though maybe he does.

'This marriage has broken my faith in relationships – *you* have – and I need to try to come to terms with that so as not to mess up the rest of my life.'

'Please,' he says. I can tell that really hurt him. In fact, I probably could not have said a more damaging thing. 'You once mentioned us going to therapy . . . We can give it a try.'

'I don't want to go to therapy,' I say. 'That implies I've got something to work on. And I don't.'

He nods. 'That's fine. I know you don't . . . I'll go. I'll go alone.'

'It won't make a difference.'

We are caught at a juncture that neither one of us imagined finding ourselves at. All I have to say is, *You're right. Okay. Let's do all of the above* . . . But instead I tell him, 'I can't do it.'

At first I'm not sure if I have actually said it, or just thought it – until I look at his face. His fallen, utterly crushed face.

'I'm sorry,' I say. 'It's over.'

He shakes his head, in a state of transparent denial.

In our living room, on Sunday night, as Ben the Budgie chirps happily by the open patio door, we tell the children.

'What?' Grace sits up sharply. 'What do you mean, *taking time apart?* You're leaving Daddy?'

I tell her that – for now, yes – I need some breathing space. I'm moving out.

She blinks, looks from me to her father. 'This can't be happening . . . This is nuts! I mean, you only just got married!' And then her eyes meet mine again. 'Is this because of me?' She presses her fingertips into her lips. 'Oh my God. It is, isn't it? It's because of me!'

'No,' I say, quickly. 'Absolutely not. This has nothing – nothing whatsoever – to do with you or Toby. This is about me and your dad.'

I glance at Joe, who is sitting with his elbows resting on his knees, his left hand cupping his mouth as he stares unblinking at the floor, like he's been cast in stone.

'But when will you be coming back?' Toby's face settles into a deep frown of worry and woe. 'When will we be able to go to the park again after school?'

'Lauren will be very busy for the next short while.' Joe finally speaks. Then he adds, 'Grace will take you to the park. And so will I.'

'But I don't want to go with you and Grace, I want to go with Lauren!'

'I know!' he says, getting up and sitting on the floor beside Toby and smoothing his hair with the palm of his hand.

I stare at the two of them. Joe sends me a look that says, *See, this is what you've done.*

Later, when they're in bed and I am putting things away in the kitchen, I am suddenly conscious of a presence. I turn around to find Joe just leaning on the breakfast bar, watching me. I have no idea how long he's been standing there.

I place the tea towel back on the hook. 'Maybe I could still see the kids from time to time.' I don't even know if it truly would be a good idea, or how it would work; I find myself clutching at some sort of straw. But there's not even a split second's contemplation before he shakes his head.

'No way,' he says. 'It's not happening.' He turns and walks away. I hear him proceed down the hall to the cupboard, the opening of the door. I follow and watch him take out his dog-walking shoes, then bend and tie his laces.

When he straightens up, his eyes are glassy with tears. 'You've made your choice,' he says. 'We will live with it. Don't worry about them. They're young. Especially Toby.' He seems to compose himself and sends me an ice-cold stare. 'In time they'll forget you ever existed.'

FIFTY-TWO

Three months later

I wheel my suitcase along the concourse, following the signs to the underground. My phone burrs. A FaceTime call. I click Accept.

'Home safe and sound?' My parents' heads are locked together.

'Just walking through Gatwick now. Flight was a bit late.' I try to juggle my phone, my handbag, a water bottle and the gloves I just unearthed from my bag so we can look at each other.

'We miss you already,' my mother says. 'Can you not turn around and come back?'

The phone bobs as I walk. I am not a lover of airports and my mission is to get through them as fast as humanly possible. 'Christmas. Remember? Isn't that what we agreed?'

'Only two months away,' my dad says. 'We'd better start writing our grocery list.'

'Tesco's Christmas pudding and Marks & Sparks mince pies,' my mother chirps up. 'That's two of them already.'

I smile. 'I'll do my best to oblige.'

'Are you going to be okay?' She suddenly turns serious.

It's a very odd question. I know I'm going to be okay, but I don't feel okay. I'd hoped that five days in Spain could have resulted in some seismic shift in my spirits, but that may have been over-reaching. 'I'll be fine,' I say.

They both look at me like they want so badly to believe me, but can't.

I tell them I should probably go because I'm coming up to an escalator and need both hands free. 'Text you tomorrow.' My feet stop. I hold their faces steady before my own. 'I love you,' I tell them.

Then I click off before I have to look at their worried, disenchanted expressions for a moment longer.

My flat overlooks a small street that's sparsely dotted with the sort of high-end niche shops that always look empty, and you're never quite sure how they manage to stay in business. On one corner is one of those civilised upper-crust neighbourhood pubs that regularly has what looks like the same half-dozen guys drinking beer outside. I can look down on to the tops of their heads, watch their breath dispersing into clouds in the cold air. And on the other corner is a small church surrounded by a cluster of trees that have lost their leaves.

When I come home after a series of busy shifts – Foundation Year 2 having brought different challenges that come with being a fully registered doctor – I'm grateful that nothing else is expected of me once I walk through my front door.

But then I'm just alone and . . . lost.

There is no one making my breakfast after a long night shift. No one to talk to about my day, or bounce my concerns off. At first it's a bit of an odd luxury to be able to take a basket around Tesco on a Saturday and pick out food for one. But coming home, eating alone and then going to bed on my own is utterly bewildering at times. I can't quite get my head around the fact that I had a marriage that lasted barely eight months. I keep thinking that as the previous narrative wasn't making me happy, this one should feel more promising. But the graph still feels pretty flat at the moment.

So, I try to keep myself busy. On Halloween night I meet Sophie at the Pig's Ear for dinner: a potent night for me, because it's also the night Joe proposed, one year ago. No fanfare. Just a dinner he'd prepared. A candle. And a question.

'Where's Charlie this evening?' I ask, as we're shown to a table in the quiet little dining nook upstairs.

'His dad's in town. He took him out for a steak.' She smiles. 'We didn't really feel like staying home and having all the trick or treating.'

'No,' I say. Tonight was the one night I was actually hugely grateful to be living four storeys up in an attic – even one I can barely afford.

'How are you doing?' she asks, once we're stuck into a bottle of wine.

'I've no idea to be honest. It's still really, really strange. Considering I was a long time single, and a very short time married, I thought it would be way easier to snap back to the me I used to be . . . I might have been a little deluded.'

'But no regrets?'

I shake my head, shrug. 'Not really.'

'There's a lot of very great guys out there, you know. For when you're ready to get back on the market.'

I snigger at that awful expression. 'Believe me, meeting some other man is the very last thing I can see me wanting to do for a very long time!'

'You never know!'

'But I think I do. Though I'm particularly looking forward to trying out my chat-up line.'

'What's that then?'

'Hi, I'm Lauren! I just got out of an eight-month marriage!' I say it perkily.

She grins in friendly despair. 'The right person won't be fazed by that. Or maybe he'll have got out of one himself!'

'True,' I say. But at this point I really could not care less.

'So . . .' she says. 'The big news, if we can call it big . . . We've been talking about using a sperm bank.'

'Wow!' I must look amazed. 'This is news!'

'It's just conversation right now. It's not like we'd be doing it tomorrow. But maybe in the next year or two . . .'

'The paediatrician who does want children after all!'

'Maybe. Or maybe the paediatrician who would like to keep her options open.'

'I get it,' I say, wondering what my options will be in that, or in any other, regard.

'I'm not sure I would go down that route if push comes to shove. It still feels a bit like a science experiment to me. A bit cold . . .'

I scrutinise her. She turns a little flat again. I tell her that once she's looked into her little baby's face I can't imagine she'd find anything cold about it at all.

When we leave, she hops in an Uber but I feel like walking. Even though it's cold I walk all the way along the King's Road to Sloane Square, to the spot in front of the church where I usually catch the number 452 bus up to High Street Kensington. My contact with Joe over the last three months has been almost non-existent – a quick email asking for my full address, no explanation as to why he needed it but I suspect it might have something to do with formalising the separation. A text with no content, obviously sent by accident; when I responded '?', it got no reply.

As I approach Peter Jones, I need to cross over to the bus stop, but out of habit I find my feet wanting to veer towards the Tube that will take me to north London. I stand there in a bizarre paralysis, not quite knowing who or what I am anymore, or even where I live, before my brain forces me to get my bearings again.

On the top deck, as the bus takes us along Sloane Street, I stare into other people's beautiful living rooms, glimpsing other people's perfect lives – a gaggle of gorgeous girls dressed as ice sculptures spilling out of a doorway, rushing down some steps to their waiting taxi; off, no doubt, to some glam party.

I'm lost in sad thoughts when my phone pings.

A text. From Grace.

There's no message, just a photograph.

Toby dressed as Edward Scissorhands, pulling a funny face at the camera.

I beam.

When I get home, the flat is dark except for the street light pouring through the window. I can hear male laughter coming from the pub. I walk over to the window and peer down at what looks like the same clutch of locals who are also eschewing Halloween for a more civilised Saturday.

I don't feel like going to bed, or watching telly. There's a glass of white left in the fridge. I pour it, then throw myself down on the sofa and kick off my shoes.

I'm just pulling Toby's picture up again when another text pops up.

Happy Halloween! You never wrote back. Hoping, therefore, that this is not out of line. Just wanted to say hello. Mel.

Just as I'm rereading it – I *did* completely forget to write back to him – a photo pops up. A sexy guy with a beard, longish greasy hair, and a guitar strapped over his shoulder. A big, endearing smile.

I stare at the moving dots that follow.

Beard is real. The rest a pale imitation.

I find myself grinning from ear to ear. Imitation of . . . ?

Jackson Maine.

Huh?

A Star Is Born.

Ah! The movie! I chuckle. Of course! More than a passing resemblance!!!

Clearly!

I'm sitting here thoroughly amused, trying to think what to say next, but then he's typing again.

Relationship ended July. Dad died Sept. First 'outing' as something other than a sad, single guy. How is your night?

Before I can reply he sends another picture of a group of guys all in varying degrees of Halloween dress-up, and looking like they're having a good time.

Sorry to hear this! I type. Sorry about your marriage, and your dad. That's rough. Then I add, My night is fine.

I try to decide if I should divulge anything else, but something stops me; it doesn't exactly feel like the time or the place. Instead I say, Hope your evening is at least pleasantly distracting.

I think he's not going to reply, but then the dots appear again.

Not bad. Anyway, sorry to appear out of the blue and . . . uninvited . . . Just thought of you and wanted to say hello.

I scroll back up to his picture. The broad smile, and twinkling eyes.

Hello, I reply.

EPILOGUE

I step out of my car. The winter ground crunches beneath my feet. I lock the door, pop my keys in my pocket and look both ways before crossing the road. The sky is thick with clouds, the kind that promise snow. Up ahead, half a dozen dog walkers congregate, hands stuffed into pockets as their mutts bark and frolic. Normally when I go for a walk, I pop in my earbuds and listen to an audiobook. But today I'm on a mission and head towards the playground, looking out for two faces.

I spot them over by the small duck pond, walking past the weeping willow that, oddly, hasn't yet let go of all its leaves.

Grace sees me and waves. She's wearing a long, dark green puffa coat and a black crocheted tam hat. Her hair falls in glossy honey tones as she leans forward and says something to Toby, who promptly lets go of her hand and runs to me.

'Lauren!' He wraps my legs in a bear hug.

Lauwen. I have missed how he says my name.

'Well, hello, little man!' I crouch down to eye level, pop a kiss on his cheek, smooth a chunk of hair back from his brow. 'Did you get new glasses? I love the electric blue rims!'

He nods. 'I broke my others in the playground at school.'

'He got into a little fight,' Grace says quietly. 'But everything's okay now.'

Before I can ask anything else, she says, 'We don't have all that long. Dad is taking us for brunch.'

'Let's go over to the swings,' I say. And then, as we start walking in that direction, I ask her, 'How is he?'

'Dad?' She sighs a little. 'He's fine . . . Well, he's not really *fine*. But you know him; he never says very much. He's not all that easy to understand.' She sends me a brief, downcast smile.

I wait for her to say more, but she doesn't.

Toby runs towards the swings the second they come into view. Joe has no idea we are doing this. Meeting. Our little secret. Toby has been sworn to not tell. Apparently, he loved that.

'I don't really want to go to for brunch,' he says. 'Maybe we can stay here instead?'

I step behind him as he climbs on to the seat, give his back a gentle push. 'How's your swimming now, Toby? Can you hold your breath under water?' I picture Joe and him in the pool together and find myself enjoying the memory.

He kicks out his legs. His running shoes have tiny cute reflectors on the heels. 'Yes!' he says. 'I can hold my breath for fifteen minutes.'

'That's fantastic!' I beam at Grace. 'A world record.'

I ask him what he's learning in school but he doesn't really want to talk about school. Grace tells me she wants to go to Tuscany to stay at her friend's villa over the Christmas holidays and her mum is fine with it but Joe doesn't think it's a good idea.

She pulls out her phone, shows me a picture.

'Nice!' I stare at the big white house set behind a row of cypress trees. 'If your dad wins, and you can't go, do you think I can go in your place?'

'Dad is not going to win, I promise you!' She grins, and the topic has a way of making me feel oddly transient and disengaged from all of them. 'Can we walk a bit? It's freezing.'

We manage to coax Toby off the swings and venture down to the pond again. 'What are you going to do for Christmas?' she asks, after we have trod on a while in companionable silence.

I don't tell her that I'm trying very hard not to think about Christmas. That, frankly, I'd prefer the holiday just evaporated. Instead, I say I've booked a ticket to go and visit my parents in Spain. And that I have to be back for work in the New Year.

Her phone pings and she stops walking. 'Hang on.' She rips off her gloves and then her thumbs fire a reply. 'We should get going,' she says, when she looks up. 'We can meet for longer next time, if you like. Maybe when it's less cold.'

I don't ask her what excuse she gave in order to come here. Or if that was her dad on the line.

'I can drop you off near home,' I say, realising that actually, I can't, because I don't have a car seat for Toby any longer. One of the last things I handed over to Joe as I left.

'It's not a long walk.' She looks slightly doleful. 'We're fine.'

I watch her take hold of her brother's hand.

'Lauren,' Toby says, when we emerge on the main street again. 'Are you going to come with us to brunch?'

I look down at him and smile. 'Not this time.' I kneel in front of him again, pull his coat up so the collar sits snuggly around his ears. 'Stay warm, little guy, and I'll see you again soon?'

'Okay,' he says, glumly.

'Bye, then,' Grace says, holding my eyes for a beat or two. I watch them turn and walk along the street.

I stand there for a while staring at their backs until they stop beside a car.

A white Lexus.

Joe emerges. I witness this tall, attractive figure in jeans and a dark three-quarter-length coat. Someone I used to love. He strides around to the passenger side; Toby clambers in the back, then Grace jumps in next to her brother. After Joe has settled Toby into his car seat, he walks around to the driver's side again and gets in.

I try to turn away from what I've just seen and start walking in the direction of my own vehicle. I focus hard on my feet hitting the pavement, a sense of loss throbbing with each step.

I haven't got far when the white Lexus rolls up beside me and stops.

The passenger door opens and Joe leans across. He looks at me earnestly, smiles. And then with a hand, he indicates the empty seat.

ACKNOWLEDGMENTS

Some people say that if you work hard, and you sit down to write every day, inspiration will always come; the key is discipline and routine. I don't believe this. There are days when you think yourself into a box and you can't see your way out of it anymore – it's almost like nothing exists outside of it and your world becomes small. You start to doubt you have a story worth writing.

This is when I generally step away and try to get on with living my life. It might be for a day, or a week. I may meet a random stranger by the beach, have a conversation in a coffee shop, witness something, overhear something . . . This is where the magic happens. My story – my belief in it – will suddenly be ignited.

I am grateful for every little thread of inspiration, no matter how offbeat the manner in which it arrives, and to everyone who helped *Between You and Me* take its eventual shape. Thanks, in particular, to my editor Sammia Hamer and to Arzu Tahsin for their patience and support, to the amazing team behind the scenes at Amazon Publishing, to my agent Lorella Belli, my friend Catherine for a timely pep talk, and friends Robyn and Andy Stroud who shared some crazy tales of raising children, given I don't have kids of my own.

Thanks to everyone who has bought, read, reviewed or recommended my books. I am truly grateful for this career.

And thanks, as always, to my husband, Tony, and my mother, Mary, for their never-ending support of all I do.

ABOUT THE AUTHOR

Carol Mason was born and grew up in the north-east of England. As a teenager she was crowned Britain's National Smile Princess and subsequently became a model, diplomat-in-training and advertising copywriter. She currently lives in British Columbia, Canada, with her Canadian husband, a rescue dog from Kuwait and a three-legged cat. To learn more about Carol and her novels, visit www.carolmasonbooks.com, her Amazon author page at www.amazon.com/Carol-Mason/e/B0045AP0NI or follow her on Facebook at www.facebook.com/CarolMasonAuthor.

Did you enjoy this book and would like to get informed when Carol Mason publishes her next work? Just follow the author on Amazon!

1) Search for the book you were just reading on Amazon or in the Amazon App.
2) Go to the Author Page by clicking on the Author's name.
3) Click the "Follow" button.

If you enjoyed this book on a Kindle eReader or in the Kindle App, you will be automatically offered to follow the author when arriving at the last page.

LAKE UNION
PUBLISHING